GUILT

❧ IS A ❧

GHOST

GUILT

✦ IS A ✦

GHOST

A Vera Van Slyke
Ghostly Mystery

by
TIM PRASIL

BROM B🎃NES BOOKS

This is a work of fiction. Names, characters, businesses, places, events, locales, and incidents are either the products of the author's imagination or used in a fictitious manner. Any resemblance to actual persons, living or dead, or actual events is purely coincidental.

DEDICATION

This novel is dedicated to Boston, Massachusetts—not the city of my birth, but the city of my heart.

CONTENTS

INTRODUCTION

The story you are about to read was put to paper by my great-grandaunt, who was born Ludmila Prášilová (1882-1965). She later renamed herself Lucille Parsell, but at the time of writing this chronicle, she was called Lida Bergson. The handwritten manuscript was very likely intended for her husband, Eric Bergson, and penned while he was off fighting in World War I. The evidence of this is a letter dated July 28, 1918, found on top of the many disorganized pages. It was an army chaplain's letter of condolence, confirming that Eric had been killed in France. Apparently, learning of her husband's death, the woman of many names stuffed the manuscript into a wooden box—one designed and labeled to display seeds for sale—and closed it for good.

Though the simile might be strained, her chronicles remained unread in that box like unsown seeds. Along with the letter about her husband's death, my great-grandaunt included several shorter tales about the supernatural investigations she had shared with Vera Van Slyke (1868-1941), a newspaper reporter who had taken up ghost hunting as something more than a hobby. The box and its curious contents passed through family attics, basements, and storage sheds until they came to *my* attention 100 years later. (Traditionally, "ová" is added to a Czech surname to indicate a girl or woman, so my great-grandaunt was a Prášilová and I'm an Americanized Prasil.) I edited the shorter cases first and made them available in a book I titled *Help for the Haunted: A Decade of Vera Van Slyke Ghostly Mysteries.*

Overlapping the first four years of the decade covered in that book, this one presents a more involved—and in many ways, more dangerous—adventure. It was titled *Guilt Is a Ghost* by my great-grandaunt herself, so I suspect she had at least toyed with the idea of having it published as a book. If I'm right about that, it is heartening to think that her century-old seed has finally sprouted.

As with the earlier book, I'm unsure where my ancestor's authentic experience stops and her creative imagination begins. On the one hand, William James was a well-known Harvard professor who combined Psychology with an interest in "psychical research" (or, as it's known today, paranormal investigation). I was surprised to learn that William B. Watts was, in fact, the Chief Inspector for Boston's Bureau of Criminal Investigation during the years chronicled. All of the books cited and many other details are also real. On the other hand, I've never found any traces of a tobacco millionaire named Roderick Morley or of the scandal involving murder and suicide surrounding him. Did my great-grandaunt change some of the names out of respect for the dead? Was she guarding against retaliation from the living?

And what do we do about the ghosts? Are they fact or fiction? Unfortunately (or is it?) the internet and other modern research tools don't supply *all* the answers.

Regardless of those questions, my long-shot wish with publishing the earlier book was that it somehow would lead to the discovery of *additional* manuscripts written by my great-grandaunt. Perhaps Vera Van Slyke—who was a journalist, after all—left records of other ghostly mysteries she had explored, perhaps without her "Dr. Watson." I'll return to this in the Postscript.

For now, let me simply say that the death of a spouse can crush a person's ambition, as it might have with Lida Bergson (née Prášilová, aka Lucille Parsell). But, as any ghost will tell you, death isn't always the end of someone's story.

ACT ONE

THE MEDIUM
(December, 1899)

CHAPTER ONE

THE SISTER WITH SENSE

"It was your *father* who died when you were twelve years old—not *you!*" insisted my mother. She spoke in Czech.

I spoke in English. "I don't think of this spirit as being *myself.* I think of her as my little *sister.* That's why I named her Marianne. She's named for Marianne Dashwood, which makes me Elinor. After all, don't I have to be the sister with *sense* all the time?"

My mother didn't speak at all. She glared.

I explained, "It's from a book. A novel by Jane Austen."

"You read too much. It gives you romantic notions." She began to pace, first gripping a handle of a pan and then of a pot—but not lifting any of them. "I still don't like it, a twelve-year-old girl who's a spirit now. It's too sad. Go back to calling your guide Uncas. These Americans like it when you summon an Indian spirit to contact their dead. Dr. Slade called his guide Owasso!"

"Yes, but that was before Dr. Slade was defrauded by the Seybert Commission. And that happened quite some time ago. These days, people like it just as well when the control is the spirit of a girl. Remember that British woman about my age—that Miss Archer?"

My mother stopped shaking hands with the cookware and tilted her head.

I clarified, "The one who conducts séances as Miss Arcati." Seeing her nod, I added, "She calls her control Daphne, and Daphne's a little girl. Marianne is no different."

My mother shrugged. "Maybe that works among the British. The Indians lived in the woods, uncorrupted by civilization. That's why these Americans like—"

5

I interrupted, "That's why Marianne is a twelve-year-old girl! Her dying young left her soul uncorrupted and trustworthy. That's what *we* Americans like."

My mother stopped fidgeting and moved to the table, slumping in the chair beside mine. She fluffed the sleeves of her charcoal house-dress. I looked at her face, always florid and offset by her black hair like a rose petal fallen on dark soil. It was a face as familiar as the smells of the chicken paprika simmering on the stove. My mother sighed significantly—and a bit melodramatically in my estimation.

Despite appearances, my claiming allegiance to the United States had not been intended as a taunt. We had journeyed from Prague to Chicago when I was five, and I felt more American than Bohemian. My birth name, Ludmila Prášilová, worked well when called upon to summon the dearly departed. Its Slavic resonance had a certain allure that many Americans found in keeping with distant realms, and it vaguely echoed the name of the famous occultist Madame Helena Blavatsky. However, when meeting people far removed from séances and Spiritualism, I had begun introducing myself as Lucille Parsell. In a way, Lucille Parsell served as a stage name in reverse—my *off-stage* name.

I confess that adopting a new name also served to free myself from my mother and the life she had imposed upon me. She had turned me into a Spiritualist medium shortly after the death of my father. To be sure, she needed a means to support her daughter and herself, as some people have been quick to tell me. But those people had not seen the excitement that ignited in her eyes after another medium approached her about contacting my father's spirit within days of his death. This recollection—my mental photograph of her enchantment with the audacity of that other medium—could still enflame me these five years later.

"Well," my mother said at last, "it would have been polite to warn me before the last séance. Why would Marianne announce her presence by beating Uncas's drum? Absurd. But you had not warned me. What was I to do? I guess we can switch to a music box or something a little girl would like."

Oddly, my mother's willingness to concede to this whim only made me feel more defeated. In truth, I did not care if my spirit guide were a noble Indian or an innocent girl. I sunk deeper into my unhappiness.

"I'm too old to continue doing this," I said softly.

"Ha!" spit my mother. "You are seventeen! And becoming so pretty now. Sometimes, I wonder if we can charge *more* because of your lovely looks!"

"But, matka, I hate *swindling* people! People who are grief-stricken! It's immoral." I felt moisture prickling my palms and a far deeper sting in my stomach.

"We provide them comfort and hope. They need consoling, and we offer that."

"*We?* All *you* do is beat a drum behind a curtain and then glide around the table in different costumes, pretending to be whoever is speaking through me! *You* be the medium! I'll go find *honest* employment." The back of my neck blazed.

She leaned forward. Now, she spoke in English. "How many timesh must I repeat? I shpeak English wid an accent, so every shpirit shounds exactly all alike. I am not young, so dey don't shee me to be pure. Dey grow doubtful and look closhly for trickery. Ish better for me to shtay in deh dark. Why you don't remember dis? I do better in deh dark." She reached out for me.

I snatched my arm back, beyond her touch. I was stymied. Certainly, she was ill-suited to play the medium, and it was true that this was a conversation that we had recited time and again. Perhaps our frequent travel had urged me to restate my plea with each new arrival. My mother's face, her pursed lips and wincing eyes, was familiar—but the frame around that portrait was ever changing.

At the time, we were spending a month in Lily Dale, a town in northeast New York State. It had become a Spiritualist colony, catering to those who practiced the same ruses as my mother and me. Along with earning profits from a multitude of grieving pilgrims, Lily Dale afforded opportunities to discover the innovations that other mediums had added to their séances. The days of Dr. Slade's table rapping and slate writing had faded. As the telegraph was becoming rivaled by Mr. Bell's telephone, rapping had become replaced by *vocal* emanations heard through an entranced psychic. Once Mr. Roentgen had made living skeletons visible with his renowned X-ray photographs, slate writing became eclipsed by fleeting but firsthand observations of life on the Other Side. Yes, Spiritualism was progressing alongside technology.

It was, after all, the final weeks of 1899.

The approaching new century seemed to add urgency to my desire to start afresh. As my mother and I sat in the cabin's kitchen, now in silent discomfort, I decided to commit to my earlier claim of being the sister with sense, the *rational* one in the family. If this career of trickery and deceit were bringing me anguish, the level-headed course of action would be to abandon it. I had come of age. I knew of other seventeen-year-old women—some even younger—who had gone into domestic service or factory work. They were self-sufficient, and so should I be. I set my mind to declining the next request to reunite the living with the dead. It was high time I became as disciplined as Elinor Dashwood, even if she were only a novelist's creation. It was high time for me to become *Lucille Parsell,* a free, mature woman of my *own* creation.

•

My resolution to abandon the Spiritualism racket led to a good night's rest, a rarity for me. The following day, the same resolve spurred me to answer a knock on our door with a confident stride. My mother rushed to hide in the bedroom in keeping with her well-rehearsed role "in deh dark." As I opened the door, a cold draft of air washed over my face.

"Good afternoon, miss. My name is Richard Brunton. I—I'm looking to hire a *medium. A psychic* they're also called—so I was told. But the, uh—the *séance* is to take place in Boston." A derby pulled low for warmth and a full beard obscured the man's face. However, his strained voice revealed an uneasiness accompanying his request. "My employer—he'll pay for your train passage. And, of course, for your, uh, *talents*. Once you're in Boston, that is. Am I addressing the—are you the correct lady for this matter?" He then chuckled at his own befuddlement.

I was charmed. I assured him that I was the correct lady and introduced myself as Ludmila Prášilova, since I was in character. As I spoke, I added a dash of the Slavic accent that had surrounded me in the Chicago neighborhood where I had been raised.

I welcomed him into the cabin. Taking his hat and coat, I saw that Mr. Brunton was a gentleman who had lived through at least sixty winters. Using his fingers to whisk the frost from his beard did nothing to change its blend of russet and silver. His cheeks were flush from the cold, and he wore a blue necktie. A distinctively triangular shape to his deep-green eyes gave him an appealing, almost elfin appearance. Mr. Brunton was a hefty elf, though, and one who would have towered over his mystical kindred.

He accepted my offer of a chair, but politely declined a cup of hot tea. On settling himself, he said, "You seem a bit young to be involved in this kind of—uhm—I'm not sure if the right term for Spiritualism is *religion* or *business.*"

"I find dat *service* is a nice compromise. Regarding my age, I have been manifesting spirits for five years now. I am a young woman, but not so much a young medium, yes?"

Mr. Brunton's lower lip protruded as he considered this fact. "Then there is someone who acts as your—uh—"

"My *mudder* has directed how I answer my calling. She is not here right now, but I am smart enough to know whedder or not I can be of help to you." This statement felt like a first step toward independence from my mother as well as toward rejecting Mr. Brunton's proposal.

"I see, I see." The gentleman nodded. "Then let me explain the situation. I wonder if you've ever heard of a man named Roderick Morley."

I had to struggle to maintain a professional demeanor. The scandal surrounding Mr. Morley had become common gossip to Spiritualists and probably anyone else who took interest in psychical research. His inherited wealth placed him on the high financial summits as other Boston Brahmins, such as the Cabot and the Forbes families. More akin to Andrew Carnegie, though, Mr. Morley had the heart of a philanthropist. His particular passion was to advance mankind's knowledge of occult subjects: hypnosis, clairvoyance, apparitions, even witchcraft. Needless to say, Roderick Morley was one of Spiritualism's greatest advocates and benefactors.

This special interest was related to the scandal. Mr. Morley's personal psychic advisor, a man named Silas Sanderson, had been murdered—a bullet through the heart, the newspapers reported—while visiting the millionaire's mansion. The crime was as yet unsolved, but the police and the press had cast strong suspicions upon those very close to Mr. Morley. In fact, he himself had been a key suspect.

"I know dat your employer is a believer in the Spiritualist cause," I explained to Mr. Brunton. "He must be distraught from deh loss of his associate, yes?"

My guest took a moment to again rub away any remaining ice from his beard. "I'm afraid he is *very* distraught, more than I've ever seen him. That's why he sent me here. He knows plenty of mediums in Boston, but he's looking for someone who *doesn't* know the local reporters. Oh dear, you aren't from Boston, are you?"

"No. I now claim Chicago as my home."

"Way out in the Middle West. Excellent. You see, the newspapers back in Boston seem to have little to discuss other than Mr. Morley's misfortunes, and he hopes to make sure that this séance will be kept secret. The entire tragedy has made him terribly skittish."

I resisted a twinge of sympathy for the millionaire. Sympathy might nudge me toward agreeing to conduct the séance. "I am pained to hear it. But whose spirit does Mr. Morley wish for me to contact?"

Mr. Brunton's eyebrows raised. "Sanderson's, of course. He was the murder victim, you know. Mr. Morley imagines that Sanderson can reveal who fired the gun that killed him—and reveal that information particularly easily, given his psychic abilities. The way it was explained to me, with Sanderson on the Other Side *in rebore* with a competent medium, and that medium *in rebore* with Sanderson's spirit—"

I felt obliged to say, "I believe you mean *en rapport*. It is from deh French."

"Thank you. Suffice it to say, Mr. Morley wants to hold a séance to find out who took the life of his friend. And he's much too agitated to arrange the matter himself."

"If I may ask, deh two gentlemen were quite close, yes?"

"Yes. *Very* close. Mr. Morley started to count on Sanderson for advice not just about his money, but also about his marriage." Mr. Brunton put a finger to his lips, almost as if he wished to restrain his mouth. "But I've been instructed to make sure that you come to the séance knowing as little as possible. My employer *is* a believer in Spiritualists, but he also knows that there are more than enough *quacks* among you."

"It is wise to let deh spirits demselves confirm who dey are," I replied. "A *quack*, as you call it, might simply repeat what had been said before deh séance."

Again, my guest's lower lip came forward, and his charming eyes drifted askance. Those eyes then shot back at me, and Mr. Brunton gave me a friendly nod. He seemed impressed by my complimenting him for being cautious. My earlier sympathy for the millionaire joined with warmth for his trusting—if somewhat naïve—employee. I knew I must act quickly if I were to do the sensible thing, forever escaping my own *quackery*.

"But I am terribly sorry, sir. My psychic gift is unluckily woven wit' an unfortunate susceptibility to nervous exhaustion. Dat is how deh doctors call it. A *susceptibility to nervous exhaustion*. Deh situation you describe is, of course, a most worrisome one, and my delicate constitution might likely to become an issue. It might make me susceptible to nervous— You understand dis, yes? You understand what I am saying?" Hearing my own voice, I became aware that I was using a quantity of words far surpassing the necessary figure. I was not in the habit of turning away business.

"Is that so?" Brunton inquired with sincerity. "So far, you've struck me as being a very self-possessed young woman—not at all the nervous sort."

I chuckled. "I am in familiar surroundings, as you can see. But I was saying that my poor nerves prevent me from accepting your—"

"If I may interrupt. I'm certain you've noticed that, when it comes to arranging a séance, I'm far out at sea. If you wish to dismiss the offer, I will certainly respect that. Perhaps you could then direct me to a medium better suited to my employer's predicament. However, while I mentioned that Mr. Morley will cover the train fare, I neglected to say *how much* he'll pay for the séance. As you know, he is a very, very wealthy man. May I tell you *that* before you send me out into the cold again?"

I had not considered what a millionaire might pay to hold a secret séance. Suddenly, my tongue felt as if coated with dirt, muddying my accent. "Why—certainly. I didn't—I did not mean to shove you out the—uhm, *de* door. A séance of th—*dis* kind would typically cost fifty dollars." In truth, I had met exactly three previous patrons whom I judged to be able to pay that high a figure.

Mr. Brunton smiled. "Mr. Morley has authorized me to pay *two hundred* dollars."

I heard a sudden clang come from the bedroom, where my mother was obviously eavesdropping.

After glancing in that direction, Mr. Brunton continued, "And I don't doubt that he'll foot the hotel bill, too. For you *and* your mother."

"Dat," I uttered, "is, indeed—*most* generous." Along with a gritty mouth, I felt the same wet palms and clenched abdomen as when pleading with my mother the previous day. Nonetheless, as I gazed into Mr. Brunton's eyes, it dawned upon me that such a sum of money would certainly ease my transition to more conventional employment. Such a sum would certainly grant me more time in securing a position suitable to my tastes rather than to my debts.

Given my situation, accepting such a sum would make—in a word—*sense*. A lot of *sense*.

"Generous," I resumed, "and certainly *more* dan adequate for any treatments to restore my nerves afterward. Yes, Mr. Brunton. Yes, I would be pleased to do what I can to help resolve your employer's predicament."

Mr. Brunton's green eyes twinkled. We finalized the arrangements, and then I helped him on with his coat. Again, the outside air chilled me as I watched him depart.

As soon as I closed the door and turned around, I saw my mother had entered from the bedroom.

In Czech, she said, "I will discover what this Sanderson looks like, then put together an appropriate costume and repaint one of the masks." Her face shone with the same giddiness that I recalled from when I was twelve years old and she met that medium offering to contact the spirit of my father.

It was the expression of a woman envious of another woman, one courageous and clever enough to live a self-sustaining life.

\backsim CHAPTER TWO \backsim

THE STAGE AND
THE PLAYERS UPON IT

A notorious murder remaining unsolved must surely cast a cold shadow upon the celebration of the newborn Savior. Their current quagmire prompted Mr. Morley and his wife to cancel their Christmas merriments. The séance was scheduled for Friday, December 22. However, before departing Lily Dale, I had wired to request a meeting with Mr. Morley at his home in Boston on the Thursday prior. I noted my desire to learn the specifics of all he sought as well as to sense the etheric vibrations of the room where we were to sit. The ploy was designed to let me plan how my mother might play her clandestine part in the séance.

The Morley Mansion was not as I had imagined. No tree-shaded drive led to it, and no verdant grounds behind it awaited a foxhunt. Perhaps my mother spoke the truth when she said that novels had given me romantic notions. Far from Charlotte Brontë's Thornfield Hall, the Morleys lived in a four-story, brick tower amid dozens of similar towers and the patchwork of cobblestone streets on Beacon Hill.

Mr. Brunton opened the door, inviting me in and taking my coat. In Lily Dale, I had assumed he was an agent for Mr. Morley, not a servant. Seeing him in this role must have startled me a bit because Mr. Brunton playfully mirrored my expression by widening the corners of his green eyes—the pair of triangles that I had found so charmingly elfin. He then smiled. "Not used to being received by a butler, Miss? Not to worry. Mr. Morley runs this house more like the son of a *farmer* than like the son of a *pharaoh*. What you see here is thanks to tobacco money."

15

"Oh?" I was caught off guard yet again. Only half-jesting, I replied, "I cannot say dat I have ever heard of a *Yankee* tobacco tycoon."

"Mr. Morley was raised in Virginia," the butler clarified, adding a bit wistfully, "As was *I* many years ago." Ushering me under an elegant chandelier and along dark wainscoting, Mr. Brunton changed the subject to the whereabouts of my mother.

"Unluckily," I told him, "my poor mother is not accustomed to deh harsh climate in Lily Dale at dis time of year. She has come down wit a terrible cold. Deh doctor prescribed resting in bed and avoiding to travel." In truth, my mother had traveled to Boston with me and was across town at the time, scouring local newspapers for information on Silas Sanderson, the psychic who failed to foresee his own murder.

We had arrived at a parlor with a crackling fire casting its glow on a prodigious stone hearth. The butler scratched his silvered beard.

"You say the climate of Lily Dale is harsh," he commented. "But didn't you mention that *Chicago* is your home? Are the winters there any milder?"

"You have been to Chicago in deh winter, yes—or no?" I asked while pulling on the brooch pinned over my throat. My collar suddenly seemed very tight.

He confessed, "No. The West seems a bit *too* wild for me, I'm afraid."

"Well, Chicago's winters are much more mild." Blatantly misleading Mr. Brunton pained me. Lying to an elf—even a giant one—must certainly be unwise so close to Christmas.

I had a very different reaction to the master of the house, though. As Mr. Morley entered the parlor to introduce himself, I knew I was seeing a man at his worst. He appeared emaciated, especially in his cadaverous cheeks and large, moist eyes. An ill-trimmed moustache drooped over thin, seemingly bloodless lips. Neither his nose nor his chin were especially distinctive. However, Mr. Morley's pale forehead, which was very high, and his dark hair, which was very sparse, both looked as if they belonged to a man older than fifty, although he was a man closer to thirty than forty. How much of this could be attributed to his recent troubles, I do not know, but the millionaire reminded me of an undertaker in a burlesque skit.

With a whispery voice, he said, "Help me to pronounce your name please."

"My fodder's name was Prášil," I said, "which comes close to rhyming with deh English word 'fossil.' As I am female, we add 'ová' to deh end. I'd lecture you regarding my Christian name, Ludmila, but the Czech language—like our sweet pastry—is best savored in small bites."

Mr. Morley, it seemed, was in no mood for whimsy. He nodded without expression. I felt myself blush from having been impertinent.

"Come," he muttered, "I'll show you where Silas—eh, the late Mr. Sanderson—liked to conduct his séances. He called it the *Dawning* Room."

As we climbed a stairway flanked by an intricately carved banister on one side and elegant paintings on the other, I asked, "Dere is more dan a pun on 'drawing room' in calling it deh Dawning Room, yes? It faces east?"

"Yes, and a small alleyway across the street grants us views of the sunrise, a rare sight on Beacon Hill. But Mr. Sanderson was being more metaphorical, of course, implying the room might play some role in the dawning of mankind's knowledge concerning eternal life."

"Very beautiful," I replied, as much to the sentiment about spiritual knowledge as to my own suspicion about why Mr. Sanderson had chosen *that* room. Séances typically take place during the evening or afternoon, almost never in the morning. A room facing east, therefore, can be made very dark. Dark enough so that sitters can be convinced they're glimpsing *actual* spirits.

Once we had climbed another flight of stairs and approached a door halfway down the hall, I noticed Mr. Morley twitch as he reached for the doorknob. Whether it was a tremor in his hand or a sudden wince of his eyes, I cannot recall. Nonetheless, people in my trade know when to act upon a hunch. We know that, if that hunch turns out to be mistaken, it's quickly forgotten—but if it turns out to be *correct*, it can appear downright clairvoyant.

I grabbed Mr. Morley's arm. Pretending to be in the first throes of a faint, I put my hand to my brow and stumbled to rest against the wall. "I—I had a strong impression. A sudden wave of terrible sadness. Tell me, is *dis* also the room where Mr. Sanderson met with *death?*"

The millionaire remained expressionless. He stared at me for only a moment before stating flatly, "Yes, Miss Prasilova, this *is* where the murder occurred. And while I'd like to think otherwise, it's entirely possible you get that information from the newspapers."

I had to think quickly. "It *is* possible I forget reading it. Perhaps. Still, dere's a strong echo of pain here, one I would have sensed—dough probably could not have explained wit'out my knowing deh details. Let us hope my knowing *some* tings about deh murder will help to give form to my impressions and make dem useful, yes?"

Mr. Morley cocked his head before nodding. It was all he was going to divulge regarding his acceptance of my psychic powers. Those two hundred dollars would not be easily earned.

He opened the door, and I walked forward.

I took inventory of the room. I first noticed one bay window, presumably facing east. In keeping with my earlier conjectures, there was a single drapery (dark, heavy, wide) that would block the entire window alcove when drawn. All around the walls of the room were bookcases (free-standing, not attached to the walls). The furnishings included two easy chairs (matching, leather-upholstered) and a desk of considerable size (positioned so the sitter can observe the whole room). In the very center of the room, upon an ornate rug (Turkish or Persian), stood a long, rectangular table. It was surrounded by six wooden chairs. None of this would be particularly helpful in making my séance anything more than a tiresome monologue.

But then I noticed a door. The door was nestled between two of the bookshelves. It stood in the *middle* of the wall, suggesting it didn't belong to, say, a closet. Instead, the door promised to afford discreet entry for my mother from the next room. I would need a closer look to confirm this.

"You say deh spirit you hope to contact had a sense of metaphor when naming dis room," I said. Beginning to circumnavigate the room, I held my palms up to the various furnishings—but without touching them. "You probably know dat dose who have crossed over often communicate wit an ethereal language, one dat is *rich* in metaphor. It is a language dat can be baffling to us on *dis* plane."

"I'm sure that Mr. Sanderson will take that into account."

As I wandered toward the promising door, I noticed a framed print on the wall that reminded me that my host had lived in Virginia as a boy. The engraving depicts a colored family leisurely gathered around the doorstep of their cottage. Spanish moss dangles from the trees. A placid river runs beside the Negros' home, and on it floats a barge loaded with watermelons and other crops. The scene's title is printed on the bottom: *Good Times on the Old Plantation*. I focused on the piece.

Mr. Morley couldn't help but notice. "Nothing more than a popular Currier and Ives lithograph, I'm afraid. My wife doesn't much care for it, but sometimes a work's value is more in the subject matter than in its execution, I think."

"And I agree. It reminds you of your days in—*Virginia?*" I asked, again hoping to evoke an air of clairvoyance.

Mr. Morley would have none of it. "Let's say it reminds me of my *family's* past there. And of those who worked so that I can play."

I suddenly felt as if the millionaire were speaking in an ethereal and baffling language of his own. Taking a step closer to the door, I hoped to divert his attention with a new subject.

"I tink I recognize some of dese books," I stated. "Yes, here is Coleman—and Sargent—and Hardinge. An *excellent* library. And very—what is your word?—*extensive!*"

"The Dawning Room was going to be a center of Spiritualist study. Mr. Sanderson suggested these shelves be brought in for exactly that purpose. We had—*grand*—plans."

Here, my host turned away and cleared his throat. I took the opportunity to observe that, yes, the bookshelves had been set in such a way that someone entering from the neighboring room could remain hidden, assuming that adjoining room were about as dark as this one. I turned quickly back to the books on Spiritualism.

"Yes," I said softly, "I *do* feel very much *en rapport* wit your advisor. The séance should go very well. Now, forgive me for raising an issue dat I know might be difficult for you. Dere is someting you wish me to ask Mr. Sanderson, yes? Someting besides deh obvious topic of, well—"

"I do have another question for him," Mr. Morley said, turning back to me. "But I'll save that for tomorrow, if his spirit appears. For now, I have a question for *you*, Miss Prasilova."

I faced him directly. He straightened his shoulders as if it were a painful act.

With careful articulation, he said, "I've lost one of the few people I could trust. I was made to think someone near me—possibly, living in this house—took him from me. I no longer can look at those people without suspicion, and I know that I would be looked at in the same way if I dared to go out in public. My faith has become very fragile. So I must ask. Should I have faith in *you*? Are you a *genuine* psychic medium?"

Instead of answering, I inhaled deeply and turned my head to the table. If I were correct in assuming that Mr. Sanderson had advised Mr. Morley to have the bookshelves placed in such a way that a confederate might creep into the room, then that advisor would conduct his séances at the end of that table farthest from that door. Even in the dark, sitters have a strong tendency to face the medium—in this case, facing *away* from where the confederate would enter and make a startling appearance. I walked slowly toward the far chair.

Upon reaching it, I sat down in that chair. I feigned having another agitating mental impression, using the spell to grope under the table. Some mediums tack wires or strings across the cross-boards supporting the tabletop from below. This clandestine clothesline offers a handy spot to hang anything from an atomizer of the deceased's favorite perfume to the gauze used as ectoplasm. But there was nothing like that there.

Despite the lack of confirmation, I proceeded with my gamble. "Mr. Sanderson sat *here* when he conducted his séances, yes?" I asked. I observed Mr. Morley blanch, if such a thing were possible with his pallor. I then nodded. "I doubt, sir, I would have read *dat* in a newspaper?"

My host raised his hand and put it against his chest. "You *begin* to restore my faith, Miss Prasilova. Thank you. With your permission, I'll ring for Brunton to show you out."

He swiftly departed, keeping his emotions poorly hidden.

I wouldn't have dared such a stunt to deceive someone longing to trust me if I hadn't been certain that this would be my very *last* time.

•

That evening, my mother and I shared what we had learned. She discovered that Silas Sanderson was only twenty-eight years of age when shot while confronting his killer. The newspapers described him as very handsome with caramel-colored hair and a well-trimmed moustache. My mother had already repainted one of the papier-mâché masks in our collection to resemble him—it was hardly the first time she had masqueraded as a gentleman. We decided against splashing red dye on the shirt over the heart to suggest where he had been shot. Doing so would have served little purpose other than to shock. However, one quotation in the papers told of Mr. Sanderson's habit of wearing a fresh, fragrant boutonniere in his lapel. This was something easily mimicked and especially useful since the sense of smell is keen in the dark.

I reported that, after Mr. Morley had fled the Dawning Room, I checked the door I had found so enticing and found it unlocked. When Mr. Brunton arrived, I asked him about possible disruptions coming through that door. He said it led to a guest bedroom, currently unoccupied. It would serve our purposes nicely. The séance was to begin at 7:30 in the evening. I instructed my mother to arrive shortly afterward. While I would be progressing into a trance state, she would explain, probably to Brunton, that she had only just arrived from Lily Dale, her cold fully cured. Honoring my insistence that the séance not be interrupted, she would request some slight refreshment in the parlor. Once left alone, she was to take the portmanteau containing the Sanderson disguise to the third floor. There, my mother would slip through the hall door to enter that adjoining guest room. The sounds of a music box would be my cue that all was in place.

We would have to hope the door remained unlocked.

I had sketched my mother a floorplan to ensure that there would be no mishaps. The next day, while riding the carriage that Mr. Morley had sent to our hotel, I mentally redrew the map over and again. I imagined my mother acting her part in our drama. So deep in thought was I that, at one point during the ride, I caught myself moving my arms as if I were a puppeteer.

The coachman had to announce our arrival twice before I heard him. I stepped out of the carriage and into the crisp chill of a clear winter evening. Wrapping my cape tightly around me, I stepped carefully along a walk shoveled clear of snow. I was suddenly struck by the muffled sounds of an orchestra coming from within the mansion, and it took me a moment to realize that someone must be listening to a Gramophone. I had almost thought that the music was announcing the start of the show, calling me onto the stage.

Again, Brunton met me at the door and escorted me up the first flight of stairs. On the way, he informed me that Mr. Morley and another gentlemen had already arrived. While on the second-story landing, the butler apologized for the climb and added that, after especially long days, he could barely climb to his room on the fourth story. Halfway up the second flight, then, Mr. Brunton heaved a heavy breath. He explained that his employer deemed having him announce new arrivals to be a pompous practice, more European than American. I understood the aging man's implication and assured him that I knew my way to the Dawning Room.

At the hall entrance, I first smelled cigar smoke and then heard a conversation between the millionaire and his guest. I paused to eavesdrop. It is an unfortunate habit among those in my profession.

"I won't deny that I found a disagreeable aroma in his methods and background," insisted the guest with a soothing voice. "But you're certainly at liberty to invest your wealth in whatever purpose you see fit."

With the raspy tone I recognized from the previous day, Mr. Morley replied, "He told me you wouldn't like my will being changed. But the popularity of your organization ensures it will remain perfectly well funded, were I to—"

"Roderick, stop this talk. You're still a young man!"

"Yes, well. I was saying that my schools are neither popular nor likely to *ever* be as well funded as psychical research," he asserted.

"And I *repeat* that such schools *are* a commendable enterprise."

Fearing I might be caught eavesdropping by other guests arriving, I created the sound of nearing footfalls to signal my presence. Upon my entering, the two gentleman rose from the room's leather chairs, extinguishing their cigars. I glanced toward the bay window to discover that the curtain had already been drawn across it. Neither the moonlight above nor the streetlights below would illuminate our shadowy ceremony.

Mr. Morley then introduced me to the other gentleman. I would have had no reason to recognize his *face*, which featured a high brow, two tufts of hair over each ear, and a bristly beard parted in the middle. From the outer ends of his eyes splayed the wise-looking wrinkles of a man nearing sixty years. His *name*, however, was familiar to me.

"Miss Prasilova, I'd like you to meet Dr. William James," said our host. "This young lady will act as our medium this evening, Will."

Boston. A séance. Mr. Morley's social circles. All combined to convince me that this was the very same Professor William James who worked with the American branch of the Society for Psychical Research. Almost certainly, that had been the organization mentioned in their conversation, the one left unfunded by Mr. Morley's will. The professor's open-mindedness regarding the occult had led to lectures on topics such as telepathy and trances at Harvard University, where he was a faculty member specializing in the new discipline of Psychology. Other universities had banished such controversies from the classroom. I had managed to read one or two of Dr. James's published essays, but I fear I gushed over another subject related to him.

After the usual courtesies, I exclaimed, "I very much enjoy your *brudder's* stories! *Deh Turn of deh Screw,* I must tell you, gave me quite a shiver!"

"Who doesn't love a ghost story, and that one is certainly becoming one of Henry's most popular," he laughed. "Have you read his novel *The Bostonians* from a few years back? No? Well, you might find it interesting. It features a lady about your age whose father coerces her to perform as a Spiritualist medium."

"Dat *does* sound interesting! Perhaps your brudder is a skeptic regarding my calling?"

"Much more so than I am, I assure you."

"Well, den, I am happy to hear deh brudder with sense sits with us tonight," I joshed.

After a gracious chuckle, the professor began, "I hope you don't mind that I've invited a friend of mine to join—"

He was interrupted by the arrival of Mrs. Viola Morley, the millionaire's wife. Her satin-and-lace gown cast a pearl sheen, an opalescence crowned with the woman's honey hair and azure eyes. She was of an age when youthful beauty was becoming sculpted slowly into a more detailed and defined handsomeness. Her overall poise was stately. Even her perfume—oil of roses, I guessed—added to her halo of beauty. I was certain that, when Mrs. Morley shared a room with other women, most men would see only her.

After introductions, Mr. Morley said, "With your permission, Dr. James and I will return to a, uhm—a *debate* we were having. I'll let you two women discuss whatever it is women discuss." He then led his friend to a separate corner.

"He often says that," Mrs. Morley explained. "I have yet to fathom what exactly it is that women discuss, however. I was told one more woman will be joining us—perhaps, she'll know. I will say this, though, I *do* like your colors."

She was referring to the costume I adopted when performing a séance. Beside Mrs. Morley's queenly regalia, my garb was that of a festive peasant. A butter-hued blouse with billowing sleeves was contrasted by an indigo vest and skirt. The hems of both darker garments were embroidered with red and yellow floral patterns associated with Eastern Europe. My headscarf, rings, and necklace added a certain flamboyance to the ensemble.

After a period of silence, I inquired, "I heard music playing earlier. You are an admirer, yes?"

"Oh," she sighed, "I certainly do enjoy an evening at the Symphony, but Mr. Morley prefers to keep his entertainments at home. The Gramophone is our sad compromise. If I must sit at home for an evening, I'd rather spend it listening to a *chorus* than a *corpse*. Oh!" Mrs. Morley's eyes widened. She opened her mouth as if to speak—but it remained agape. Next, she grabbed my hand. But still she seemed unable to speak.

"I take no offense," I allowed. "Chorus. Corpse. You are most quick witted."

She found her voice again. "A crude pun—stupid. It was rude of me to say such a—and to a *medium*. Please—I—I confess I've been attempting to avoid this—can you forgive me?"

Before I was able to respond, Mrs. Morley hurriedly sat down in one of the chairs at the table. She seemed unduly ashamed of her comment. I wondered if the stately poise she had shown only moments ago had been girded with nothing stronger than the satin and lace she wore.

This left me by myself. It was then that the final sitter arrived, entering the room unseen by the others. I noticed her height first. She was almost six feet tall. Her auburn hair was very curly and clearly a challenge to arrange. Her eyes were brown, the brows a bit thick and the mouth set seriously. It was a forthright face, but one that revealed almost nothing about the person's age. There was also something untraceable about her apparel—a plain white blouse under a green velvet jacket and matching skirt—that evoked the quality of being slightly disheveled or of wearing clothes that were one size wrong in either direction.

"Hello," I said, offering my hand. "You are here for deh séance, yes? I'm Ludmila Prášilová, deh medium."

"A pleasure to meet you. I—I'm—I'm not very strong with names," she responded.

"Oh, I will not ask you to remember *my* name. But may I please ask for *yours?*"

"Well, yes. That's exactly it, isn't it?" she answered with a giggle.

I pressed my lips together tightly. I then asked, "You cannot remember your *own* name?"

"Oh, that would be ridiculous, wouldn't it? I wonder if you're familiar with a journalist named Nellie Bly? It's the same as that. Nellie. Of course, my surname is different from hers." The woman then smiled politely and blinked twice.

I found myself grappling to find a courteous way of asking if she might happen to remember her surname. With a sense of consternation, I turned slowly to look to the others and found Professor James hurrying our way.

"This is my dear friend—Miss Nellie Hudson," he announced as much to the group as to me. "She's in from New York and takes a deep interest in ghosts as well as spirits. I see you've met our young medium. Come, let me properly introduce you to the others."

Mrs. Morley stood and stepped toward us, resuming her stately attitude as quickly as it had crumbled. "Ghosts *as well as* spirits?" she asked. "Is there a difference?"

Dr. James formally introduced the two women.

"I believe there are," replied Miss Hudson, "in the colloquial meanings of those words, at least. *Ghosts* linger in the physical realm of their own volition. They haunt a place. *Spirits,* on the other hand, visit our realm only when called upon to do so."

"It's a useful distinction, perhaps," stated Mr. Morley, stepping toward the group. "And do you believe in such things?"

Dr. James next introduced the tall woman to the millionaire.

Miss Hudson raised two fingers to her jaw, as if contemplating Mr. Morley's question. "Let me answer this way. I think that ghosts are like cats. They're quite real—but they rarely come when called."

The others chuckled at the comparison, and Mr. Morley began a discussion of how those who've crossed over are working strenuously to prove their continued existence to those left behind. Rather than pay close attention, I glanced at a clock on the mantle to see that we were soon approaching 7:30. I pictured my mother waiting outside in the snow. Though eager to suggest we begin, I then noticed Miss Hudson wander in the direction of the curtained bay window. It was as if she were curious what might be behind it. She took a peek to find that no one was concealed there. She then stepped to the center table, standing now on the side farther away from us.

Miss Hudson then suddenly pointed to the Currier and Ives lithograph depicting the contented family on the plantation. She gasped, "Impossible! Did something in that picture *move*? The boat seems to be *bobbing!*" She thrust her pointing finger forward.

All heads but my own spun to witness the impossibility. The hesitation this woman had betrayed while stating her name had tickled my suspicions, and I turned only enough that I could maintain a sidelong eye on her. In doing so, I discovered that she was deliberately *diverting our attention.* Very swiftly, Miss Hudson removed the single candle standing in its holder on the table, and in a well-planned move, replaced it with another candle she had been harboring under her green jacket. This, then, explained my earlier impression that something was askew with her clothing.

And yet *why* would anyone prefer one candle over another? I suddenly recalled that some mediums use candles prepared with certain ingredients that flash and flicker as the wick burns toward the bottom. The effect was used to suggest the supernatural must surely be present. Yes, I convinced myself, *this* explained the woman's machinations. She was ensuring that I would not be allowed to commit the same trick. I privately snorted at the futility of her actions.

And I decided that she deserved some small punishment for the attempt.

The gentlemen assured Miss Hudson that she had been misled by a flicker in the gaslight—or perhaps the illusion could be attributed to a ripple in the glass over the print.

"Of course, of course," replied the tall woman with only a hint of embarrassment. "I apologize for being so easily fooled." She then turned to me. "Don't let such a silly woman as myself get in your way. Shall we turn down the lights and begin the séance?"

All agreed to the suggestion.

CHAPTER THREE

WHY SHE SWITCHED
THE CANDLES

Mr. Morley shut off the gaslights while Dr. James lit the candle on the table. Clearly, they'd performed these duties on a number of occasions, since I hadn't asked them to do so. Of the six chairs available, I claimed the one that once belonged to Mr. Sanderson, the one that would steer eyes away from the door to the guest room. Dr. James pulled out the chair on my immediate left for Miss Hudson, keeping a hand on the chair beside her to claim as his own.

Mr. Morley stepped to the chair on my immediate right and pulled out the next chair down for his wife. However, Mrs. Morley appeared to be utterly perplexed in her decision of which chair to take: the one beside her own husband—or the one on the end directly opposite to me. In response, what little was left of Mr. Morley's vigor appeared to drain out of him, as a mostly empty bottle still dribbles when turned upside down.

"Viola?" Dr. James offered, holding his hand to the chair across from himself and next to the millionaire.

Only then did Mrs. Morley come forward to sit as guided, though she gazed at the empty chair while doing so. Back in Lily Dale, Mr. Brunton had divulged that Mr. Morley consulted his psychic advisor regarding his marriage. Mrs. Morley's reluctance to sit beside her husband seemed to be a symptom of this trouble. And yet, much as she had upon Miss Hudson's entrance to the room, the beautiful woman instantly shifted from dark distraction to bright attentiveness upon settling into her seat.

"Let us join hands," I requested. I waited until all had done so. "I shall now enter into a trance state. Deh time required for dis is uncertain. At times, I need an entire hour before my spirit guide is able to speak t'rough my voice. Her name is Marianne. Her spirit became attached to me when I was quite young, and we are now as close as sisters. You will listen for her girlish voice, yes? Sadly, Marianne died when she was but twelve years old."

Dr. James sniffled at this point. I wondered if my story had touched his heart the way his brother's fiction could stir readers' emotions.

"If all goes well," I continued, "I am hopeful dat Marianne will be able to locate Mr. Sanderson's spirit. I ask dat you carefully follow the instructions of Marianne, my protector, once I am at deh deepest and most vulnerable level of my trance."

I had to make entering my trance a lengthy process to ensure that my mother could perform all of her small deceptions—arriving late, asking to wait in the parlor, locating the guest room, and putting on the costume—that preceded our grander ones. A stalling method employed by some mediums is to open a séance with hymn-singing. I was never so daring as to mix blarney with blasphemy, however, and it is with shame that I touch upon the histrionics that signaled my entrancement. I breathed heavily with intermittent stops. I swayed in my seat. I stamped my feet and worked my elbows like a fledgling readying for flight. I twitched my head around—to this angle and then that angle, again like a bird—increasing to movements so spasmodic that I inadvertently strained a muscle in my neck. At that point, I returned to the nest, so to speak, and cooed until the pain passed.

Very gradually, I melted into catatonic silence, my head drooping slowly downward. I held this pose for what felt like an interminable time. While holding my position, I heard Dr. James sniffle a few more times. Apparently, my tale of poor Marianne had *not* been the thing that was disturbing him.

I managed to hold my position even when the gentleman's sniffling became joined with clearing his throat.

"Excuse me, Miss Hudson," he rasped, "but I desperately need my handkerchief."

Presumably he dropped her hand and attended to his nose. I produced a soft gurgle, suggesting the broken circle had disturbed my psychic connections. With some embarrassment, I disclose that I always enjoyed inventing a response to these unpredictable moments. Departing from a script, if only on a small scale, grants one the adventure of entering uncharted territory. Perhaps it is the exhilaration of finding freedom. The feeling was short-lived, though. The melodic tinkling of a girl's music box wafted into the room. I was being called back to my obligations, much as little Marianne had been summoned to return to the corporeal plane. I lifted my head.

Replacing the Slavic accent with the pitch and cadences of a child, I said, "Did I hear someone with the sniffles? How te'wible! Oh dear, look—it's wintuh outside. I *do* hope no one has caught a chill!"

The group remained quiet, if not slightly flummoxed.

Finally, Dr. James responded, "Do we have the pleasure of speaking to Marianne?"

"Yes, that's co'wect."

"Are you aware, Marianne, that there's a heavy curtain hanging in front of the window?"

"Oh, yes."

"But you're able to see that—*and* see that it's winter outside?"

Giggling, I said, "Yes, that's also co'wect. I fo'get that you cannot!"

"What a *clever* girl she is," Miss Hudson exclaimed. "*Very* clever."

Something lurking in that comment—was she praising Marianne or the medium?—reminded me of the woman's secretive swapping of the candle. I recalled I had promised her a slap on the wrist.

"Vewy kind of you to say so. Did you know, Miss Hudson, that a spiwit is standing behind you? She says that you call to her in you' dweams. Do you miss you' gwandmamma?"

But for the childish inflection, the ruse was a part of my routine. However, the tall woman's indeterminate age added some risk to the assumption that at least one of her grandmothers would be deceased.

"Hm," Miss Hudson uttered. "Well, I never knew my *mother's* mother."

"Was that gwandmamma fah away?"

"Yes. In Ireland."

"Oh, yes—I see an emerwald radiance suwwounding you."

"Ah," Miss Hudson replied. "Perhaps that's the pork I ate on the train. It tasted a bit past its prime."

Hearing the group snicker, I unshielded my sword. I asked, "But do you miss your *fatheh's* motheh, Miss Hudson?"

"Yuh—yes, I do," she answered, now with a serious tone. "I miss her very much."

"You shouldn't feel sad that this gwandmamma is gone— because she's *not*. She's still with you. She keeps an eye on you fwom the Otheh Side." My sword was in position.

"That's a lovely thought—if not a slightly *unsettling* one."

The group laughed.

"But your gwandmamma died with a secwet. Something that she wants to tell you because it weighs on heh *soul!*"

"Something—she wants to tell—*me?*" replied Miss Hudson, as if uncertain why she had so quickly stolen the spotlight in a séance intended for others. "Well, by all means, do release your burden, Grandmamma."

"She wants me to tell you that she and your gwandpapa neveh eveh ma'wied."

"Neveh eveh ma'wied? I'm afraid I don't understand—"

"They neveh legally *wed*."

I had thrust my sword forward.

All except Miss Hudson responded by either gasping softly or shifting in their seats. The woman herself drew her lips inward, as if to keep them closed between clenched teeth. Her honoring me with the description of "clever girl" now felt justly earned.

"I think it best that we *move on*, Marianne," Dr. James strongly suggested.

"Yes—yes, please, darling girl," added Mr. Morley. "I wonder—I very much hope that you're able to summon the spirit of Silas Sanderson."

"Silas Sande'son?"

"Yes, he crossed over very recently. And—and in this very room! I'm hoping he hasn't journeyed far away. Of course, I know distances aren't measured in the same way on your plane."

"Wait please," I said with Marianne's voice. I dropped my head forward to give the impression that she had left my body in search of the desired spirit. Again, I heard Dr. James sniffle.

"Forgive me," he whispered. "I was fine before we sat down."

"I'd blame my perfume," Mrs. Morley said apologetically, "but my eyes seem to be reacting to something in the room, too. Tomorrow, I'll ask Brunton to have the chimney cleaned."

"Will and I have been in this room since dinner without a problem," Mr. Morley stated. "It isn't a problem with the flue."

At that instant, I realized who the *clever girl* in the room truly was. With my head still hanging down toward my chest, I remembered the candle. The candle that Miss Hudson had made certain would be lit. The candle that had been set aflame by Dr. James and that was burning a bit closer to him and to Mrs. Morley, the two people feeling the affliction.

Miss Hudson hadn't switched the candles to prevent me from dazzling the group with a trick. No, she had a trick of her own. Something in the fumes of that candle triggered an allergic reaction. And I came dangerously close to kicking her under the table for it.

And I realized that my mother was walking into a trap! The fumes of the candle naturally would rise above those of us sitting at the table and then hover above us. This, of course, would be on the same level as my mother's head.

A pulsating panic, such as I had not felt since performing my very *first* séance, drenched over me. It was not the candle alone that terrified me, though. It was something that I had been ignoring—refusing to consider—all along. Much as eavesdropping is one of a medium's finer skills, so is *evading*. Usually, it involves dodging specifics when speaking as a spirit. For instance, I knew that when the spirit of Mr. Sanderson was asked to name his killer, I would proclaim that he was barred from meddling in earthly affairs—but that the killer would be revealed in time. I wonder, though, if Dr. James' Psychology might be able to explain how a person's own *mind* can evade other subjects, even subjects crucially important to that very person's safety.

Picture this: a seventeen-year-old girl is attempting to bamboozle a powerfully influential man with great resources to prosecute should that girl be caught committing *fraud*. Across from that powerful man sits a Harvard professor, whom the seventeen-year-old is also attempting to *fool*. Vanity, I suppose, had coaxed me into believing I was immune to those dangers. However, at the precise moment I realized the candle was designed to induce an allergic reaction, the other terrible dangers that surrounded me in this room also rushed upon my thoughts.

In fact, until that very moment, the idea hadn't dawned upon me that I might be sitting in a room with a *murderer!*

Was Miss Hudson, for instance, hoping to disrupt the séance to prevent even the slightest chance that the murderer's name might be revealed? I remembered her quip about ghosts being as real as cats—but not responding when summoned. Had this been as much a diversion as her farfetched claim to see something moving in the lithograph? Did she have a dark reason to be fretful that, contrary to a cat, Sanderson's spirit might actually *come when called?*

Dr. James had claimed that Miss Hudson was his friend. Was she also the professor's confederate, to use the jargon of swindlers? I could infer from the fraction of conversation overheard before I entered the Dawning Room that Dr. James disliked Mr. Sanderson. It seemed the psychic advisor had convinced Mr. Morley to revise his will, taking funds away from psychical research—Dr. James' cherished subject—in favor of some kind of schools. Was this motive enough for ruthless revenge?

Now, Mrs. Morley had been acting very strangely, vacillating between confidence, even defiance, on one extreme and complete submission on the other. She even admitted that she had wanted to avoid this séance. Were these clues that she was dreading having Sanderson's spirit aim his finger at her with the same prophesy of doom that the Ghost of Christmas Future implies when pointing to Scrooge's headstone?

Could it be, instead, that her wish to be elsewhere came from knowing a terrible secret about her husband? Oddly, the man I least suspected of committing the crime was the very man who *appeared* the most criminal. Was Roderick Morley's bodily deterioration—his pale complexion, his gaunt figure, his sickly voice—less a result of *grief* and more of *guilt*? Was his careful organization of this séance a deeply distorted scheme to confess his sin? Or, perhaps, to beg for forgiveness from the very man he had killed?

After these speculations had been unleashed in my mind, I began to silently plead that little Marianne would *never* return from her search for the murdered psychic. But a heaving convulsion shook my body when, at long last, I again heard the piercing plink-plink-plink of her music box. I had to raise my head. I had to speak.

I had to continue to enact my role.

"I've found the spiwit!" I said in the childish voice. "He's so sad. So te'wibly sad. But he says he wants you to see that he lives still! *Look! He walks among us!*"

At that moment, the outline of Silas Sanderson glided into the room, though a close observer might see that he was smaller—his hands more delicate—than in his physical life. Mrs. Morley must have caught sight of him first, since she spun her head. Her whimper alerted the others, and I saw Dr. James jolt upon recognizing the figure.

"I can smell his boutonniere!" whispered Mr. Morley.

I had to squeeze the man's hand with all of my strength to keep him from rising.

"Of *course*—of course, I know *better* than to approach," he muttered to me. He then turned to the figure. "Silas? Are you able to communicate with us?"

Slowly, the figure put forth its hands and rotated its palms upward.

Marianne explained, "He is not able to let you both see *and* heah him. He tells me this pains him."

Dr. James sniffled before saying, "Ask your questions through the *control*, Roderick. Marianne will convey his answers."

"Of course! Marianne, please ask Mr. Sanderson if he can tell who held the weapon that killed him."

I repeated the question. As Mr. Sanderson swayed his head from side to side, Marianne explained that he was forbidden from sharing this information. My mother continued to move her head, pulling it backward as if looking at the ceiling. I noticed her hands. Her fingers were curling into tight, trembling fists.

Miss Hudson's candle was working as intended.

"Is it *real*, Will?" Mr. Morley asked painfully. "Can this *really* be Silas?"

"I'm not sure. Ask your second question. That will let us know if it's him."

Mr. Morley spun to face the figure. "Silas! I must know about the *schools*! Will they do more good than—"

"*Where are they,*" Dr. James urgently corrected his friend.

"Yes—yes, *where* are they being built?" Mr. Morley asked. "Please ask him *where* the schools are being built, Marianne."

I did so while seeing my mother take a step backward. After a pause, I answered, "He says you awe to have faith that he *is* Sande'son and—and he wants you to have faith that the schools will do much good—*much* good once they awe all built."

Dr. James insisted, "But, Marianne, ask Mr. Sanderson *where* they're being built."

"He says he's sow'y he must go now. He wants to tell you mo'e, though, and he will come back if you—"

I was interrupted by the sound of a throaty inhale followed by an abrasive *hiss!* My mother had finally succumbing to a tremendous and irrepressible need to *sneeze!*

But that was not the greatest catastrophe. Simultaneous with the sneeze—as if slapped cleanly off his spirit skull—the phantom *face* of Silas Sanderson came hurling in our direction! It jumped the dimensional divide with ease and bounced onto our table. It slid, spun, and stopped nearest Mrs. Morley.

It was the mask, of course.

Everyone at the table was instantaneously frozen. After a dramatic pause, my mother fled the room through the door from which she had entered. I should have done the same, I suppose, but bewilderment caused me to simply gaze at the mask. Mrs. Morley was doing so, too, though she managed to whimper once or twice. Dr. James sniffed hard and then grunted harshly. Mr. Morley was the first to reach toward the mask—but his twitching hand was unable to touch it.

At long last, Miss Hudson spoke. "Spirits shouldn't *sneeze*, should they?"

She then let go of my hand and patted it gently.

❦ CHAPTER FOUR ❦

MY *TRUE* NAME

"My *true* name is Lucille Parsell," I told the group without accent or inflection. Although I heard a *ring* of truth in this statement, I still felt compelled to confess, "And that was my mother pretending to be the spirit."

No one had asked me any questions. We were still at the table except for Dr. James, who was lighting the gas. Miss Hudson slid the candle by its holder closer to her and blew out the flame. Mrs. Morley was looking down at her interlaced fingers, her cheeks and mouth suggesting that she was struggling between a smile and a scowl. Devoid of expression, Mr. Morley was still gazing at the mask. He had become courageous enough to fiddle with the edges of it.

"Your own mother?" Miss Hudson inquired gently. "I've seen this arrangement before. Always with the daughter, though, never a son. How long have the two of you been in the Spiritualism racket?"

"Five years."

Mrs. Morley leaned forward and raised her eyebrows. "Five years. So this is how your girlhood was spent? How it was *ended?*"

I nodded, longing to remain silent now. I felt that my words had been false enough that evening.

The tall woman lifted the candle from the holder. "My father was a chandler. He experimented with adding various fragrances to his candles by mixing different plants with the wax. He knew that goldenrod is reputed to cause the hay fever. Instead, he tried ragweed." She replaced her special candle with the original, which she retrieved from inside her green jacket. "The ragweed turned out to be worse—or perhaps should I say *better*—at making people sneeze. I never forgot this and have since improved the formula."

"Gracious!" I exclaimed. "Your *father*. Can you ever forgive me for—for that *horrible* thing I said earlier about your family?"

She laughed. "My father was a brilliant and gentle person. Just the same, you're hardly the first to suggest that he was a *bastard*, my dear."

Again, the group of sitters became motionless. As motionless as the subjects sitting on the porch in Mr. Morley's beloved lithograph.

The tall woman continued to converse, though. "Oh, and you'll be pleased to hear that I also have a *true* name. It's Vera Van Slyke, not Nellie Rivers."

"Nellie *Hudson*," Dr. James amended quietly, almost absent-mindedly, while resuming his place at the table.

"As I said before, I'm not very strong with names," conceded the now-talkative woman. "Hudson. Rivers. A natural mistake for a New Yorker, I guess. A cardinal is a scarlet tanager to the bird-fancier who's forgotten his spectacles. But I'm much more interested in learning about *your* particular story, uhm—"

"Lucille. Lucille Parsell," I repeated, feeling slightly dizzy as much from my dilemma as from trying to keep up with Miss— *Van Slyke*, as I now knew her.

"You see, as my stunt with the candle reveals, I take a special interest in Spiritualists. Warning my readers against these séances is something of a campaign of mine."

"Your *readers*?" asked Mrs. Morley.

"Yes. I work as a journalist back in New York."

The millionaire's wife stood suddenly and spoke quickly. "Perhaps we'd be more comfortable in our parlor. I could have Brunton serve us hot drinks, and we could all calm down before deciding what our next step ought to be. How does that sound, Miss Parsell?"

"I feel as if I—it is a very generous offer. I will agree with—with whatever you feel is appropriate."

"Excellent. Are we all agreed, then?" invited our hostess.

I saw Miss Van Slyke stand, too, before I attempted to do so myself.

"How *dare* you?" Mr. Morley shouted abruptly, slapping his palm against the table top. He grabbed and glared at the mask.

I shook from his intensity and tumbled back into my seat. I hadn't thought him capable of such volume. My tears starting to well, I searched for the proper words.

"I—you must understand," I pleaded. "I was prepared to—to *quit* séances! *Forever!* Until your butler told how much you were willing to pay, I was on the verge of refusing—"

"Not *you!*" the millionaire scolded. He spun to Dr. James. "You brought a *reporter* into my house? Undermining my trust in Silas is one thing—but blatantly defying my wish to keep this séance private? Oh, I could have tolerated finding out I've been duped by a charlatan. It's hardly the first time I was misled by a pretty *face.*"

Mr. Morley flung the mask in the direction of his wife. She raised her arms to protect herself. The mask fell to the floor, missing its mark. Nonetheless, Mrs. Morley stepped backward as her countenance resumed the attitude of helplessness that washed over her with unsettling regularity.

"How *dare* you, Will?" repeated the devastated man.

As if not knowing what else to do, Dr. James yanked on the cuffs of his suitcoat. He wet his lips. At last, he said, "Why don't—uhm, yes. Why don't you women go ahead down to the parlor? I'll, uh—I will need time to explain why I invited my friend here to debunk this—*well, yes.* It's best that you women go along now."

I managed to lift myself from the chair. As we left the Dawning Room, I felt Miss Van Slyke place a guiding hand on my elbow. The strength I derived from its gentle pressure was probably the only reason why I neither wept nor fled—nor fainted into merciful oblivion.

•

As I say, I hadn't fainted. Yet I do not remember descending the stairs to the parlor. I recall nothing until Mr. Brunton handed me a cup of tea there. The cup was extraordinarily delicate, porcelain as fragile as a wafer. I gingerly put it and the saucer down on the table beside me, imagining that I would certainly break it. I was able to do so with no cracks, though.

It occurred to me that my mother probably had been served tea in the same parlor—possibly, the same chair—about an hour earlier. Where had she gone? In her flight, had she managed to snatch her dress, her coat, or the portmanteau that had hidden the suit and mask? Had she abandoned any of those items—or *all* of them—in the guest room? And was she now skittering around Boston wearing nothing other than the gray suit of a gentleman? It was a picture as distressing as it was ridiculous.

"Miss Parsell? Did you hear me?"

It was Miss Van Slyke.

"I'm very sorry. I'm afraid that the situation—" I stopped there.

After a moment, she responded, "I see. I was explaining that I'm in the midst of a writing project. I have a decade of experience at exposing mediums, and certainly that's enough to fill the pages of a book. I wonder if you might meet with me sometime—after a few days pass, of course—to answer some questions about the tricks to your trade."

"That's right," I murmured. "You mentioned that you're a journalist. Like Nelly Bly."

She chuckled. "Nelly's a dear colleague. I don't think she'd mind my having borrowed her name earlier. After all, it's actually no more than her *pen* name."

"What a wonderful thing," Mrs. Morley interposed. "To be a woman who makes her own way in the world." There was a hint of envy in her voice.

Only then did I become aware that our hostess was sitting across from us on a crimson-cushioned divan, one with enough upholstered curves and wooden curls that one might call it feminine. On one side of her, a fire blazed under a massive, mahogany mantelpiece that displayed figurines carved of jade. On the other side, the ornate horn of a Gramophone splayed like an enormous, bronze blossom. I imagined that Mrs. Morley spent many hours lounging in that spot—looking beautiful.

"Well," Miss Van Slyke resumed, "no need to answer right now. I simply wondered, since you had said that you were on the verge of quitting séances earlier."

I sat up. "Oh, yes! I am *more* than eager to find a new livelihood. I would be pleased to answer any questions you might have, Miss Van Slyke. *Very* pleased. Of course, that depends on what the gentlemen upstairs decide is my future. If that future is what I fear, you'd be very welcome to visit me in prison."

Mrs. Morley rose from her divan and rushed toward me. She knelt on one knee and took my hand. "You mustn't worry about that, young lady. Roderick's not going to prosecute. He's had more than his fill of public scandal and the police. Rest assured, he's far angrier with Dr. James than with you. My husband feels both pain and compassion very deeply—in regard to *some* people. However, women such as you are not among those who evoke his passions. Indeed, I barely qualify for that honor myself."

"Who, then, *are* the people who stir his deeper feelings?" asked the reporter, apparently unaware that such a question might be more befitting a trusted friend.

With a heavy sigh, the elegant woman rose. Straightening her dress while wandering back to her divan, she explained, "Those schools that he asked about during the séance. They're being built throughout the South. They're intended to educate the colored children there."

Miss Van Slyke cocked her head. "Well, that's certainly noble of him. Now, what's the name of the black gentleman from

Alabama who's organizing the movement to educate his people?"

"Booker T. Washington, isn't it?" Mrs. Morley replied.

"That's the man. Is your husband part of that effort?"

"To tell you the truth, I'm not certain about that. He's a very private man, my husband. Oh, and I wouldn't say that his motivation is exactly *noble.*"

Without discretion, Miss Van Slyke asked, "If not noble, then — *what?*"

Mrs. Morley's eyes drifted away from us. "I guess *guilt-ridden* would be the best way to explain it. His wealth and leisure were earned by 'the sweat and blood of slaves,' as he phrases it. But, you see, he left Virginia and was sent to be schooled here in Boston once he came of age."

"Ah ha!" Miss Van Slyke clapped her hand together. "A Southern boy sent to be educated in the same spot where abolition once reigned supreme! That's a bit like rearing a wolf cub among very righteous sheep!"

Mrs. Morley chuckled. With that same glimmer of envy as before, she commented, "I must say I've never heard *that* expression before."

"Oh, they seem to tumble out of me," replied Miss Van Slyke, shrugging her shoulders and joining her hostess's laughter.

I could not laugh with them. I could barely pay attention to their conversation. As I stared into the fire, images of my mother pervaded my thoughts.

With difficulty, I sat forward and raised a finger. "I beg your pardon," I uttered, "but it's possible my mother left a case — a portmanteau — in that guest room beside the Dawning Room. I'll understand if you'd prefer I remain here until the gentlemen join us, but would it be possible to have that checked? You see, my mother's dress and coat might be with that case."

The two other women turned to one another, very likely realizing that this meant my mother might be wandering around while still in male attire. Again, they laughed.

"Of course, young lady. I'll call Brunton to run up and take a look."

"I hate to bother him," I said quickly. I had caused enough pain. "He mentioned earlier that the stairs take their toll on his legs in the evenings. Is there someone else?"

"What do you say, Miss Van Slyke—can we trust our pretty, young medium to not hop on the next train out to the territories?"

"She strikes me as trustworthy. And, if I'm mistaken, I'll keep an eye on the front door, if you keep the *back* one under close scrutiny!"

The two newfound friends laughed again. Mindful of the delicate teacup beside me, I cautiously pushed myself up from my seat. I managed to smile and to give them each a curtsy.

They replied with sympathetic snickers.

•

Ascending those stairs weighed on me in a manner that I'm certain Mr. Brunton never suffered. During that simple journey up to the guest room and back down to the parlor, I would be shaken by *two* frights. The first almost sent me tumbling down the first flight of stairs.

Of course, I had no idea when Mr. Morley and Dr. James might finish their talk and leave the Dawning Room. This being the case, as I was arriving at the second-floor landing, I jolted upon seeing a pair of men's gray trouser cuffs skirt by my eyes. However, those legs were not headed my way, and so I strained to quickly climb the remainder of those stairs. I wanted to see if this might be my disguised mother.

"Matka?" I hissed as I finished the climb. *"Matka!"*

I was certain I had been loud enough to catch my mother's attention, if it had been her. Instead, I glimpsed the door of a nearby room quietly shut. For all I knew, it might have been Mr. Brunton or, perhaps, even the coachman who had driven me here. What if it had been Mr. Morley, though? The mere chance of having the latter gentleman open that door stirred too much humiliation for me to attempt knocking upon it.

It occurred to me that my first order of business was to confirm whether or not my mother's dress had been left behind in the guest room. I scurried to the next set of stairs and climbed again.

Creeping along the third-floor hallway, I heard the two gentleman we had left in the Dawning Room. Though their words were muffled, Mr. Morley's whispery voice was still agitated, and Dr. James' rich one was still attempting to calm and console him. I hurried along to the adjacent room and opened the door.

Here was my second fright. It was much more a matter of lingering uneasiness than of startling surprise, however.

Despite the dim light that filtered in from the hallway, I easily located my mother's case on a canopy bed. The portmanteau was gaping open—but its mouth was empty. It had nothing to tell me. Furthermore, I could spot *neither* a man's suit *nor* a woman's dress in the vicinity of the portmanteau. I found no coat, either. Not on the bed. Not on the floor. Not on the dressing table. I found some comfort in the notion that my mother might have retained enough presence of mind to have grabbed her dress and coat during her escape. That comfort vanished, though, as soon as I pictured her changing back into female clothes in some deep shadow on the snowy streets of Beacon Hill.

I then spotted a window, a twin to the bay window in the Dawning Room. Perhaps it was the promise of a few more rays of light that drew me further into the room to make a final survey.

In this way, I found my mother's dress. It was in a heap on the floor on the far side of the bed. It was reassuring that she appeared to have her coat, but as I lifted the dress, I discovered that it had been torn. Two rips ran from above the waistline to about halfway down the skirt—gaping slashes—making the dress unwearable without repair. In her flurry, had my mother ripped the dress and thrown it aside to make her escape? What could have caused such damage?

My perplexity was interrupted by a passionate outburst from the next room. I quickly stuffed the dress into the portmanteau. Avoiding the noise of snapping the latches, I lifted the case and kept it closed under my arm.

I then scampered to the stairs and started down them. Knowing now that my mother was, in fact, most likely dressed in a man's suit—and that Mr. Morley remained in the Dawning Room—I found the courage to gently tap on that second-story door I had seen close earlier.

"Matka?" I inquired with a cautious volume.

There was no answer. No sounds came from within the room, though I had seen someone enter it only a minute or two earlier. Rather than raise suspicions by remaining absent too long, I returned to the parlor.

•

Mrs. Morley and Miss Van Slyke expressed curbed amusement upon learning that, almost certainly, my mother was returning to our hotel in a man's suit under her coat.

"Let's consider it *suitable* retribution for her hoax," Miss Van Slyke offered with a smirk. "And if that's too harsh, remember that the boutonniere adds a touch of refinement."

Only then was I able to succumb and join in with their chuckling. I remembered having deemed myself as being "the sister with sense" in my relationship with my mother. But, given the costumes that I too had worn that evening—costumes designed of both cloth *and* voice—I relinquished any claim to that title.

This lesson in humility was followed quickly by Dr. James wandering pensively into the parlor. We three women quieted. Mrs. Morley returned to her divan, I to the chair where I had left my cup of tea. Miss Van Slyke stepped toward her friend.

"And how did it go?" she asked him.

Dr. James took her hand. "Oh, you did wonderfully, Vera. I knew I could count on you, and I apologize for asking you to misrepresent yourself."

"By now, I'm accustomed to attending séances under a false guise," Miss Van Slyke assured him. "I meant, though, how did your conversation with Mr. Morley go?"

"Ah. Yes. Well. He's asked for some solitude for the time being. He said he'll join us once he's had time to think. I fear, however, that my prescription was grievously mistaken." The doctor turned to Mrs. Morley. "I had hoped to cure Roderick's depressed state by dousing it with the cold water of Truth. I knew it would be hard on him, but that was the point—to spur him to struggle rather than surrender. And yet *now* I fear I've only made matters worse—permanently worse."

"But he's always suffered from melancholia," Mrs. Morley offered. "Or what's the medical name for it these days?"

"Neurasthenia." Dr. James nodded and then tilted his head. "This is something new. Beyond the reach of medicine. This is something in the realm of *religion*, and I'm not sure a scientist such as myself is qualified to address it. Heavens, how I wish science would expand its sights to encompass the full range of human—"

A shattering blast erupted! It had sounded through the ceiling and echoed in the stairway. I saw Miss Van Slyke quake in response and then heard the saucer and teacup beside me rattling. Next, Mrs. Morley appeared to, not lift herself from her divan, but to float up from it languorously. She and Miss Van Slyke then took unnaturally slow steps in the direction of the staircase. In tandem, they stopped. And I noticed Dr. James frozen entirely, his eyes squeezed tightly together. Somehow, the scene before me had melted from actors on a stage to figures on a canvas.

Eventually, loud footsteps came pounding down the stairs, seeming to correct the sluggishness of motion that had suffused the room. A man I hadn't seen before stumbled toward us, headlong and breathless. I noticed that he was wearing *a gray suit!* My first thought was that this must be the gentleman whose trouser cuffs I had caught sight of as I was climbing to the second-floor landing.

Later that night, I learned from the police that he was Mr. Morley's valet. About the time I had witnessed the gray trouser cuffs, the valet had been in that hallway to set out his employer's sleepwear. He claimed he hadn't heard my calling to my mother and he hadn't heard a later tapping on the door of what turned out to be Mr. Morley's bedroom.

At *this* moment, though—the moment he came scrambling into the parlor—I learned that the valet had bolted down those stairs to tell us what would become the next day's shocking headlines:

MILLIONAIRE TAKES OWN LIFE
TWO DAYS BEFORE CHRISTMAS!

~ ACT TWO ~

THE MURDERER
(October, 1903)

❧ CHAPTER FIVE ❧

AN UNLIKELY FLOWER

On occasion, against all unlikelihood, the flower of friendship takes root and thrives.

Shortly after the tragedy at the Morley Mansion, I was reminded of Vera Van Slyke's belief that, while *spirits* ignore the summons of psychic mediums, *ghosts* truly do haunt the living. Upon my arrival to be interviewed for her book debunking Spiritualism, she astonished me by asking if I'd join her on a ghost hunt not far from Boston. I agreed, and during that investigation, affection between us budded.

Our friendship fully blossomed a year later, when Vera's constant quest to investigate and report the news led her to settle in Chicago, the city I considered home. In the years when Ida Tarbell exposed the corrupt management of Standard Oil for the pages of *McClure's Magazine* and Upton Sinclair researched the meatpacking industry's cruel treatment of immigrant labor for his novel *The Jungle*, Vera was also using the power of the press to spark social reform. On one end of the spectrum, she decried the backwash of problems that came from having reversed the direction of the Chicago River. On the other, she heartily supported the determined boys of Garfield School who organized a strike for more time during recess. Within a year of her move, her book was published with the fitting title *Spirits Shouldn't Sneeze: A Decade of Defrauding Mediums*.

In the meanwhile, I had found only modest success at securing a paying alternative to flimflamming the grief-stricken. Learning of this, Vera offered me a position as her assistant. She was, after all, very successful as a journalist—one of the few professions in which a Nelly Bly or an Ida Tarbel could win respect and renown. *Women* reporters were a rare novelty, however, and I sometimes wondered how Vera managed to afford a personal secretary. To be sure, the rooms she had taken at the Hotel Manitou—which served as both her residence *and* office—were hardly the elegant accommodations found on Lake Shore Drive. Still, I couldn't help but think that Vera's finances were bolstered by a substantial inheritance. She never spoke of it, though, and so I never raised the issue with her.

There is another matter that I am wary to raise for fear of my reader's reaction. I refer to the ghost hunts that my friend and employer managed to conduct with some frequency. I am not embarrassed to admit that Vera Van Slyke pursued specters in dilapidated houses and pristine churches, rural bridges and metropolitan theatres, noisy schoolhouses and silent graveyards. Plenty of others have similarly gone in search of phantoms.

Rather than hesitate to say that *ghosts were hunted,* my reservations grow from declaring that *ghosts were beheld!* Yes, Vera Van Slyke very often *found* the ghosts she hunted! I know this because, ever since the investigation she had invited me to in Boston—the one that germinated our friendship—I have witnessed them firsthand. No doubt, if that first experience and the those that followed had been more terrifying—more nightmarish—I would have struggled far more to accept the reality of ghosts. I might have attributed my experiences to delusions arising from the darkest depths of my mind. However, while some hauntings certainly *are* frightening, more often they pose an intellectual mystery. They become a puzzle to challenge the mind rather than an aberration to freeze the blood. Suffice it to say, since becoming Vera's assistant, I now stand with the believers in regard to the ghost question, the same topic one sees debated in popular magazines and even in academic circles.

Adding to the ghostly puzzle, those determined to return from the Other Side manifest and communicate in ways that are widely diverse—yet are often severely limited. For example, a ghost might groan while being incapable of conveying what causes the groan or what would relieve it. The process is often terribly frustrating for both the ghost attempting to, say, resolve unfinished business as well as for the courageous few who seek to understand and assist them.

In 1902, Vera's supernatural investigations came to include far-ranging travel when she ran an advertisement announcing her offer of "Help for the Haunted" in newspapers throughout the nation. At times, we were deluged by replies to the advertisement, so many that we were unable to investigate them all. Vera did her best to send her advice by letter at least.

The following year, in October, a man named Herman W. Childers solicited Vera's help, for he found himself among the haunted. At first, the question of whether Mr. Childers contacted Vera because of her advertisement—or because he knew that she had played a part in the suicide of Roderick Morley—remained a matter of debate.

You see, as Fate would have it, Mr. Childers' haunted residence had formerly served as the Morley Mansion.

•

I barely glanced at the envelope before opening it at my small desk in the Hotel Manitou. I was well into the story told by the letter inside before being stunned by its connection to my earlier life. We saved this letter, and so I am able to copy it here exactly as it had appeared that day with its sprinkling of misspellings, some corrected and others missed by the man who wrote it.

—

Sunday, Oct. 4, 1903

Dear V. Van Slyke:

I wonder if, in your encounters with ghosts, you have ever dealt with one motivated less to frighten and more to irritate those ~~who's~~ whose house it has invaded? That is my situation, and I am requesting your aid in banishing this specter at your earliest convenience.

I have counted three distinct performances by the ghost. I have learned that you probably refer to these as <u>manifestations</u>. I will describe them in order of increasing irritation. The first involves the removal of common items, such as a pen or a handkerchief, from one location to a spot where it is highly doubtful that it would have been left abcentmindedly. I view this as the ghost not wanting to cause harm but to simply make its presence known.

The second manifestation, however, reveals a more destructive side of the ghost. I have discovered shirts slashed, bed linen ripped, even draperies sliced in such a way as to suggest the entity is subject to fits of rage. Neither my staff nor myself have ever witnessed the destruction as it occurred—only the results of it afterward. Does this suggest we have a vengeful ghost, I wonder?

I raise the question because of the third way we know that something supernatural visits us. A sudden blast of what sounds like gunshot is heard through the house at ~~unpredictible~~ unpredictable times, be it daytime or night. Of the three manifestations, this is the most jarring, and it makes keeping a maid in the house difficult. However, it is also the most revealing in that it points to two events, both very tragic, witch occurred in the residense a few years ago.

Perhaps you recall that, some time back, a well-known man named Roderick Morley committed suicide. He had inherited great wealth from his father's tobacco fields, but the loss of a close friend, a victim of murder, took its toll and led him to commit that terrible deed. Both of these murders—the friend's and the self-murder of Morley—involved gunfire and both occurred in the house I now occupy. Though I am not able to connect these deaths to the first two manifestations, the sound of gunshot seems to hold conciderable relevance to them.

Please inform me of your opinions on this haunting and your willingness to investigate it. I will agree to any ~~reasonible~~ reasonable terms.

Sinserely yours,
Herman W. Childers

—

58

On finishing the letter, I quickly scanned the envelope, perhaps on the foolish assumption that, along with his spelling errors, Mr. Childers had made some mistake about his own house's history. No, the sender's address was the very same as the one I had been given four years earlier for my preliminary meeting with Mr. Morley. And the very same address where I had held my final séance. And, yes, Vera was being asked to investigate the very place that *I* had left haunted.

After deciding against simply tossing the letter into the flames, I steeled my nerves, stumbled twice on my way to Vera's desk, and found the words to summarize the case being offered.

"If memory serves," Vera said as she took the letter from my trembling hand, "*you* were not responsible for the suicide. *I* was! Didn't that unfortunate fellow say that he was accustomed to dealing with phony mediums—but that it was my friend having smuggled in a reporter that so upset him? It's true that I cannot call forth the name of, say, the man's pretty wife, but I *do* remember the key events of that evening." She leaned back in her chair and looked at me with her head at a tilt.

Vera held her hand out to the chair facing her desk. Instead of sitting in my usual spot, though, I remained standing. Silently, I ran my fingers along the edge of her desktop, as if checking for splinters.

Eventually, I replied, "That's kind of you to say, and I know it's probably not very logical—but it's not how I *feel* about the situation. I thought that the shadow of Mr. Morley's suicide was my burden—my penance for those years of defrauding people. But now *this?*"

Vera rose. She stepped from behind her desk to take my hand away from the cold sharpness of the desktop and to put it into the warm softness of her own hand.

"Here's what I propose. As I often say: lunch before ghosts! Perhaps today we'll have an *early* lunch, during which we can decide if this particular ghost is worth our effort. Now, let's get our coats. The wind off the lake is growing chilly!"

On the cab ride to The Foiled Gelding, our favorite public house, Vera carefully studied the letter. At one point, she put the letter in her lap and placed two fingers against her jaw.

"Like almost everyone," she commented, "Mr. Chilton—"

"Childers," I corrected.

"—makes the same handful of writing errors over and again. He's improving on words that end with *able*, but he confuses *s* with soft *c*. The schoolmarm's advice to sound out a word isn't always beneficial."

Still lamenting the prospect of returning to the scene of my greatest humiliation and horror, I remained quiet. I did manage to point to a specific line of the letter, however.

"Ah ha!" Vera nodded—but then shrugged. "He spells *which* as *witch*. Simple homonym confusion. It's the *there, their, and they're* dilemma that befuddles so many. But the wrinkles in a bridegroom's suit wouldn't be a problem if it weren't for the wedding."

At times, Vera's colorful expressions were more enigmatic than enlightening. I communicated this with a throaty sigh.

"I mean that his spelling problems are not of concern. As I say, they're quite common. However, isn't it a touch odd that someone with, let us say, a *commoner's* education has taken ownership of a *millionaire's* mansion? Certainly, some members of the upper class graduated at the bottom of their class. But they can afford to hide the fact. Mr. Vanderbilt grew up with almost *no* education, but when he endowed that university, I wager he had a staff member or two who could proofread his correspondences."

Vera refolded the letter, slipped it into the envelope, and placed them into her handbag. She then looked up at me, presumably for my comments.

I abstained.

She continued, "One answer is that the notoriety of the murder and a suicide sent the mansion's sale price plummeting. In addition to that, a mere rumor that a house is haunted can make it terribly difficult to sell. This is all a minor mystery, I suppose, but we have so little to ponder at this point."

I knew that Vera was chatting about trivial puzzles in order to lure me out of my dark mood. Indeed, she was beginning to accomplish her goal.

"But isn't the *major* mystery," I said, "the three distinct manifestations of the ghost?"

She pursed her lips. "Ghost or *ghosts*. Remember, there were *two* deaths in the mansion. We were present during the death of—uhm—you know—"

"Roderick Morley."

"But that resulted from the earlier death of the fellow whose spirit he wanted to contact. The fellow whose spirit suffered from what a physician might term *a dislocated face*."

After stifling a chuckle, I clarified, "Silas Sanderson. Are you suggesting that we should look for the ghosts of *both* men?"

"Merely that we should keep it in mind. They seemed to've been very fond of one another and, so, were perhaps drawn together on the Other Side."

"Mr. Morley was certainly fond of Mr. Sanderson. So much so that he agreed to change his will. But was the psychic advisor as fond on his client?"

Vera scratched her neck. "Very astute."

Once we had arrived at The Foiled Gelding, I recounted what I had overheard about the will before the séance. I also noted how, after my being exposed, I discovered my mother's ripped dress. I then allowed Vera to digest the clues' importance as I nibbled a bit of my pot roast stew.

"That ripped dress fits the second manifestation that Mr. Childers describes," said Vera while chewing the first bite of her salmon. "This suggests Sanderson's ghost is the one who tears cloth. After all, Morley was still among the living while you went to that room, correct?"

"Yes."

"Our first significant piece of evidence in the case. But now

I must ask you the vital question, my dear. Are we to *accept* this case? And travel back to Boston? Back to that house?"

It was one of those moments when one's words charge ahead of one's thoughts. "These manifestations are very likely an attempt to communicate something about the tragedy that we stumbled into—or brought about ourselves. If we were *not* to accept the case, I fear I would become as restless as its ghost. Or ghosts."

I took a sip of water.

I lifted my napkin to dry my lips.

At long last, I said, "We *must* take the case, Vera."

•

That evening, I had returned home to Chicago's Pilsen neighborhood. My mother was finishing dinner, and I set the table as I savored wafts of meaty scents from the kitchen. Across the rooms, I explained to her why I would be returning to Boston for an undetermined time. Oddly, my mother did not scoff at my returning to the house where I had found the motivation—it can hardly be called *courage*—to never again perform a séance.

Instead, she set her sight on a different target.

"Vera Van *Slyke!*" she fired from the kitchen. She continued her assault in Czech. "She convinces you to believe in ghosts! She takes you on crazy pursuits! She makes you stay awake all night in abandoned houses, where there might be robbers or *worse!* She—"

I halted her there. "She pays me so that you and I can afford to live in comfort! She pays me so that you and I can eat!" I spoke in English. It had long been our custom when arguing, perhaps only to escalate our disharmony.

"I take in money! My Sunday sittings take in money." Her anger was tinged with agony now.

"Oh, those poor widows you charge to chat with their husbands barely cover the cost of the tea you serve them."

"Who else do I have for conversation? *You* go off to serve Vera Van Slyke all day—and then she drags you along on these trips so I have no one to talk to for most of a week!"

"Matka! We live across from Sýkora Bakery! Next to them is Novák's Butcher Shop! Most of your neighbors are Czech! Get out and meet them! Sokol Hall has been accepting women for years now. And the Church has for *centuries!*" Hearing myself speak snidely about the Church, I suddenly softened my tone. "Why don't you start attending St. Procopius with me?"

Her lips pursed, she brought in the roasted duck with dumplings and cabbage. Her already rosy cheeks were made even more flushed by heat of the oven—and of her temper. Only after sitting down did she answer my question. She used English to do so. "I heve to make ready for my Sunday sittings. I heve spent too much time in deh dark. I have no place at Church services."

We were not a family for discussing the deeper subjects, such as religion. My father, for example, had been a lax Catholic, visiting the Church only for the occasional baptism, wedding, or funeral. I was much the same, but renouncing my career as a swindler had nudged me to brave the weekly confessional. I found its comforts limited.

Perhaps, like my mother, I felt my soul was too sullied to ever be entirely forgiven. Perhaps, like her, I had spent too much time "in deh dark."

We ate without speaking. I had finished so little at lunch, I fear that I pounced upon my meal like a tiger.

At one point, my mother put down her knife and fork. Returning to Czech, she said, "Sometimes, I wonder if you want to replace me with Vera Van Slyke. Maybe you want Vera Van Slyke to be your mother now."

I smirked. Using the same language, I replied, "She is not *old* enough to be my mother. Or, to be correct, *barely* old enough."

Again, we ate in silence for several minutes. I listened to the wind hiss against the windows, as if it were vexed by the tight seals there.

My mother then said, "I am thinking that I should return to

Europe. Perhaps to Prague. I could earn enough money to support myself there. I cannot do so in this small enclave."

"You have mentioned this previously. You have been telling me about this plan for a few months. As I have said before, you might look for a more honest job than performing séances here. The bakery is always hiring."

She shook her head and put her hand to her chest. "I am too old for that." She looked up at me. "And you are now twenty-one years old. Mature enough to take care of yourself. Room and board are easy to find."

"As you have said. And, again, I agree. But is there a rush?"

After a pause, my matka looked down again. She said something she hadn't ever said before. "I want to be buried in my homeland."

I shivered. A draft of October air must have found a chink in the windows. As Vera had mentioned, the wind across Lake Michigan had become chilling. At least, that was my feeling.

All I could think to say was: "And you *should* be buried there. But that won't be for many, many years. Perhaps I could come visit you in Bohemia. I have such dim memories."

I saw that her eyes were now fixed on her fork. She was rubbing her thumb repeatedly against its handle, as if laboring to clean away a blotch there.

"I will probably leave while you are in Boston. Would it not be easier that way? I will probably leave while you are gone."

I rose to clear my plate. On my way to the kitchen, I gave my mother a kiss on her cheek, a gesture less of farewell and more of forbearance. You see, I didn't put much stock into these statements she made. My mother had announced her plan to return to Europe and assume the role of the psychic medium there so many times that these proclamations sounded very much like idle threats. At the time, I assumed that—when I returned from Boston—she would be waiting for me, cooking another delicious meal.

I now know I had been wrong. I never saw my mother again.

After I came back from Boston, instead of a meal, I found a letter from her explaining that she had booked passage on a train to New York and a steamer bound for Southampton. Once arrived, she would find another ship to Bremen. Back on land, she planned to work her way toward Prague.

Not until the following summer was I to learn that she had lived on the Continent for only a few months.

She lies buried in her homeland.

ᥫ CHAPTER SIX ᥫ

THE CLIENT AND THE COP

The Monday we strolled along Beacon Street was a fine example of a New England autumn, a cool breeze swaying with warm sunshine. The leaves in Boston Common were gold and orange and burgundy. The Frog Pond there reflected the cloudless sky, and I imagined the ducks were calling me over, eager to chat about the weather.

However, we turned away from the Common for the maze of streets found in Beacon Hill.

On the long train trip from Chicago, I had exhausted myself with worry over how I might react upon seeing the Morley Mansion again. I had chosen a new collection of tales, Mrs. Wilkens' *The Wind in the Rose Bush,* for the journey, and I must have read and reread its first paragraph two dozen times before surrendering. Instead, I gazed through the window and repeatedly stopped myself from gnawing my fingernails.

My anxiety was made still worse when, in Cleveland, Vera informed me that we would be *residing in the mansion* for the duration of our visit.

"Other than one maid-of-all-work and a fellow who acts as both chauffer and groom, our client lives alone," she had explained. "There are several unused bedrooms available, and don't you agree that it makes sense for us to investigate the haunting by being at the site as much as possible? As long as we're *both* there, I assume propriety will be observed."

I had agreed while privately wishing for some kind of refuge if my memories became overwhelming. Nonetheless, actually coming to the building proved somewhat less daunting than I had anticipated. Was the crisp air acting as a tonic? Was it the passage of years and the growth from a seventeen-year-old to a woman of twenty-one?

Vera paused on the steps. "It occurs to me that you might have some reservations about revisiting this house. You had quite an unsettling evening here long ago. Will you be quite all right?"

Instead of asking why she had taken so long to ask, I simply shrugged. Moving the valise I had been carrying to my other hand, I quietly conceded, "As you say, it was *long ago.*"

As quickly as she had halted, Vera proceeded up the rest of the stairs and pressed the doorbell. There were, after all, ghosts awaiting us!

The door was answered by a well-rounded woman with dark hair and a long, single furrow across her brow. She appeared to be in her late-twenties, and I attributed the wrinkle to experience rather than to age. The woman smiled, her dark eyes sparkling in the sun. However, she did not speak.

Vera assumed command. "Good morning, madam. My name is Vera Van Slyke, and this is my assistant, Lucille Parsell. We're here to see what can be done concerning the spectral annoyances. I believe we're expected."

The crease in the woman's forehead vanished. "S'funny," she said. "He told me to expect two ghost hunters, but I pictured you'd be gentlemen! S'a pleasure to see you both. Please, do come in!"

I confess to feeling some jitters once I stepped in and found a strange discord between what I recognized and what had been added. The front hall with its dark wainscoting seemed somehow narrower—the chandelier somehow lower and heavier—than I remembered them. Formerly, Brunton had deposited all outerwear in some discreet closet, but now there was a conveniently placed coatrack and umbrella stand. The central stairway and its ornate banister were largely the same, of course, but the portraits had been removed.

The maid interrupted my survey of the house by gesturing

to take my coat and valise. She chuckled. "I'm grateful you've come. The agency let me know that previous maids had run off from the noises and whatnot. They said I would be a better fit because of my steel. S'all very flattering, to be sure, but still isn't it a strange thing to see cloth has been torn when there was nothing to tear it and to hear a gun get shot when there's no gun at all and to find—"

"Sophie? Won't you please direct my guests into the parlor?" The nasally voice had come from further within the house.

The single wrinkle resurfaced in the woman's brow, but it was matched with a tight-lipped grin. "Come right in, please. Mr. Childers likes to make an impression."

As we entered the front parlor, I again felt the dissonance of old mixed with new. The jade figurines were missing from the mantelpiece. Mrs. Morley's crimson divan remained, though, and the Gramophone beside it might well have been hers. I could not remember if the chairs and tables were the same, but I knew that, if so, they had been rearranged. It seems that when Mr. Childers acquired the house, some of the furnishings were included.

Perhaps the most out-of-place feature of the room was Mr. Childers himself. He was a fairly short man with hair of a reddish-blond color, a trace of which was going white and some of which had gone missing. He seemed to be in his forties, but there was a boyish quality that came from the freckles sprinkled across his nose and from his front teeth, which were large and uneven. I suspected that, were his face completely relaxed, those teeth would protrude into view.

More than anything, his clothing suggested he was decidedly not a member of the American aristocracy. His tie was off to one side, as if it had grown bored with standing guard at the Adam's apple and opted to slouch against a clavicle. That tie's silver-dots-on-black pattern might have complimented the pin-striped blue trousers if not interrupted by a clashing chestnut-brown morning coat. A mustardy kerchief in the breast pocket completed the hodgepodge palette. Though the separate pieces appeared expensive, the whole did not suggest the brash fashion of a dandy. No, this was a man without a valet to advise him on how to combine such costly pieces. If his Beacon Hill neighbors did not deem him eccentric, they probably dismissed him as "nouveau riche" — a vulgar social climber. That is, if they paid him any notice at all.

For me, the incongruity had a certain appeal. If Herman Childers was wont to make an impression, it was one comparable to a pigeon in a pen for peacocks. This made another odd bird — one hatched in Prague, fledged in Chicago, and currently roosting with a ghost hunter in Boston — feel like one of the same breed.

Our client approached Vera and me with a welcoming smile and shook our hands warmly as we introduced ourselves. He offered to have his maid-of-all-work prepare some refreshment, but we declined. He then invited us to sit.

"I hope your trip was a pleasant one," began Mr. Childers once we were settled. Along with its nasal tone, his voice was fairly high, reinforcing the impression of youthfulness.

"Uneventful," Vera stated flatly. She was never one for niceties.

I attempted to soften the mood by interjecting, "I thought the meals were especially well prepared."

Vera raised an eyebrow. "Were they?"

"I thought so."

"I should've paid more attention," she lamented. "You see, Mr. Chitters—"

"Childers," I corrected. It had become habit.

"Forgive me. You see, sir, my mind was preoccupied with what your ghost might be trying to communicate with the three manifestations you described in your letter. If indeed it's attempting to communicate at all."

Mr. Childers leaned forward with wide eyes. "Yes, I've

gathered something of the sort from my reading! At times, a haunting is less about completing unfinished business and more simply the reenactment of a significant act—usually, a terrible one. The gunshot strikes me as along those lines."

Vera turned to me with a proud smile. "It's a rare delight when a client has done his own research." Turning to Mr. Childers, she added, "May I ask what books you've read?"

"Only one, I'm afraid. *Footsteps on the Border of a Different World*. I forget the author's name."

"I think you mean Robert Dale Owen's *Footfalls on the Boundary of Another World*. That's a fine book. Of course, if you're curious about such things, Mrs. Crowe's *The Night-Side of Nature* is my recommendation."

To this day, I have been unable to follow the patterns in the mosaic of Vera's memory for names.

Mr. Childers replied, "I must see if that's in the library, too. When Mrs. Morley oversaw the selling of the property, she made it quite clear that she had no use of the books her husband left behind in the library upstairs."

I realized Mr. Childers was referring to what formerly was called the Dawning Room, and my throat clenched.

"Your purchase of the property," said Vera, "is something I wanted to discuss, sir. Did much time pass between the previous owner's death and your acquiring the house?"

"Well, let's see." Mr. Childers' gaze drifted in the direction of the rug. His misaligned teeth revealed themselves. "I moved in on August of last year, so that would mean—"

"Two-and-a-half years?" I felt my face go warm at my sudden mathematical proficiency. "Is that correct, I wonder?"

Vera tapped her fingers together before nodding. "Well done, Lucille. When did you first notice the manifestations, sir?"

"Right off. There were no traditional hooded figures or ghastly groans, so it took some time before I suspected the supernatural might be at play. The previous maids were the first to jump to that conclusion. I sought more physical explanations until I had to yield to the ghost theory. And that's when I contacted you."

"In response to my newspaper advertisement?"

"Yes. My groom brought your ad to my attention once I had abandoned solving the puzzle with science. You see, I'm an inventor! When Benjamin Franklin failed me, however, I bowed to Cotton Mather." He chuckled.

There was something in his delivery of this witticism that made me wonder if it had been his own invention.

"An inventor, you say!" Vera grinned. "Clearly a successful one to afford to live in this luxurious abode."

Mr. Childers chuckled again. "I'll let you in on a secret! There is a certain—shall we say, *wizard*—in New Jersey. He has found far *greater* success by paying other inventors for their patents and then taking credit for those inventions. In my case, he pays handsomely. But I must ask you to be discreet regarding my arrangement with—uh—"

"Thomas Edison," Vera stated, nodding. "Now, *that's* a name I'd like to forget. Oh, he did fine with the electric light, I suppose, but I wish he had stopped there."

"In some ways, Vera pines for the last century," I said. "In others, she's at the forefront of this one. But we certainly will be discreet in your arrangement with the Wizard of Menlo Park."

In the wake of his failure to conceal Mr. Edison's identity, Mr. Childers knit his brow and again shifted his gaze to the rug. Perhaps my description of him as a pigeon in a pen for peacocks was wrong. At this point, the impression he was making was that of a potato in a patch of peonies.

Vera continued, "That answers one of my questions. Another concerns the house not being sold for two-and-a-half years. Do you know if Mrs. Morley resided here during that time?"

Rebounding quickly from his indiscretion, Mr. Childers explained, "It is my understanding from the agent that she had abandoned the house shortly after the death of her husband."

"Have you spoken to her about the manifestations?"

"I've barely spoken to her at all."

"Reasonable. This raises the question of why it remained unsold for so long?"

Mr. Childers seemed somewhat pleased when declaring, "The reputation of the place made it difficult to sell. A murder. A suicide. Neighbors gossiping about ghosts! After two-and-a-half years, I took advantage of an unfortunate situation, I admit."

Vera glanced my way again, this time with a wink. Her earlier conjecture had proven correct.

Putting two fingers to her jaw, she tilted her head and muttered, "It would be useful to learn if the manifestations were present after the widow left and the inventor arrived."

Seeing that Vera's thoughts had wandered away from the client, I asked him, "Do you happen to know if a caretaker was assigned to look after the house?"

"Yes, there was. And I can tell you exactly where he is. He's my groom now, but he served as the Morleys' butler."

"Your groom is *Mr. Brunton?*" I exclaimed.

Vera's head rose immediately.

"Yes, that's the fellow," said Mr. Childers, clearly surprised by our reaction. "Do you know him?"

"I—I met him once. It was long ago."

Vera slowly stood. She paced as she spoke. "Who would know the maintenance of the house better than the butler? It follows that he would remain as caretaker rather than learning to oversee some entirely new house. And yet you say he lingers here to care for the horses? One doesn't raise *orchids* to flavor a cake with the seeds!"

Mr. Childers opened his mouth to reply—but then he pursed his lips and knit his brow.

I explained, "Miss Van Slyke means that it's odd that a butler would accept such a demotion."

"I agree entirely. When I told Brunton I had no use for a butler and, in fact, couldn't afford one, he pleaded with me to keep him in *any* capacity. I needed a groom, and he had been raised with horses. He explained that his first position with the Morley family had been as stable boy."

"In Virginia," I said quietly.

"Of course, I asked Brunton about any manifestations in the house between Mrs. Morley leaving and my arriving. He said he *did* have some odd experiences. But he refuses to discuss them in detail with me. At times, he's a sly fox, that one."

"We'll have to investigate this, Lucille. Beforehand, sir, my assistant and I must visit your city's Police Headquarters. Your theory that the manifestations in this house are linked to its violent history is virtually certain, and though the murder was never solved, the detectives involved surely learned a *few* things. In addition, on the train, I wrote a detailed letter to a newspaper colleague of mine, requesting backgrounds on the chief participants in that history. The man—Vitellius Berry—is a tenacious bloodhound at digging up information. I had the good luck of fostering a friendship with him while investigating a series of fires set by spectral hands in Pittsburg."

Mr. Childers stood. "This is very exciting! Clearly, I've hired the right ghost hunter!" he cheered, his large teeth unveiled.

I stood, too. "We must remember to post that letter, Vera."

"It's in my coat pocket. And we must remember to bring our valise, my dear." She walked back to the front hall to retrieve her coat.

"Before you go," said Mr. Childers, "should I have Brunton fetch your baggage from the station, or will it be delivered?"

Vera was busy putting on her coat.

"It will be delivered," I said. As I hurried to get the valise and my own coat, I added, "But can you inform us where we might post that letter?"

Mr. Childers walked with us to the front door. "I hope you'll let me take some small part in the investigation and allow me to have it posted for you. And may I provide you with directions to Police Headquarters?"

Vera answered yes to the first request and no to the second. She then departed without a word. Quickly, I informed Mr. Childers of when we were likely to return and wished him a good day—and then rushed to rejoin Vera. Fumbling to open the valise as I walked, I found a map that had the Boston Police Headquarters marked.

Along the way, Vera commented, "You know, to terminate the haunting, we might have to solve the murder."

"That had occurred to me."

"Have you ever solved a murder, my dear?"

"I regret that I have not. As a matter of fact, I thought *The Hound of the Baskervilles* would end with the revelation that the culprit was, indeed, an unearthly canine sent by the Devil. I blame that mistake on your having introduced me to the reality of ghosts."

Vera halted us for a moment. "Are you saying the hound *isn't* the culprit? *Despite* the title?"

I smirked. "Despite the title."

"Well, that's entirely misleading!" Disappointed with Sherlock Holmes, she resumed our walk while resuming her original subject. "No, I've never solved a murder, either. I imagine our first step is to enjoy a good lunch."

"The preliminaries of ghost hunting ought to apply equally in this investigation," I teased.

Rather than grin, though, Vera cocked her head in the direction of the valise. With a serious tone, she declared, "It's good that we remembered our oboes."

If, during my previous time spent in Boston, someone had suggested that two oboes might play a role in solving a murder, I would have deemed it absurd. Life with Vera Van Slyke had, indeed, altered my comprehension of reality.

•

Although she had never solved a murder, Vera had reported on several—that is, when her editor recognized that a "girl reporter" could manage the subject without an undue number of fainting spells. Her experience had revealed that the police were often unwilling to share information about such cases with newspapermen—of either sex. With that in mind, Vera had a plan devised to inspire cooperation. The oboes were key to this plan.

After lunch, approaching Police Headquarters, we noticed a group of uniformed officers and civilian photographers gathered around an automobile. It was one of the popular Stanley Steamers, so named because of its running on steam, not gasoline.

"These horseless contraptions are becoming a plague," Vera spit. "And from the looks of it, the Boston Police Force plans to battle the plague by *adding* to their numbers!"

We asked a gentleman—one dressed as if he were a businessman passing by after his own midday meal—if he knew what had drawn the small crowd. He confirmed that the motor carriage had been purchased to apprehend reckless automobilists who could effortlessly outrace a policeman on bicycle.

"Progress," muttered the gentleman, moving his head from side to side.

"Progress," repeated Vera in a tone as disdainful.

The gentleman turned to her with a glint in his eye and a grin on his lips. He was a man of medium height and solid build. He wore a trimmed and curled moustache, and the gray in his temples suggested that he was around fifty years of age. If he had any distinguishing feature, it was his hazel eyes and the fleshy eyelids crowning them. He looked as if losing sleep had become routine.

He asked, "Do you ladies have business here at the station? If so, I might be of some assistance."

"We do," answered Vera. "Would you be good enough to direct us to the detective or detectives who handled a murder case and a suicide from four years since."

"The murder of Silas Sanderson," I clarified. "And the

suicide of Roderick Morley that followed shortly after in the same house."

The gentleman's eyebrows raised. "I remember *those* crimes very, very clearly. Do you have new evidence related to either of the deaths?"

"Not as yet," Vera responded. "However, we're hoping to discover information that might explain—uhm—certain *subsequent* events occurring at the millionaire's mansion. And these might harken back to reveal something about those deaths."

"I think I follow you. I'm particularly interested in hearing about those 'certain *subsequent* events.' My name is William B. Watts. I'm the Chief Inspector of the Bureau of Criminal Investigation."

Vera and I exchanged blank faces, then turned back to the Chief Inspector.

"Kindly lead the way, sir," said Vera. As we entered the building, she murmured to me, "And what did I tell you about the benefits of—*lunch?*"

I hoped my giggle did not reach Mr. Watts' ears.

We found the Chief Inspector's office to be a spacious one, adorned with portraits of police officials and furnished with a single roll-top desk, several chairs, and cabinets that looked to me like card catalog drawers from a library. Mr. Watts pulled over two chairs and tapped them to signify that they were for us. He then repositioned the desk chair and sat before us without a word.

Vera put her plan into play. "I propose what might seem, at first, a roundabout strategy for uncovering a secret or two that died with the millionaire and his psychic advisor. You're welcome to scoff at us—but I ask that you also *humor* us on the mad chance that it works. Of course, should this strategy reveal the murderer of Cypress Salesman—"

"Silas Sanderson." I interjected.

"—we will gladly grant full credit to yourself and your office. You have nothing to lose and much to gain."

Mr. Watts placed his elbow onto his chair's arm and his chin onto the knuckle of his forefinger. "I am not averse to using—*controversial* methods if the end result is punishing the guilty. Please continue."

Vera glanced at me, inhaled deeply, and proceeded. "My assistant and I have been asked by the current owner of the mansion to investigate—and eliminate—its *ghost*. The haunting there is corroborated by the owner and members of his staff, and it appears to be a direct consequence of the murder, the suicide, or both."

Vera paused, appearing to await some response from Mr. Watts.

However, he remained as stone.

She continued. "The ghost—possibly, *more* than one ghost—appears to be doing its best to communicate something about the deadly events that occurred there four years ago. Items are moved from place to place. Sheets, clothing, and other fabric articles are found ripped and shredded. Phantom gunshots ring through the four stories. I propose we treat these manifestations as *clues,* and see where they lead. Perhaps—nowhere. What *if,* however—what *if* these clues, when combined with the information your detectives gleaned back when the case was fresh, lead us to the murderer?"

The Chief Inspector sat silently. His hazel eyes drifted to the side. He rubbed an eyelid with one finger. His eyes drifted back. "Shortly after being stymied by the Sanderson murder," he explained, "I had a hand in bringing a certain huckster to justice. He went by the name of *Francis Truth,* believe it or not. The rascal claimed he could cure *any* disease—not with medicine—but with his divine powers. Patsies from across the nation answered his advertisements in hope of a miracle. For those miracles, he charged five dollars a month. That might sound trifling, but one estimate put Truth's earnings at about 30,000 dollars *a month!* Needless to say, I have very little faith in faith healers. Now, Miss Van Slyke, are you asking me to share police files—with a *ghost hunter?"*

Vera did not flinch. "Curiosity, not currency, motivates my interest in the supernatural, sir. I followed the Francis Truth story closely, and I applaud your exposing his fraudulence. While I have accepted an honorarium or two as a ghost hunter when a client can easily afford it, the bulk of my income is earned as a newspaper reporter."

I observed Mr. Watts wince.

"In that capacity, I have myself defrauded many a huckster—most often of the Spiritualist persuasion."

And then I winced, too.

"But *you* know that convenience and criminal justice are rarely close companions. You illustrated that lesson when you persevered in the investigation of Jack the Slugger—"

"Jack the *Ripper?*" I offered without allowing enough time.

"No, she's correct," Mr. Watts interrupted, leaning back in his chair and facing me. "We preferred to call him simply 'The Slugger.' The man committed a string of street robberies here last year, using a wrench, an axe, or some other blunt instrument to incapacitate his female victims. Two of them died from their wounds."

Vera said, "I followed *that* story, too. Remind me who the prime suspect was? The man who had been in and out of asylums for the insane. There was even a witness—a trolley conductor, wasn't it?—who placed him in the vicinity of the crime!"

"Alan Mason." Mr. Watts had assumed my usual role of Keeper of Names.

"You could have easily stopped there. You had all the pieces of the puzzle. But they did not quite fit together. Remind me who the other man was? The one finally convicted."

"George Perry." Mr. Watts again rubbed his eyelid while shifting in his chair, as if he were tiring of the conversation.

"I hope," said Vera, "that you'll use that same tenacity to explore every avenue to find the killer of four years ago, whose actions led to not one but *two* deaths."

"But, Miss Van Slyke, imagine if the newspapers caught wind of this. The Boston Police cooperating with *a ghost hunter?* Why, we'd be the laughing—"

"Oh, it's *old* news, sir. The affair has gone stale! No reporter is going to show any interest in—"

"Well, then, I have *personal* qualms about working with a ghost hunter! Sure enough, I've heard reports of the disembodied voices at the Granary Burying Ground, the Lady in Black roaming George's Island, the haunted lighthouse off of Cohasset. By God, half the officers in this building have some spooky tale to tell about when they were assigned night duty. But I *personally* have yet to glimpse even the vanishing buttocks of a ghost."

Vera slowly grinned. This was exactly what she was anticipating.

"I assume you have a room in which you interrogate suspects?"

"Of course."

"Does it have windows?"

The Chief Inspector sighed. "Are you suggesting that we have a ghost here in the station?" He had humored us, as Vera had requested, but I sensed that he no longer found us humorous.

"I cannot tell you *that.* However, I can easily discover if a ghost would have *access* to your station—access from the spirit realm. You see, my assistant and I have stumbled upon a phenomenon that has significant ramifications for the exploring the reality of ghosts. You might say, it is a sign of progress in ghost hunting."

Mr. Watts now rubbed both eyelids. "*Progress,* you say?"

"Progress," Vera conceded. "But not in physical mechanics. No, this is a step forward in *dimensional harmonics!*"

•

The windowless interrogation room was much starker than the Chief Inspector's office, and it was considerably smaller. Vera, a tall woman, seemed gigantic in relation to its low ceiling.

The only fixtures in the gray-walled enclosure were two gray chairs positioned for parley across a gray table. The lighting was electric, not gas, and it was particularly glaring. A smell in the room made me think of old mushrooms covered with slime.

It was perfect for our purposes.

I immediately removed the two oboe cases from my valise and began to assemble each instrument on the end of the table. Meanwhile, Vera tapped on the chair nearest the door to signify where the Chief Inspector was to sit. He did so. She then crossed to the other side of the table, taking the stance of a professor in a very disheartening classroom.

"We learned of this phenomena when a friend of Lucille explained that he had observed glowing rings floating around the room where he lived. He was a musician and—at night, with the gas turned off—he played phonograph records. A master of many instruments, he would occasionally harmonize along with these recordings. Do you remember the recording he played, my dear? The composition that led to his discovery?"

"Braham's *Violin Concerto*. The second movement opens with a solo for oboe. My talented friend played it as a *duet*, though, improvising the accompaniment on his own oboe."

"Now, whenever this musician matched a B flat with a high G, his darkened room became suffused with what he called 'little, purple halos' that skittered through the air! We were intrigued enough to witness this wonder that very evening, and—lo and behold—it was no dream. No hallucination. No optical illusion. The room was swarmed by violet-edged *holes!* They wobbled and floated around us as if they were luminous jellyfish. Or, rather, the outer *edges* of jellyfish, since there were neither centers nor tentacles trailing behind them."

Again, Chief Inspector Watts remained as still as a statue.

"Understandably, these violet circles made me curious— and *foolhardy*. I approached one hole and managed to jam a nearby violin bow into it. When we relit the lights, we discovered that the length of the bow that had passed into the hole had *crystalized.* Turned to sparkling dust easily blown away. Therefore, they pose a danger—but only so long as they're visible. Once Lucille and I are playing our notes, I bid you to remain very *still.* The holes seem to shy away from physical bodies *if we keep still."*

Mr. Watts nodded. He narrowed his eyes, though, and I imagined he might be pondering whether he would require *one* pair of handcuffs or *two* to subdue us before our trip to the sanitarium.

"The only scientific explanation I can offer is that, somehow, the harmonics produced by oboes playing B flat and high G pull at punctures between our dimension and the invisible one, tugging them into our visual spectrum. Violet, of course, is at the far border of that spectrum of visibility, and so we can see the outer edges of these punctures as glowing circles."

The Chief Inspector shifted in his chair. "There are *punctures* between our dimension and another one?"

Vera tightened her lips for a moment. She then sat down in the chair on her side of the table. "We have consistently discovered these holes at sights said to be haunted. The punctures seem to allow those in the spirit realm access to our physical realm."

He looked as if he were chewing the inside of his cheek.

"And we've learned something more. *Guilt.* Strong feelings of *guilt* is what tears these holes. That's why I wanted to try this experiment here in the interrogation room. I figured it's a *hub* of guilt."

Mr. Watts, yet again, rubbed one of his eyelids. "As I understand you, then, if the station *does* have a ghost, this room is the transom it would have to wriggle through."

Vera clapped her hands together. "An excellent metaphor! I knew the moment we met that you had a poetic side."

He slowly cocked his head.

"However," Vera added, "even if this dimensional transom were open, it doesn't necessarily mean it's been used for passage.

In other words, the violet holes indicate guilt, not ghosts. What do you say—shall we see if the transom *has* been pried open?"

With very measured enthusiasm, Mr. Watts admitted, "You've piqued my interest."

Vera stood, and I handed her one of the oboes. Once she had set her fingers to produce the note she routinely played, she threw me an inquiring look. I checked her fingers and nodded. I then walked with my own oboe to the electric light switch.

We were plunged into complete darkness. I heard Vera give a count of three. I inhaled deeply and blew my high G in harmony with her B flat.

For as long as we could sustain those two pitches, that dank, compact room became inhabited by phosphorescent purple rings that wavered and swam and, in some cases, coalesced to form larger shapes. I heard the scrape of a chair and, in the dim light, saw the figure of Mr. Watts recoil. Vera and I ceased our drone, and the room went black.

"Perfectly still, sir!" Vera commanded with what breath she had left. "Let's have one more look. Lucille? One. Two. Three."

Again, we sounded our whining harmony, and again, the rubbery bands of violet light appeared. The glow they cast was very dim, but I managed to see that—though the Chief Inspector remained seated—he was *not* keeping perfectly still. Frozen with indecision, I kept a sharp ear on Vera's note. We both soon ran out of breath.

"Would you mind switching on the lights again, my dear."

As my eyes adjusted, I followed Vera's gaze to Mr. Watts' gaze, and from Mr. Watts' gaze to a short club he held before him. It had been the kind of short club common to policemen—but this one looked even shorter than usual.

This was because one half had become crystalized dust. Like cigar ash, the club's end had fallen to form a small pile on the table.

"I—I couldn't stop myself," he uttered. "I figured this must be a trick. But if what you said about the violin bow—and I always have a billy on my belt. So I—well. *Look!"*

His hand trembled, and more of the crystalized end crumbled away. His breathing was hard and irregular, and a bead of sweat dripped from his brow.

Vera sat in the empty chair, looking closely at the club. She raised her hand as if to take it. We all jolted from the sudden *clack* of Mr. Watts dropping it. Vera caught the club's handle from rolling off the table.

"To return to my question, sir," said she. "May we have your cooperation in our investigation of the murder of four years ago?"

The Chief Inspector rubbed his eyelid. He remained mute for approximately a full minute.

"You may," he answered at last. "Of course, you may."

⟲ CHAPTER SEVEN ⟲

RODERICK MORLEY
PURCHASED THE GUN

Following an afternoon of taking notes on the police files regarding the Sanderson case, we arrived back at our client's house. We shared what we had learned with Mr. Childers, and he expressed profound fascination with it.

"Were there no fingerprints on the gun?" he inquired.

"Other than smears, only the victim's were discernable," said Vera. "This is intriguing—why did the victim handle the gun prior to it being used on him?—but it's also not very helpful. Of course, fingerprinting is still in the developmental stage, and I assume it was even more rudimentary four years ago. They might've missed something."

"It would have been very odd if the gunshot wasn't heard by anyone," continued our host. "A blast in that room would have resounded throughout the house—just as the phantom gunshots do now."

"In fact," I explained, "it *was* heard. The murder occurred on a Sunday morning, so most of the staff was at church or elsewhere. However, a cook rushed down from her room on the floor above. She was first to enter the room and find the body. Mr. Morley rushed up from *his* bedroom on the floor below and entered next. His wife then entered from her accustomed spot in the parlor."

"If she had been in the parlor," Mr. Childers speculated, "then Sanderson must have come in through the back. Unless she was facing the other way and occupied with her thoughts."

"Or occupied with her Gramophone," I added. "He could have tiptoed right behind her."

"There's another puzzle regarding comings and goings," Vera stated. "By the time any of the house's residents had arrived—assuming none of the house's residents were responsible—the criminal had vanished. It's uncertain how exactly."

"The police were unable to *confirm* any specific escape route," I noted. "That's what led them to believe the crime was committed by someone in the house—or familiar with it."

Vera stated, "Of course, drain pipes allow more than rainwater to escape. I once reported on a burglar who had hunched and hid inside a dumbwaiter for over an hour before absconding when safe to do so. I suspect the killer *could* have fled in a way as humdrum as that. Perhaps, after dinner, we could go upstairs and envision possible paths out of the house."

Mr. Childers nodded, and his misaligned teeth then became very noticeable as he bit his lower lip. "All of this reminds me to ask where you two might claim a bedroom for tonight." He then offered us a choice of sleeping accommodations.

There was the Pink Room, a second-floor bedroom once used by Mrs. Morley. Mr. Childers carefully noted that only a door stood between this and his own sleeping quarters—designated the Blue Room—which had formerly served as Mr. Morley's bedroom. Our other option was the third-floor guest room. This was the one beside the Dawning Room, where my mother had disguised herself as a man—and then fled back to and away from—on that tragic winter night. With my consent, Vera told him that we would share the latter room—called the Green Room.

"It's more central to the house, and that might prove useful should a manifestation occur," she said. The wink she gave me afterward suggested she was equally concerned with social convention.

I had only seen the guest room in darkness, and upon entering it fully lit to prepare for dinner, I felt a disharmony similar to when I entered the mansion that morning. On the one hand, it was delightful to see the golden light of a setting sun cast upon the pine-green color scheme of the furnishings, to hear the homeward-bound horses and pedestrians on the street outside, even to smell how the room had been aired for our use. On the other hand, I knew my mother had suffered deep humiliation here—and the memory of my discovering her ripped dress made me a bit woozy. I told myself to do my best at remaining *unhaunted* by this haunted house.

On a whim, I wandered to the door leading to the Dawning Room. I gazed at the doorknob and then slowly curled my hand around it. I could almost taste my dread. Still, I found the strength to give it a twist.

I discovered the new owner kept the door locked. I was partly grateful for that. Yet I was also partly pleased that I had *attempted* to enter the room behind it.

At dinner, however, I felt myself droop under the weight of our visit. The maid-of-all-work, earlier called Sophie by Mr. Childers, was a fine cook. However, she also seemed to be a disgruntled employee. A strained and barely muffled exchange between herself and her employer made its way from the kitchen to the dining room, and Mr. Childers explained afterward that the additional duties brought about by our presence in the house—joined with the ghostly manifestations—were pushing this woman closer to quitting. Nonetheless, Sophie remained very pleasant towards Vera and me.

"Let's show this woman that we depend on her contribution to resolve this haunting," Vera said quietly after Mr. Childers had excused himself yet again to attend to the maid's complaints. "If we make it clear we don't think she is beneath our dignity, she might find comfort in not being the only woman in the house for a while."

"That's very understanding of you."

"I guess it is. Sometimes, I surprise myself." Then she added, "And, no doubt, she's an ideal source of information. Now, we'll also have to arrange an interview with the former butler, of course. Would you prefer I do that myself? I know the memories of your evening here must be terribly burdensome."

With Vera Van Slyke, compassion is like a moon circling a planet, and the planet is called Concentration. Clearly, her thoughts about the haunting were revolving to the back of her mind, allowing her sympathy to rise.

"Thank you," I replied. "I must say that I am *curious* to see Mr. Brunton again. He seemed like such a kind man. But I haven't seen him around. You don't suppose he's avoiding us for our role in his former employer's suicide?"

"Oh, probably out running errands. Let's devote tomorrow morning to interviewing both the maid and Mr. Brunton. We'll want to spend as much time *here* as we can in case of a manifestation, but I'd also like to return to the files at Police Headquarters. I can't help but feel there's some tasty licorice amid all that tar."

"What shall we do this evening? Stay here and hope for ghosts?"

"I'm *forever* hoping for ghosts, my dear. Yes, let's make it a quiet evening. Oh, let's compile a list!"

"A list?"

"Of murder suspects."

"Well. Then a *quiet* evening it will be."

•

After dinner, we excused ourselves to begin work on the haunting's probable history. Vera, who liked to wander while thinking, spread our notes of the police files across the bed. She used the green and white stripes on its coverlet to help organize the notes into piles. Meanwhile, I pulled over the chair from the dressing table for myself.

"Three distinct manifestations, and three prime suspects," Vera began, as if to herself. She turned to me suddenly. "Oh! Are we agreed that there are *three* prime suspects?"

"Yes, three. Agreed"

"I believe I can identify them by name at this point. There's the millionaire, Roderick Morley."

"Well done. Agreed."

"The wife, Mrs. Morley. What was her first name?"

"She enjoyed music."

Vera pointed at me. "Viola! Excellent trick."

"Agreed."

"And, of course, the third suspect is undoubtedly Mr. Brunton."

"Excuse me? *No!* Not Mr. Brunton!"

Vera halted in arranging the notes on the bed and turned to me. "He lingers here. At the spot where the murder took place. *Despite* his fall in professional status! Is that *not* suspicious?"

I had to consider this a moment. "Well, he seemed like such a nice fellow when he came to Lily Dale in search of a medium. And, though my experiences with him here in Boston were brief, he only affirmed my first impression. Besides—"

"Yes?"

"He looks like a giant elf." I chortled upon hearing my own ridiculousness.

Vera chuckled, too. "I'll be sure to scrutinize that claim at tomorrow's interview. But we're much closer to Halloween than Christmas this time round, and it might help us to think of these suspects more as *goblins* than elves." She seated herself on the edge of the bed. "More importantly, who was *your* third suspect?"

"Oh, uhm—your friend. Henry James's brother. The professor."

"*William James?*" she asked with her eyes wide and her brow knit. "Are you suggesting that *William James*, Professor at *Harvard University*, is currently evading prosecution for *murder?*"

"I overheard Dr. James say that, when Mr. Morley had diverted money away from psychical research and into schools for colored children, it was because of Sanderson's influence. '*Undue* influence,' he's quoted as saying in one of those reports. I sense that Dr. James thought Sanderson had his friend under a sort of hypnotic spell." I shrugged. "Not much of a motive for murder perhaps, but do we have any motive for our other suspects?"

"But—but William is an old colleague," Vera rebutted quietly. "He's the one who told me about that haunting near here, the *first* case you and I investigated *together*." She stared at the floor with a pout. After a time, she nodded. "So that makes *four* suspects, agreed?"

"Agreed."

She resumed piling papers on the bed. "Let's begin with the only suspect the police actually charged with the crime. Roderick Morley. They didn't have much of a case against him, though."

"Well, he had purchased the gun shortly before the crime."

"Suspicious only on the surface. He was far from secretive about having done so. It's likely all of our suspects knew about the weapon being in the house." Vera scanned the notes that, at this point, covered the top of the striped bedspread. "The matter at hand is—does his role in the tragedy relate to any of the three manifestations occurring in this house? The sound of a gunshot? Certainly! But what about ripping fabric and moving doodads?"

After pacing from one side of the bed to the other and back again, Vera decided to apply her skills as a reporter. In this instance, she was no longer a *collector* of information, but now a *collator* of that information. A typewriter was one of the few machines she valued, and along with our oboes, her Remington Portable was a key item among our luggage. When she placed the machine on the dressing table, I was obliged to abandon my chair for a bay-window bench cushioned in the same green as the curtains.

Vera began the first draft of a biographical sketch of Mr. Morley, something she would do again with each of the suspects. She revised and expanded these histories as new facts were gathered—be it our continued study of the police files or the return letters she received from Mr. Berry, her fellow journalist in Pittsburg with a talent for unearthing *old* news. Mr. Brunton provided details about Mr. Morley's life in Virginia and Boston. Dr. James and Mr. Morley's widow both added insights into his marriage and his dealings with Silas Sanderson. Below is the final product that was eventually shelved among Vera's small library on ghosts. Her marginal notes—mostly questions she would have pursued if the investigation continued—appear bracketed at the end of the paragraph to which they were nearest.

—

Roderick Augustus Morley (1861-1899) was born on the 17th of May in Virginia exactly one month after that state seceded from the union and nine days after Richmond became the capital of the Confederacy. His father, Jefferson Rolfe Morley, owned a residence in Richmond, but sensing trouble on the horizon, he had wisely relocated his expectant wife to the family plantation down in Lunenburg County. Roderick's mother, born Rosalie Ravenna D'Evereux, was the daughter of a well-to-do cotton broker from Natchez, Mississippi. [Ask the butler how the parents met? Probably irrelevant.]

The Morley patriarchs had grown tobacco in Virginia since Colonial days. After the passage of abolition and General Lee's surrender, Jefferson strategized to remain financially stable. Seeing the world's economy moving from agriculture to industry—and knowing the South was lagging in that transition—he sent his son to be educated in the North. There were rumors that Rosalie was displeased with the decision.

In 1879, Morley entered Harvard University, where he met William James (W.J.) in a class covering the relations between Physiology and Psychology. W.J. remembers him as being an intense, if somewhat moody, student. Morley had a keen interest in German literature and philosophy, and he and W.J. would meet socially to discuss the emerging developments in Psychology that were being published in that language.

In 1881, Morley met Viola, his wife-to-be. He was at a fraternity frolic on the Cambridge shore of the Charles River. Morley enjoyed telling people that, when he first saw Viola, he was by himself, appreciating the reflection of the moon on the water, when he spotted Viola swimming—in a stylish evening gown—toward the brightly lit festivities as if she had come from the Boston side of the river. Viola would then assure listeners that swimming such a distance would have been impossible for her and she had slipped from a sailing club's dock not far upstream. Regardless, Morley rescued the drenched damsel, who would become his bride.

During these years, his widow recalled, Morley never developed close friendships with his classmates. His Southern origins frequently made him the target of lampooning, one of many spurs to his brooding spells. Try as he might, he could not lose his accent.

In 1883, Morley graduated from college and, promptly thereafter, married Viola. Honoring his father's wishes, he began to invest in manufacturing industries that promised a profitable return. His father's wealth safeguarded any failures as he learned the Stock Exchange business. [Perhaps Morley's own attempt to predict the future prepared him to hire a psychic investigator later. Unknowable.]

Four years passed before the couple gave birth to their first child, a girl. The father said he chose his daughter's name for its musical quality: Dorothy May Morley. [Why four years?]

The wheel of fortune turned in 1890, when the influenza epidemic of that and the previous year found its way from Russia to the eastern seaboard of the U.S., taking the lives of thousands, including both Jefferson and Rosalie in Richmond. Their son inherited the family's wealth, which he increased by selling the business and properties in Virginia. It was shortly after this time that he moved into his Beacon Hill mansion, and Brunton—whom Morley had known from his childhood in Virginia—accepted his offer to act as butler. [Lucille notes the difficulty of severing ties to home. Regarding Virginia—did Morley inherited all the family wealth? Any Siblings?]

1893 saw a national economic depression from exactly the kind of financial speculation that was Morley's profession.

Hiring Spiritualist mediums, Morley began to seek contact with his deceased father for guidance. Many patrons of séances seek emotional relief, but some hope to profit from those in the spirit realm, the belief being that they are able to perceive the future. Morley combined the two with a longing for his dear father's guiding hand. [Confirm this. The poor economy pushed R.M. to mediums—not the next catastrophe?]

The summer of 1896 brought an unprecedented heatwave to the eastern U.S. Outdoor laborers, kitchen workers, and residents packed into poorly ventilated tenement housing suffered especially, both adults and children dying from heat exhaustion in alarming numbers. Seeking relief, Morley took his wife and daughter to the isle of Martha's Vineyard. While the family was bathing at South Beach, Dorothy May strayed from her parents. A strong wave tripped and dragged her beneath the water. This time, Morley was not the rescuer. The nine-year-old girl drowned. [How well I remember that summer. New York suffered at least as much. Horrible.]

The brooding student became a guilt-ridden man. The weight of losing both parents at once was multiplied by feeling that he had been a negligent father. He spent silent hours alone in what had been Dorothy May's nursery first, then her play room, and finally the Dawning Room. The guest room beside it once had served as sleeping quarters for her nanny. [When did R.M. hang the lithograph in that room? "Good Times on the Old Plantation." Ironic reminder of those who suffered for his benefit.]

Not long thereafter, Morley received a letter. The writer first denounced any Spiritualist mediums who might have appeared uninvited at his doorstep (and, indeed, several had) and next explained that, while he offered similar comforts, he would only do so after at least a month had passed. That length of time, the writer explained, would allow for sounder decisions to be made. The patience and respect shown in this letter impressed Morley, and after that month had passed, he contacted the sender: Mr.

Silas Sanderson.

Though a young man, Sanderson was articulate and prudent. His handsome features and smart suits—punctuated with a fresh boutonniere—were counterpointed by a warm, even deferential demeanor. Despite his charm and allure, he was never known to woo young ladies nor to court a favorite. After the shooting, Morley told the police that Sanderson had shown only polite interest in the beautiful Mrs. Morley. Instead, the psychic medium devoted his energies to his Spiritualist "calling" with a devotion that was nearly monastic.

In that same interrogation, Morley divulged that Sanderson had advised him to alleviate his guilt by becoming a major supporter of the movement to provide colored children in the South the educational opportunities that neither Reconstruction had provided nor subsequent state-regulated racial segregation allowed. Morley had barely seen slavery, but he knew that his life of ease and elegance had depended upon it. Furthermore, while he knew that the North was hardly free from race prejudice, his priorities were with the land of his birth.

Sanderson's suggestion had so enthused the millionaire that he contacted his lawyer to alter his will. The grand house would be left to his wife, but his other rich resources would go to the schooling of the grandchildren of slaves. Whether this were his own or his psychic advisor's idea, Morley did not remember.

However, such generosity struck some of those closest to Morley as impetuous and irresponsible. The psychic had reported having an overwhelming vision of sinister forces plotting against Morley, though no faces were discernable. It was unfathomable to the millionaire that leaving his money to charity would incur a violent response—but Morley had indeed garnered sharp animosity and strong objections from his wife and his few friends. He agreed with his advisor's urgent proposal that he protect himself with a gun. Having a weapon at hand—and letting its presence be generally known—might be an effective block against any dark machinations. Thus, Morley purchased a pistol.

Sanderson was murdered with this gun on the morning of July 23, 1899. Morley was sleeping late in his bedroom after having spent the previous night enjoying Sanderson's company. Brutally awoken by the gunshot, he was the second person to come upon the corpse. He was the first, though, to notice the weapon had been placed on the forward edge of the desktop.

The same gun was found lying beside Morley's corpse six months afterward.

—

As Vera was typing her first draft of this biographical sketch, I was slouched on the bay-window bench, resting my eyes. Once I realized the clacking of the typewriter had ceased, I opened my eyes to find Vera pacing the room with the pages in her hand. She was not reading them, but presumably she was contemplating the story they told. At last, she shrugged, handed me the manuscript, and asked if I could spot any links between what she had written and the supernatural manifestations occurring in the house.

After reading it, I confessed that—apart from the spectral gunshots—I could not make any connections.

Resuming her wandering, she stated, "The ripping of fabric is the most confounding of the three. I've never run across anything like it. Does the specter want to convey a crucial point— but is unable to do so in anything other than a symbol? What does ripped cloth suggest?"

"Tearing up the will?" I offered.

"If so, tearing paper would come closer to the mark. And if our spook can do one, he would seem able to do the other."

"If it's symbolic, perhaps Mr. Morley is expressing his being *torn* from his Virginia home—and from his parents."

"And his daughter." Vera tilted her head.

"And his daughter," I muttered. "I certainly cannot forget his daughter."

She sat beside me. "Is there something in particular troubling you about the drowning? The waves—ripping at her clothing?"

"No, not that," I whispered. "Do you remember my spirit guide? Her name was Marianne."

Vera chuckled. "I dimly recall she had some very salty things to say regarding my grandmother!"

"If Dorothy May had lived, she would have been almost exactly the same age as my imaginary Marianne. Neither of the Morleys said a word about that—before or after the séance. Understandably so. But my point is—I don't know who killed Mr. Sanderson, but I certainly aided and abetted Mr. Morley's death with my horrible chatter about a dead girl."

Vera leaned against me, and I mirrored the token of affection.

She said, "I was going to suggest that we check for violet ruptures in various rooms to see if one if most likely to be the source of supernatural intrusions. But those punctures are caused by intense guilt."

"We'd find them in any room I enter."

"Purple holes would be bubbling out of both your ears."

I nodded. "And I doubt very much that the maid would find the moaning of two oboes very soothing."

Then I spotted something. I sat up straight. I rose—then I took a few steps forward.

"Vera?" I said. "You know that tin for your spare typewriter ribbon? The one you keep in your Remington case? I don't suppose you very carefully balanced it on top of the doorknob that leads into the Dawning Room, did you? Perhaps while I was asleep. Even though I'm very certain I never fell asleep."

I felt more than saw Vera come to stand beside me.

To be sure, my eyes were not deceiving me. Vera also gaped at the small, lightweight tin almost floating on that round knob.

"I was typing the entire time that I was—*typing.*" Vera stuttered. "This appears to be our first manifes—"

At that instant, a short but thundering explosion filled the room! It shook the walls and knocked the ribbon tin off its precarious place on the doorknob. I realized I had grabbed Vera's arm and then saw that she had clenched her fists and lifted them, as if to ward off any assault.

She then gently patted my hand, which was squeezing her arm tightly. I dropped my grasp, and side-by-side we ventured out into the hallway door.

We heard Mr. Childers charging up the staircase before seeing him arrive on the landing.

"No need for panic!" he shouted. "Please remain calm. This is our ghost! I hope you're both all right. It's only our ghost being a nuisance yet again." He stopped on the landing and leaned against the bannister, catching his breath.

We walked to him.

"We're fine—perfectly fine," Vera replied. "It did catch us unawares, but no damage done."

"Thank you for your concern, sir," I added. "I hope Sophie isn't too upset."

"Ah, well. I imagine I'll have to have another talk with her."

Vera surveyed the hallway as she raised a finger. "The gunshot seemed to have come from a room adjoining ours. Perhaps the room above, below, or beside. Have you attempted to determine where the sound is heard the loudest?"

"I wish I could help you there. I *have* tried to track the source, but as soon as I think I've got it pinned down, it comes from someplace else the very next time. It's infuriating."

Her study of the hallway at an end, Vera stated, "Perhaps there's significance in its roaming."

Mr. Childers nodded as if impressed with that comment. "Well, I'm sort of pleased that you observed a manifestation on your very first night here. Now, you're less inclined to think you've entered the home of a madman." His smile unveiled his teeth, not deranged but certainly disarranged.

Vera also grinned and then jested, "It's as if the ghost were saying 'Pleased to meet you, Madam Ghost Hunter.'"

As the two chuckled, it occurred to me that Vera was not

mentioning the displaced typewriter ribbon tin that we had discovered only a minute earlier. Not knowing the reason for this, I also remained quiet about it.

"Well," resumed Mr. Childers, "I'll let you get back to your typing."

"We weren't too loud, I hope," I apologized.

"Not at all," said our host as he gave us a curt wave and turned to descend the stairway. "It's a much better sound than gunfire, I'll tell you!"

We said our goodnights and strolled back to our room. Vera had her look of contemplation, so I remained quiet. Once back in the room, she stood still.

I gave her a good while before asking, "Why didn't you tell Mr. Childers about the ribbon tin being moved to the doorknob?"

She looked up at me and resumed walking. "None other than my thoughts were elsewhere. My little joke about the ghost introducing himself wasn't *entirely* meant to be droll."

"I see. But do you think the ghost—or ghosts—are pleased to meet us? Or—something else?"

Placing her fingers to her jaw, Vera said, "Ay, there's the rub, Macduff."

Amid numerous habits, Vera Van Slyke always had a surprise in store. Rather than correct her Shakespeare, I went to work at gathering our notes from the police files and removing them from the bed. Vera meditatively ambled to the dresser where, prior to dinner, we had deposited our clothing.

After very little time, she grunted, *"Hmmh."*

I turned to see that she was holding out her nightgown at arm's length. It was plain beige with routine ruffles on the sleeves and neckline. I wasn't certain what she wanted me to notice.

Until I saw the three long rips running diagonally along its side.

~ CHAPTER EIGHT ~

THE SINS OF THE FATHERLY

The next morning, as we ate breakfast with Mr. Childers, Vera mentioned the relocated spare ribbon tin and the ripped nightgown. Our host noted that he had never known all three manifestations to occur in a single evening before, adding that he would appreciate our not upsetting Sophie with this news.

"Of course," Vera said. "I did notice something peculiar about the nightgown. The damage seems to be less *tears* and more *slashes*. The cuts don't start at the edge and aim toward the center as if I had asked you to rip this napkin. Instead, the three cuts begin and end in the middle, if you see my meaning—as if the garment had been lacerated with a bullwhip."

With his mouth slightly open, Mr. Childers nodded slowly. He then whispered, "A switch to switch a witch."

"Sir?"

"Oh, a phrase ol' Grandpappy used when describing what he'd use on me when I misbehaved. Similar to being punished with a belt. 'I'll go cut me a switch,' he'd say, 'a switch to switch a witch!' I never knew exactly what it meant."

Vera blinked a few times before explaining, "I imagine it meant a tree branch that, if whittled clean and applied to a witch's backside, would smart enough to change her ways. A very, uh—*poetic* phrase."

Mr. Childers chuckled.

Vera resumed, "However, if I promise to be discrete, may I ask the maid for a needle and thread? I can mend the gown myself."

"Of course," said our host. "I'll mention it to her before I leave." Apparently, Mr. Childers caught something in our reaction to his leaving. "Leave—for my workshop."

"I see," said Vera. "For some reason, I assumed you did your inventing here in the house. You have so much space. But it makes perfect sense that you have a special facility for such things."

He grinned. "For many years, my workshop *was* where I lived. I slept on a cot and boiled beans there. Once my inventions began to earn money, I was pleased to keep my work in one place and my rest in another."

"I've never seen an inventor's workshop before," I submitted. "Is yours at all close by?"

"Not close enough for *your* convenience!" He said this very suddenly, a bit loudly. He quickly smiled and slowly bowed his head while retaining the unsettling grin.

His protruding teeth suddenly reminded me of a snarling dog's. I sensed that his workshop was no place for prying women. Perhaps he simply had projects that he kept secret or— like an artist—felt his work should only be seen at a formal unveiling.

He then added, "Brunton drives me there in the morning and then fetches me in the evening. In fact, that's his main duty, so if you need him to take you to Police Headquarters this afternoon, you have only to ask him."

"To be honest, I enjoy walking to Pemberton Square," said Vera. "The brisk air helps me think."

"But thank you for the offer," I amended.

"We also would like to chat with Mr. Brunton this morning."

"If that's convenient."

"Excellent idea. He knows much more about the house and its history than I do. As I mentioned yesterday, he admits to having had strange encounters when he served as caretaker. But he's reluctant to discuss them. You might have more success at getting him to talk if you exercise your feminine wiles."

Vera laughed. "Or simply tell him that my own strange encounters have been vastly stranger, I'd gamble!"

Our breakfast soon ended and the start of our Tuesday was organized. After Mr. Childers left, we found our way into the kitchen. It was spacious and well-supplied with hanging pots and utensils. The oven was enormous. Clearly, the room was intended to prepare meals for many more than three.

After some polite debate, Sophie allowed us to help her wash the breakfast dishes. We learned her full name was Miss Sophia Marchelli and she was born in Boston's North End. Finishing with the dishes, Vera let our new friend know about the ripped nightgown and insisted on mending it herself. Vera added that we wanted to treat the maid to lunch at a restaurant sometime. Miss Marchelli kindly invited us to join her at the table where she and Mr. Brunton took their meals. She became a compendium of ghostly anecdotes regarding not only the Morley Mansion but also the spectral experiences sworn to by other maids and by her relatives.

Miss Marchelli telling her tales and Vera repairing her nightgown occupied our time until Mr. Brunton returned. When he entered the kitchen through the backdoor, his movements and his eyes gave hint that he had been informed that Vera was awaiting him. Expectation was followed by recognition, but upon seeing me, recognition led to confusion.

"I remember Miss Van Slyke from her height and her curly hair," he said. "But I didn't expect to see *you* by her side. Weren't you—the—"

"Yes, I *was*," I confessed. "But I am no longer."

We reintroduced ourselves, and I might have squirmed when I said my name is Lucille Parsell. Mr. Brunton looked exactly as he had four years earlier—the same silvered beard and the same triangular eyes—but I noticed a pronounced limp as he walked toward us. He asked how I came to be Vera's assistant.

"It's a complicated story," I explained.

"I have an inkling of that story." Mr. Brunton put a book he had been carrying onto the table. "Did you share your secrets for this? I live back in the coach house now and fetched it before coming in. I wonder if Miss Van Slyke would be kind enough to put her signature on it."

It was a copy of *Spirits Shouldn't Sneeze.*

As quickly as Vera consented, Miss Marchelli was off to retrieve a pen and ink well.

"Indeed I did bare my soul for that book. And I'm very grateful Vera—uh, Miss Van Slyke—didn't mention my name."

He turned to the author. "And I'm very grateful you didn't mention anybody's name in your references to the sad events that transpired here. Mr. Childers informed me that you're seeking information about the ghost and what might be behind it. Let me hang up my coat, and I'll sit with you."

As he did so, Vera asked, "I understand that it was *you*, Mr. Brunton, who passed my advertisement to your new employer. Did I hear that correctly?"

"Yes, that's right. You introduce your book by saying that, while you're skeptical about the Spiritualists, you hope the book won't hinder investigation in *other* branches of psychical research. I believe you even admit to finding promise in ghost hunting." His coat hung now, he hobbled back to us. "When I then spotted an offer of help for the haunted from 'V. Van Slyke,' I had a notion it was none other than the author of this book."

"Sound detective work," Vera said.

"And I thought it would be fortunate—if not fateful—if you could help *this* haunted household." Mr. Brunton eased himself into a chair with a muffled moan.

Anxious about how Mr. Brunton felt about *my* returning to the house, I entered the conversation with some trepidation. "I had wondered if wild coincidence or, as you say, the hand of Fate explained why we were contacted to return here. But your explanation of the matter makes it all seem far less predestined."

Miss Marchelli returned with the writing implements, and as Vera signed the book, Mr. Brunton turned to me.

"I'm still taken aback by *your* being here. I must say I was very ashamed for having hired a—"

I cleared my throat. "A *fraud?*"

He reached out and rested his fingertips on my arm. "I recall you were in cahoots with your mother. I was going to say that I was very ashamed for having hired a young lady who had been led astray."

Vera added, "Since we're slicing the bitter pie, I deserve a wide piece, too!" She slid the book to him.

Mr. Brunton nodded. "Adam succumbed to Eve, who succumbed to the serpent. Who's at fault? Poor Eve usually bears the brunt, but I contend that all *three* carry the blame."

As if to blow away the dark clouds, Miss Marchelli joshed, "Well, s'never going to keep *me* awake nights! I was nowhere in the vicinity!" Collecting the pen and ink well, she explained that she had fireplaces to clear and prepare for the coming night.

At this point, I began to wonder if Miss Marchelli truly was the skittish mouse that Mr. Childers had suggested. She hadn't expressed any desire to quit her position to us. To the contrary, she seemed like a confident and capable woman.

Once she had gone, Vera began her interview. We learned many things about Roderick Morley's past. For instance, we heard about the earliest time when young Roderick's moodiness became apparent, according to Mr. Brunton. The adolescent had developed an infatuation with the daughter of one of this father's former slaves, and his mother's stern admonitions about the relationship had broken his heart.

"Forbidden fruit," commented Vera, "is never out of season. I don't suppose there was ever talk about these star-crossed lovers bearing a child, was there?"

"*Vera!*" I protested. "That's a very bold thing to ask!"

Calmly, Mr. Brunton turned to me. "Oh, such things happened more often than someone of your age and experience might realize, miss. *Before* and *after* the War." He then turned to Vera. "But I very much doubt it was the case here."

Undaunted, Vera proceeded. "How did the *father* feel about the son's flirtation with miscegenation?"

"He was more sympathetic than his mother. Of course, this was a man who had worked—and worshipped—beside Negroes all his life. He understood them better than the mother. Jefferson Morley was no abolitionist, mind you, but he didn't seem very bothered when the President freed the slaves. He was very good at knowing which way the wind was blowing."

Vera put two fingers to her jaw and knit her brow. I wondered if she had never envisioned a slave owner cast in such a light.

I thought it best that I assume the role of reporter. "When Mr. Morley was in Virginia, did he ever show signs that, one day, he would devote his fortune to the uplift of colored people? That decision seems to've caught many people off guard."

"No signs that I can recall. I think that came about from his experiences here in Boston. To see the scope of a place, one often needs to be distant from it."

Vera nodded. "Very astute."

"I read that somewhere, I'm sure."

After a chuckle, Vera said, "Speaking of catching people off guard by revising his will, how would you describe Mr. Morley's marriage with—with the woman who enjoyed music. Don't tell me. *Viola!*"

Mr. Brunton placed both palms down on the table. He then brought them together. Next, he laced his fingers together. "Now, remember that I'm an old bachelor, so I'm hardly qualified to say. Nonetheless, their marriage—their marriage struck me as a very troubled one." He squinted his green eyes.

I attempted to set him at ease. "Even in the brief time that I spent with Mrs. Morley here, I felt that there was trouble. And yesterday we learned that their daughter wasn't born until four years *after* the wedding. I thought that might be the sign of— certain problems—right from the start."

The elfin giant grinned with his lips, but his eyes and posture became crestfallen. "Dorothy May. What a delightful scamp she was! And what an *atrocity* to turn her playroom into a center for Sanderson's pet project. The *Dawning* Room—ridiculous. But forgive me. Yes, as you say—certain problems from the start. I wasn't alone in thinking Viola married Roddy for his money."

Vera asked, "Why do you think that Roddy married Viola?"

"Oh—" Mr. Brunton's hands were now in prayer position, the tips of his fingers touching his chin. "Perhaps to please his father. Perhaps to maintain his place among the wellborn. A man of his social circles is under terrible pressure to keep up appearances, and in that regard, Boston is as strict as Richmond or any other Southern city."

"How did Viola feel about Silas Sanderson?"

Mr. Brunton placed his hands down on the table again. "There is one thing I never told the police when they asked the same question. I don't see how it could do any harm to tell you—*now.* I know that letters were passed between Roddy's wife and Sanderson. One of the maids—the one tasked with delivering those letters—had been sworn to secrecy about them. But her conscience got the better of her, and she confided in me."

Vera and I glanced at one another.

"For all I knew," Mr. Brunton continued, "Mrs. Morley was chastising Sanderson for his control over Roddy—or even begging him to temper that control. That is *exactly* what I would have told that cad!" He sniffed hard. "But it wasn't my place to do so. So I told the girl to continue to pass the letters with a clean conscience."

Vera leaned forward. "Might the letters have had a very different purpose?"

I clarified, "Silas Sanderson, after all, was a very charming and handsome man."

At this point, Mr. Brunton's hands were tight fists. "That possibility was exactly why I never mentioned them to the police. If Roddy *had* discovered that his wife and Sanderson had been—you know—well, combine that with his purchase of the gun! It would have looked very, very bad. You see, a Southern man's code of behavior is very clear. Very strong. It's why dueling lasted longer down there than up here. A man's honor is a serious matter where we're from. *Deadly* serious."

"And the green-eyed monster passes freely over the Mason-Dixon line," I interjected.

"Nicely phrased, Lucille. But, sir, you were saying that you didn't mention the letters to the police to safeguard Mr. Morley, correct?"

"Yes. Another of my rash choices that plagued me after his death. Please understand that, when Roddy was born, *mine* was the very first hand his father shook. I watched that baby become a young man, and when he needed help running a house after his parents passed on, he came to *me*. I had very fatherly feelings for Roddy."

I felt compelled to say, "And who's to know what was in those letters? They might have been, as you said, not letters that betrayed the husband but intended to protect him."

"To know *that*," Mr. Brunton declared pointedly, "you would have to ask the woman herself."

"Is she still in Boston?"

"Yes. Remarried now. To a prominent gentleman named Ernest Lapham. I can get you her new address—or, at least, the address she had when the house was sold. Why don't you let me arrange a time when you can meet her?"

"We would very much appreciate that," said Vera. "I fear my next question won't be any easier for you to discuss. We were told that—while you were acting as caretaker for the house—you had strange experiences that relate more directly to the haunting. Could you describe these experiences? Remember, there's little I *haven't* heard about ghostly goings-on."

Mr. Brunton remained silent. It was time for me to reach my fingertips to his arm. He patted my hand.

"As I mentioned," he said, "I felt very ashamed for the part I played in Roddy's suicide. The months following his—death— well, it was a gloomy time for me. Living here alone."

"Is it that you don't wish to discuss those months at all?" I asked.

"Not quite," he said with a clack of gravel in his voice. "It's more that I doubt what I saw. I was disturbed about Roddy taking his own life—and ready to believe that he hadn't done so. That it had all been an insane mistake. Did I see his ghost? Or did I convince myself that he hadn't died? It's all such a muddle."

"Perhaps another time, then," Vera said softly. "One final question—and a much more pleasant one. I haven't tasted a beer since leaving Chicago, and I know that Boston must have a tavern that's steeped in local history. Unfortunately, two unaccompanied women in such a place might raise eyebrows, if we're allowed to enter at all."

"You're a *beer* drinker?" he asked with raised eyebrows.

"We're *both* beer drinkers," I answered.

"That being the case," Mr. Brunton laughed, "I'd be delighted to drive you up to the Warren Tavern—if it's history you want. But if it's local *flavor* you want, I know a preferable place."

In unison, Vera and I responded, *"Local flavor!"*

•

We spent that afternoon at Police Headquarters. Mr. Watts spotted us and asked if the ghost hunt was advancing at all. Without naming Mr. Brunton as her source of information, Vera mentioned the clandestine letters passed between Mr. Sanderson and Mrs. Morley. She also told the Chief Inspector that the ghost, while cooperative, was also very selective in sharing what it knew. Mr. Watts nodded as if he were familiar with such a situation.

On our walk back to Beacon Hill, we discussed our reactions to what Mr. Brunton had revealed in the morning's interview.

"Does your giant seem any less elfin?" asked Vera.

"He clearly didn't care for Mr. Morley agreeing with Mr. Sanderson's plan to convert the playroom into a space for séances and a library of the Supernatural. Hardly reason to commit murder, though."

"True, true." Vera slowed her pace. "Those letters are of interest. If Mr. Morley *had* discovered an illicit relationship between his wife and Sanderson, there's a motive for murder. You spent a bit more time with the millionaire than I did. Did he seem capable of that kind of outburst of jealousy?"

"He struck me as a *sensitive* man, but not a man of action. To be sure, it doesn't take *much* action to pull a trigger. And I know nothing about a Southern man's code of honor."

"I wonder if Mr. Morley did. The more I study him, the more I perceive him to be a 'man caught between.' When he fell for the daughter of the former slave, he was caught between the *racial* divide. Even after he settled in the North, he was still caught between the *regional* divide. Then he started frequenting séances and searching for those he had lost. Caught between the *ultimate* divide."

"So you discount Mr. Brunton's comment about the code of honor?"

"As it applies to Mr. Morley. But what if the fatherly butler knew *more* about those letters than he admitted? The same letters he failed to mention to the police. What if Mr. Brunton took it upon *himself* to defend that Southern code of honor? He had spent much more time steeped in Virginia tradition than his 'Roddy' had. And the police records show he had no solid proof of where he was when the murder was committed."

The logic in this was unsettling. I found myself resenting Vera's earlier advice to picture our four suspects as Halloween goblins. With a splash of vinegar in my voice, I asked, "Is there *anything* in that line of reasoning that helps us sort out the three manifestations?"

Vera halted but remained looking forward. She sighed. "The tearing of fabric to suggest ripping up the *letters* is no more convincing than ripping up the *will*. You make a good point."

"Shall we pay a visit to Dr. James sometime soon?" I asked. As soon as I had spoken, I realized that I was implying that Vera's colleague should be treated with as much suspicion as my own least-likely suspect.

Vera seemed not to infer that, though, and she resumed our stroll. "He's informed me that late Thursday is the earliest he can meet with us. Mid-semester is a busy time. I'm more interested in Mrs. Viola Morley at present. Let's hope Brunton is able to arrange *that* interview."

I remained quiet for the rest of the walk, wondering if Vera would allow for the possibility that Dr. James might be the culprit.

Later, after another of Miss Marchelli's delicious dinners, I also wondered if Vera had exercised her "feminine wiles" when asking Mr. Brunton about a place to drink beer. Indeed, once we had arrived at the tavern he had suggested, she was able to get him to drink—and to speak—freely.

The tavern was among the wharfs of Boston Harbor, the salty air outside blending the smell of steamed clams and smoky cigars within. It was called The Pitcher and Coach because of the history of its location. Back in the days of stage coaches, the site had been used for watering horses and "watering" passengers. A modern building now stood there, and on its first floor, the tavern was as welcoming to financiers as to fishermen. I was pleased to spot several women among the customers, since it seemed to be a place where Vera and I might return before our investigation was over.

"An ideal setting for a beer!" Vera cheered as we entered. "I wonder if the locals ever gather to play music here. You know, sea shanties and a melancholy air or two?"

Mr. Brunton scratched his beard. "I've never known that to happen. This is a waystation between a long day's work and a restful evening at home. The place is usually empty by nine o'clock. But you'll see all manner of Bostonians here."

Vera cocked her head. "Oh well—chilled or spilled, it's still a pilsner." She led us to a table in a quiet corner.

The first round was spent discussing how Vera and I moved

from debunking séances to expunging ghosts. Mr. Brunton also revealed why he remained working at what had been the Morley Mansion, a mystery that Vera deemed suspicious.

"Primarily, it's my aches and pains," he said. "Any more than a single flight of stairs feels like Pike's Peak these days, and houses that employ butlers invariably have several flights of stairs. I confess, though, that I also feel beholden to the memory of the Morleys. It's why I encouraged Mr. Childers to hire you two. So long as Roddy's spirit cannot rest, neither can my own."

While I felt a touch of triumph in this answer, I saw the bridge of Vera's nose wrinkle. Whether she found a stink in his answer—or in the cigar of the gentleman at the next table—I was not sure.

"Besides, my schoolroom back in Virginia was the Morley planation stables. I grew up tending horses. So you see, my life has gone from livery to *livery*," he said, tugging his lapels to suggest the dignified apparel of a butler, "back to livery."

Vera and I smiled politely.

Mr. Brunton shrugged. "That comment might be more deserving of a laugh in England, where footmen and butlers wear livery more regularly."

Vera and I raised our glasses to his attempted witticism, and he took a satisfied swallow of beer. My aversion to thinking of this man as capable of murder deepened. He seemed too ordinary, too companionable.

The second round of beer was spent discussing Mr. Brunton's childhood in rural Virginia and its contrasts to my own in metropolitan Illinois. Typically reticent about her early years, Vera sidestepped the subject to relate a few of the more bizarre cases handled by her ghost-hunting mentor, Harry Escott. These are tales for another time, of course, but my love of reading nudges me to note that one supernatural mystery involved Mr. Escott meeting the great author Edgar Allan Poe!

The third round of beer started with Vera resuming her discussion of Mr. Escott.

"Harry was a believer in ghost-seers," she explained. "The theory is that one sees or otherwise perceives a ghost because the witness is *en rapport* with the specter in the way that a medium makes contact with a spirit guide or a mesmerist does with a subject. In other words, Harry felt that some people simply have a knack for spotting ghosts—but there are degrees of being *en rapport*. It's possible, then, for anyone to witness a ghost depending upon the affinity they share with it."

Remaining expressionless and silent, Mr. Brunton took another swig of beer.

"Harry might have attributed, for example, your encounter with Mr. Morley's ghost while you served as caretaker—not to the longstanding *affection* you shared—but to the psychic *affinity* you shared. Even strangers can share this affinity. Now, my conjecture is that, if all of this were true, there would be no way to tell if your ghost was real or merely a delusion. Do you have any thoughts on that, sir?"

Mr. Brunton gave his beard a slow stroke. "I may be a country boy, Miss Van Slyke, but I'm a *large* country boy. You'll need more than two beers to dupe me into telling you what I saw during that time."

Turning her face down, Vera said, "Sometimes, our eyes certainly do fool us—but, sometimes, what you *think* you saw is *exactly* what you saw. I hoped that, with my experience, I might help resolve whether you saw a ghost or only *thought* you did."

I added, "And this information might help release Mr. Morley from whatever keeps him earthbound." Mr. Childers had compared Mr. Brunton to a sly fox on the matter of his ghostly encounter. However, I wished to free—not trap—my giant elf.

The large man closed his eyes and kept them closed. "It *would* be good to break Roddy from his chains."

Vera looked up with her lips pressed tightly together.

The large man took one more swig before nodding and then leaned forward. He eased into telling his tale. "Have you ever had the experience of being in the dark and *thinking* you see a face—perhaps even a body—but you're just not quite sure? You stare and stare at it while your thoughts scramble to determine what odd pattern in the wallpaper or the woodgrain—or the moonlight shining on the hanging coat—accounts for the illusion. And all the time you wonder: but what if it's *not* an illusion?"

We replied that we knew that experience. Of the many accounts of ghostly manifestations I had heard since meeting Vera Van Slyke, the one then related by Mr. Brunton was among the most uncanny.

"Well," he began, "I had that experience—more than once—when I climbed by the third floor at night with only a candle. My room was still on the fourth floor, you see. This was only a few months after Roddy had taken his life—and approaching a year from Sanderson's death. I was living alone in the house.

"The first time I spotted it, the figure was about midway down the hall at the very brink of my candle's light. I couldn't be sure, but it seemed to be crouching—facing me, but hunched with its hands on its knees. Not leaning back against a wall. Just crouching there in the hall and somehow remaining perfectly still while staring back at me. Patiently staring back at me. 'Is there someone there!' I demanded. It didn't move.

"That posture is what paralyzed me, I think. The motionless crouching. If it had moved even slightly, then I might have known how to react. I would have inched closer, or I would have *fled*. I raised the candle, lowered it, shifted it from left to right, all in the hope that light cast from a different angle might expose the illusion. Or expose the intruder! No. It remained crouching.

"If I *had* thought it was Roddy come back, I was growing convinced it could not be. Why would he be appearing in this ludicrous position? No, this—this *thing* struck me as something that might *never* have lived on Earth. Especially when I moved the candle and noticed there was absolutely no glint in its eyes. It *did* have eye sockets, that much was certain! But where the eyes *should* have been, there were only dark, empty smudges.

"That first time, I did the cowardly thing. For fear it would pounce at me if I approached, I went back downstairs. I coughed loudly. Then I climbed the stairs again, pretending that nothing was amiss. I didn't go so far as to whistle, but I'm not entirely sure I could have whistled. Even so, the crouching figure was gone now. I had a uneasy laugh at my blunder.

"But it was back a night or two after. As I climbed those same stairs at the same hour, I glanced down the same hall. The figure was now crouching beside the door to Dorothy May's playroom. The so-called *Dawning* Room, where Sanderson's corpse had been found. Perhaps the scoundrel should've named it the *Dying* Room—wouldn't *that* have been—oh, forgive me. This time, I noticed the door to that room was *open*. I always kept it closed. 'I'm only the caretaker!' I heard myself shout. 'If you're here to rob the place—' At this instant, the vision retreated—but not into the room. It retreated into its own—I don't know how to express it. More than simply shrinking, the figure *receded in size*. Imagine watching a caboose disappearing into a tunnel. Vaguely like that. But with no tunnel around it."

Whether it was time for the tavern's patrons to head home or it was an effect of my third beer, Mr. Brunton's baritone voice was steadily becoming the *only* sound reaching my ears.

"And yet, this night, I saw the door swing almost to the point of closing. And then it swung open—and again almost closed—and opened again. It continued, and I spoke to it again. 'Are you here to *taunt* me!' The prospect that I was being mocked gave me courage. This night, I intended to prove to myself that there was nothing supernatural happening, even if it would cost me a cracked skull!

"I approached the door. Of course, there had been no fires on that floor, and it was still early Spring, so it was naturally cold. But the temperature noticeably dropped with each step toward the Dawning Room. A *prickly* cold, almost like a lightning storm was approaching—but very much colder."

Mr. Brunton took another swallow of beer. The quivering

foam in his glass showed that his hand was trembling.

"Once I reached the doorway, the swinging had stopped with the door wide open. Was I being *invited* to enter—or was I being *dared* to enter? As I say, I was feeling ridiculed as much as terrified, and that was enough for me to take that last step into the room. The temperature changed markedly, from prickly cold to downright *balmy*. It made no sense. There had been no fire, and it was nighttime. But this felt like the warmth of Virginia in that season, not Massachusetts!

"As I raised the candle to survey the room, I saw the crouching figure again, the same hollow eye sockets. It was beside the bay window. I stared back at it until, in the corner of my eye, I became aware of something—*materializing*. As if dust were being drawn together to form a mass. I turned, and I jolted when I saw—not something *else*—but the very same crouching figure staring at me there beside the door to the guest room. Turning back to the first figure, I discovered it had vanished, but now there was another dim mass in the other corner of my eye. Yes, there was the crouching figure *yet again* beside one of the bookcases on the other side of the room!

"I knew then that I was not being taunted. Not ridiculed. I was being *tormented*. I don't know by what exactly. A demon? It was *that* possibility that reminded of the phrase 'Get thee behind me, Satan.' I was too, too horrified to say the words, but their meaning must have given me strength. Inching backward, step by step, I began to remove myself from that damned room. And everywhere I looked, *there* was the crouching figure. At last, I made my way free—and I've avoided that room ever since."

We sat silently. Indeed, the crowded tavern had become emptied but for only a few customers. Mr. Brunton lifted the glass of beer toward his mouth, but put it back down on the table instead of sipping from it.

"Did you ever see the figure again?" I whispered.

He managed to take another sip of beer before he nodded. "Twice more, and both times, it tried to lure me into the room again. The first time, I sat down on the steps, refusing to look back at it, for what might have been close to an hour, and when I finally pulled myself up, it had gone. The last time, I barked some rather uncivil words and did my best to ignore it. What is your diagnosis, Miss Van Slyke? How *real* was my crouching ghost?"

Vera hadn't touched her beer, which was a worrisome thing. She grinned as if it hurt to do so. "Though not unheard of, it's rare for a ghost to 'torment' the living. Typically, *they're* the ones tormented. What happens if we flip the coin? What if, instead of a tormenting demon, your crouching ghost were a protector? Your beloved employer? The psychic advisor? I don't know, but I cannot help but think that there's a vague message regarding the Dawning Room here."

I couldn't help but interject, "And *we* were given a similar message—a similarly *vague* message—when Vera's typewriter ribbon tin was weirdly placed on the doorknob leading from the Green Room to *that* room! That room holding all that history!"

"Very astute, my dear," Vera said. She turned to Mr. Brunton. "Your encounter strikes me as similar to a warning dream. Now, ghosts have been known to communicate a warning—or simply an important memory—usually, to someone asleep or under a trance."

"But I was wide awake, I assure you!" Mr. Brunton insisted.

"Precisely. Before I decide if it was a ghost or a hallucination or even some combination of the two, I must consult a book or two. Unfortunately, most of my resources are back in Chicago."

Mr. Brunton leaned backward, almost growling.

"Perhaps, there are some useful volumes in the—uhm, in what is now Mr. Childers' library," I suggested with a glance towards Mr. Brunton. "He mentioned that many of the books Mr. Morley purchased remain there. I too have been avoiding that room since my return—due to my own demons—but those hollow eyes you described will now haunt *my* dreams! Even a blind person's eyes reflect candlelight!"

Mr. Brunton gave me a sympathetic smile as Vera put two

fingers to her jaw.

Our companion leaned forward again. "Unfortunately, that library has become Mr. Childers's sanctum. You might not know him well enough, but he is a very private man."

"Yes—we know," I said, recalling my implication about visiting his workshop and his pointed aversion to it.

Mr. Brunton grinned. "I fancy he scribbles down some of his inventions while he's in there, which is frequently. The point is— he keeps it *locked.* He'll tell you the locks prevent the many maids who have paraded through the house from rearranging things when they clean. I can't imagine, though, that he would mind if you borrowed a book or two."

"But we should ask permission?" I inquired.

"You should ask permission," Mr. Brunton answered.

All the while, Vera's two fingers tapped against her jaw.

ᗡ CHAPTER NINE ᗡ

THREE DOCUMENTS
OF A SINGLE MORNING

At breakfast the next morning, Vera informed Mr. Childers of what we had learned from Mr. Brunton. First, she admitted that coaxing him to relate his ghost story had required a touch of wiles, but she maintained that they had been journalistic, not feminine. She also mentioned the alleged letters passed clandestinely between Mr. Sanderson and Mrs. Morley, letters that—if located—might establish a motive to commit murder, both for the husband and for the butler with deep emotional attachments to the husband.

"Of course," said Vera, "this is a gray gull feather floating on the gray ocean."

I clarified, "She means it doesn't have much weight. It's indefinite."

"Oh yes!" said Mr. Childers. "I understood the metaphor perfectly. How wonderful that the investigation is succeeding swiftly!" This morning, his smile was not a snarling dog's. It was a lighthearted boy's.

"Returning to Mr. Brunton's ghost story," Vera said, "it is markedly different from the manifestations you've experienced. I'm not fully convinced of its authenticity for that reason. However, if authentic, it indicates we *aren't* dealing with a phantom locked into recreating some trauma—say, the trauma that ended in death. Instead, the ghost seems to be doing his best to convey some message. There's unfinished business in this house, in other words."

"It's like a puzzle in the back of a magazine!" Mr. Childers exclaimed.

Vera nodded. "And our task is to solve that puzzle. There are certain books that can assist us. You mentioned that you have Owen's *Footfalls,* and I never travel without Crowe's *Night-Side.* May I have permission to see if there are any other useful resources in your library?"

I had known Vera long enough to recognize a particular angle of her head—a particular directness of her gaze—when she was doing more than simply asking a question. She was scrutinizing exactly *how* that question will be answered.

Mr. Childers' giddiness was unruffled. "Without a doubt!" He dug into a pocket in his trousers, retrieved a ring of keys, and removed one of them. "It'll be good to get some use out of those dusty books. I'd have gone ahead and replaced them with my own long ago, but the ones I really need all belong at my workshop."

Vera raised an eyebrow. "But I'm told you visit the library here with some frequency. And you keep it locked."

Mr. Childers laughed as he passed the key to Vera. "You'll think me a bit silly, I suppose. You see, back in Tennessee, I grew up in a tiny house—a cabin, really—where I shared a bedroom with *three* brothers! It's a pleasure to have one room that's mine and mine alone—not even invaded by a maid."

"We all would like to have a private *sanctum,*" I agreed, borrowing Mr. Brunton's word.

"Exactly! And I find the desk there very useful for figuring household finances and whatnot."

The pursing of Vera's lips and her fiddling with the key let me know that she had been hoping for something a bit more revelatory.

After breakfast, Mr. Childers departed for his workshop, and Vera and I headed to the third floor. She told me that she would understand if I didn't want to join her in the library. My desire to avoid the room, though, was eclipsed by an impulse to see it again.

I was astonished upon entering.

"It's *exactly* the same!" I hissed. "He hasn't just left the books in place! That's the same table. The same chairs. The same desk and the same dark curtain over the window."

"Even the same lithograph hanging there," Vera added. "We mustn't snoop too much, but let's take a glance at the desk."

True enough, there were ledgers along with receipts from the last few weeks. Everything was as Mr. Childers had said, but so much remained the same that I had a feeling of stepping backward in time. It was unnerving, and I quickly excused myself while Vera began to scan the books.

Only a short time passed before Vera returned to our room with an armload of books. She went to work, rifling through the books and typing a biographical sketch of Mr. Brunton. I was left with nothing else to do. I stared through the window as people outside bustled to work. I then attempted to read the collection of tales I had failed to read during the train trip east. Meeting with similar frustration, I tossed the book aside and rose to pace.

I wanted to see the Dawning Room again.

It was a strange compulsion, one which I did not understand and which I labored to resist. However, before long, I had discreetly taken the key that Vera had placed beside her and strolled silently into the hallway. After only a moment's hesitation, I unlocked the door and wandered in again.

Quite quickly, I realized that my earlier astonishment at seeing the unchanged room might have been inflated. Mrs. Morley did not share her husband's fascination with the Supernatural, and it followed that she would be glad to be rid of these many books. Mr. Childers had kept many of the Morleys' furnishings, and his own library was at his workshop. Still, as I brushed my fingertips along the backs of the chairs around the séance table, I couldn't help but sense that something was amiss. Unlike the rest of the house, virtually *no* changes had been made here.

I sat in the same chair I had occupied almost four years earlier. I recalled my first meeting with the late Roderick Morley.

My ruses to convince him that I was trustworthy. My playing the part of little Marianne, a role I had coerced my mother to accept against her wishes. My snide retaliation for Vera switching the candles. My having agreed to perform one last séance because the *payment* would make acting on an ethical decision far less burdensome.

I began to cry quietly.

I'm not sure how long I sat there before Miss Marchelli knocked softly on the door, which I had left open. I quickly wiped the tears from my cheeks and pretended that nothing at all was the matter.

"Forgive me for interrupting, Miss Parsell," said she. "I didn't realize you were—. Two letters arrived for Miss Van Slyke, and I hear her working on her typewriting."

"Oh, thank you! Here, I'll take them to her. That's one of my duties. As her assistant, I mean."

The maid turned to leave, but she turned back slowly. "Do you think the three of us might have our lunch today? Mr. Childers dines near his workshop, so I won't have to feed him. And I know of a restaurant in the North End that I think you'd both enjoy."

"We have no plans for lunch. I'd be happy to ask Miss Van Slyke about your offer."

Miss Marchelli thanked me, and after lifting her hand as if wishing to give me a comforting touch, she dropped her arm and left the room. I inhaled deeply, struggled up from the chair, and reached for the key. I had placed it on the séance table near where I had sat, but it was not there now.

"Oh, you pesky ghost!" I spit. "Where've you put that key?"

I searched the floor around the table, checked the seats of each of the chairs, scanned the desktop, then scoured the bookcases. And there it was, on one of the bottom shelves. It was leaning upright, the bit of the key resting between the spines of two adjacent books. With a moment's inspiration, I wondered if the ghost were dropping another hint. I noted the two books: Sir

Walter Scott's *Letters on Demonology and Witchcraft*, which was an old volume, and Joseph Glanvil's even older *Saducismus Triumphatus.*

I locked the door behind me with the two letters in hand. Vera was still working, so I opened her correspondence, read it, and prepared to summarize it, exactly as I would at the office back at the Hotel Manitou. I then waited for Vera to finish her biographical sketch.

"Here," she said, handing me her work. "It's rough and incomplete, but why don't you read this while I read the letters on my own? You'll see that the last couple of pages can be passed along to Mr. Brunton, since I attempt to make sense of his crouching ghost there."

"Fine, but before I forget—I know of some evidence, if it's not mere happenstance."

"Is it that, despite our client being a private man, he disclosed that he's from Tennessee? This house certainly seems to attract sons of the Confederacy, doesn't it?"

"Yes, I noticed that, too. But my discovery involves a couple of books."

I guided Vera to the two volumes, explaining what—or *who*—had led me to them. After replacing the ones she had borrowed, Vera stayed in the library to consider Scott's and Glanvil's books along with the two letters. I returned to the comfortable, pine-green cushion by the bay window in our room to read Vera's biographical sketch of Mr. Brunton.

This chronicle continues with that sketch—again with Vera's jotted side comments in brackets—followed by those two letters.

—

Richard Elijah Brunton was born in the Commonwealth of Virginia, in the year of 1837. He described his life as moving "from livery to livery, back to livery." In other words, his father managed the horses for Jefferson Morley's tobacco plantation, and Richard spent his boyhood assisting in the livery stable. When old enough, he advanced to the main house as a footman. Eventually, Mr. Brunton rose to the status of butler, a position he continued in Boston when hired by the younger Morley. However, as age—and stairways—took their toll, he accepted the profession of his father, albeit on a much smaller scale.

Mr. Brunton held a deep sense of duty to Roderick Morley. This and his Southern code of honor are matters of concern. He resented the influence exerted by Mr. Sanderson on his employer and, especially, the advisor's success in reassigning the playroom to serve as a center for psychical study. Add to this the police reports, which explain that Mr. Brunton was unable to confirm his location on the morning of the murder. On his way to worship, said he, the warm July sunshine reminded him of his younger days in Virginia—and he decided to give praise under the sky of Boston Common rather than the roof of the cathedral. Despite the park being crowded, Mr. Brunton knew of no one to corroborate this.

Though under suspicion in the case, Mr. Brunton has become one of its most valuable sources of clues. His secondhand knowledge of private letters passed between Mr. Sanderson and Mrs. Morley introduces—however tentatively—a motive behind Sanderson's murder for two suspects. The letters are quite likely destroyed by now. Their value lies mostly in steering further investigation. [If merited, ask Brunton the identity of the maid who fretted over delivering the letters? Could Watts locate her for us?]

While acting as caretaker of the mansion, Brunton experienced an unusual ghostly manifestation: a crouching figure with dark "eye sockets." It appeared four times near and within the Dawning Room. Unfamiliar with such sightings, he interpreted them as hostile and demonic. Greater familiarity with such subjects leads this writer to a choice of very different possibilities:

   a) it was merely the hallucination of a sleepy man alone in a
      house with his painful memories, or
   b) the figure was struggling to communicate an important
      message.

Regarding the latter possibility, a stark contrast is provided in T.M. Jarvis's <u>Accredited Ghost Stories</u>, which recounts a number of cases of what I term "chatty phantoms." Francis Taverner, for instance, was approached by a ghost who bid him to clear up a matter with his will, and when Taverner failed to comply, that ghost became quite vociferous, threatening to "tear him in pieces." The ghost of a woman mistreated in life by Lord Lyttleton returned to warn that man—in a plainspoken manner—that he best repent his sins or die at midnight in three days. Jarvis's most telling narrative is of the "hour and three quarters' conversation," in which Mrs. Bargrave reminisced with her old friend, Mrs. Veal, a woman who was afterward revealed to have died prior to the chat. This reporter has met with one or two "chatty phantoms" in person, but they are woefully rare.

More typical is the ghost with severely limited means of communication. Catherine Crowe exemplifies this type in <u>The Night-Side of Nature</u>. The case involves a man named Dorrien, a conscientious man who died with an unpaid debt. His guilt regarding the debt was great enough that Dorrien returned from the spirit realm to convey it to colleagues at the college where he had tutored. After some preliminary sightings by various witnesses, one smart professor theorized that Dorrien had left behind an unpaid bill. As brave as he was clever, the man waited for the ghost and then asked if his conjecture were correct, to which the specter was observed to draw a hand across its mouth while holding a pipe. The professor deduced that Dorrien's debt was to the tobacconist, but this proved incorrect. Crowe then says that the dark apparition of Dorrien finally "presented another sign or symbol, which seemed to represent a picture, with a hole in the middle, through which it thrust its head." When asked for clarification, Dorrien could only mutely shake his head—but he repeated the same symbol to different members of the faculty. Combining their intellects, the professors at last hit upon the solution: Dorrien "had obtained, on trial, several pictures for a magic lantern, which had never been returned to their owner."

Once the pictures were returned, Dorrien's debt-free ghost was never seen again.

The haunting at hand is similarly a case of unraveling what has been fittingly termed a "cryptogram." If Mr. Brunton's visitor were struggling to communicate—in the way that Dorrien had while gesturing with the pipe—we must consider it alongside the subsequent three manifestations. The first notable feature of the apparition is its crouching posture. Mr. Brunton assumed this to be a prelude to pouncing, a sign of danger. However, crouching also suggests an attempt to hide oneself or, generally, someone being secretive. This led the writer to wonder if there's a warning here. A simpler interpretation, though, is that the ghost is referring to someone noticeably shorter. [What was Sanderson's height? Who in this case is short?]

Another outstanding feature is the figure's eyes or lack thereof. Mr. Brunton reported that no candlelight was reflected by them, and Lucille noted that blind people's eyes still reflect candlelight. This, in combination with the figure appearing in various spots in the library, suggests that the symbol might be of a person thwarted in locating something there. [Something hidden in the library? The letters? Why C. keeps it locked? The timing is wrong.]

Upon passing from a frigid hallway into the library, Mr. Brunton reports he felt unseasonable warmth. Following the hallucination theory, this could have been a misinterpretation of his own bodily responses: the chill of "perceiving a ghost" and the heat of becoming excited. (The latter might have added to his interpreting the phantom as hellish.) If authentic, however, the temperature increase could be a clue of a warmer climate—and, oddly enough, the mansion has been owned by at least two Southern gentlemen. Indeed, perhaps the ghost was hoping to remind the former butler of his Virginia home.

One final note: Mr. Brunton's guilt for having had a hand in Mr. Morley's suicide might have punctured the membrane between the dimensions, allowing for the ghostly activity. The ruptures can occur from the Other Side, however, and if Morley shot Sanderson, his suicide may well have been incited by the same emotion. The challenge, then, is to connect either of these men to 1) the searcher in the library, 2) the ripper of cloth, and 3) the prankster who moves small items. [Stray phrases from a front page article yet to be written!]

—

Oct. 20

Dear Miss Van Slyke,

My late husband's butler, Mr. Brunton, visited to inform me that you've returned to Boston and that you would like to speak to me regarding your investigation of a ghost lurking at the Beacon Hill mansion. What a remarkable woman you are!

I was unable to give him an immediate answer, which is why I send this letter instead. I trust that you will understand my hesitations in complying with your request. When I find myself shaken by memories of those years, my current husband advises me to picture my life as a symphony: the adagio gloom of one movement now finished, and the next, a lively minuet, begun.

A cheerful setting, though, might permit me to answer your questions without much agitation to my nerves. I shall wait for you tomorrow afternoon (Wednesday) beside the Ether Monument in the Public Garden. Let us say 2:00 4:00.

Mr. Brunton says the unfortunate girl with us on that tragic evening serves as your assistant now. You were kind to take her under your wing. I look forward to meeting you both again.

> With my sincere admiration,
> Mrs. Lapham

P.S. It now strikes me that this letter will not arrive until Wednesday morning. I hope you are able to meet me at the alternate time above. If you do not arrive, I will understand. If you discover that I am not there, I hope <u>you</u> will understand.

—

Bureau of Criminal Investigation
Boston Police Headquarters
October 20, 1903

Miss Van Slyke:

I hope your investigation is going well. Since our meeting on Monday, I have been amused by the similarities of hunting ghosts and hunting criminals. You guard the laws of Nature. I guard the laws of Man. I bow to the duty you show to your vocation. I trust you will grant me the same courtesy regarding the duty I show to my avocation.

I need not remind you of another similarity between your work and mine. As I understand it, your theory is that strong guilt breaches the barrier separating us from the next world. Guilt is something I know very well. I know that it can lend a hand in apprehending a criminal. A few years since, I was searching for some freight stolen from a railroad company. Imagine my surprise when two large crates containing much of that freight were dropped here at headquarters. A letter arrived the next day with a promise to repay the railroad for the missing goods. True to his word, the anonymous writer paid the sum in full, though he was only able to do so in installments! This shows us how guilt can haunt some criminals.

We learn something about Sanderson's killer in the fact that the crime was committed in the Morley home instead of a darkened alley or even Sanderson's own residence. This was an impulsive act, not one of cold-blooded premeditation. The murderer, therefore, is likely troubled by some degree of guilt for the rash deed. (How the passage of four years might dull this guilt is impossible to say.)

Some criminals are drawn back to the place where a crime has been perpetrated. Is it guilt that drives them? Is it to confront that haunting regret and to master it? Why they risk doing so is a mystery to be solved by a detective smarter than me. My plan, though, depends on the culprit's guilt being excited by a return to the place where the crime was committed. More on this shortly.

Now, I have no idea if guilt acts like a crowbar, allowing ghosts entry into our world. I cannot doubt, though, that your use of oboes to tug these alleged punctures into our visual spectrum was more than impressive. I found it disarming. I think anyone would do so.

With this in mind, I propose that we gather our key suspects in the same room where Sanderson's body was discovered. You and your assistant will then perform your trick with the oboes, explaining your theory. I have confidence that the sight of those purple rings—compounded with being again at the scene of the killing—will so shake the murderer as to trigger a landslide of remorse. This landslide, in turn, could end with a full confession to the crime.

If this plan fails, we lose no ground. If a success, it closes a case left open for too long. That benefits me. It will also crack the whip regarding the first phase of your ghost hunt. As you said, solving the Sanderson murder will take you a far way toward evicting the supernatural tenant. That benefits you.

I have already dispatched officers to "invite the guests," and I will personally request that Mr. Childers grant us the use of his residence on Friday evening at 8:00. By that time, the room in question can be made dark enough for your purple rings to shine their brightest and, with luck, expose our culprit.

> Cordially,
> William B. Watts
> Chief Inspector

CHAPTER TEN

WOMEN WHO HAVE TRUDGED THROUGH MUD

"Buongiorno, come posso aiutarla mia bella signorina?" asked the gentleman behind the bakery counter.

Flustered, I replied, "Anglicky?"—the Czech word for English. I spun to Miss Marchelli for rescue.

Laughing, she explained that the clerk had assumed I was Italian, and upon hearing of his mistake, he repeated the very same explanation in his best English. Miss Marchelli then ordered a dessert, her gift to us for having treated her to lunch across the street. Meanwhile, Vera and I took a table by the window.

Since we had a private moment, I said, "You seem very quiet. Was the ravioli not to your liking?"

Vera blinked several times before turning from the street view to me. "Oh. No—no, I liked it very much. I guess I'm in a brown study because of that letter from—from—"

"Mr. Watts? Is it his proposal to use our oboes to shock and shake a confession out of the murderer?"

Vera nodded and returned to gazing outside. "Our 'trick with the oboes,' as he terms it. Does it strike you as one step short of strong-arming a confession? Illuminating the holes between the dimensions should be a means to study the reaches of reality!" She turned back with a sneer. "Not a—what did he call it?—a *crowbar*! Certainly, not a tool to force a confession!"

"I do wish the Chief Inspector had *proposed* his proposal rather than stating his intention to execute it."

Vera crossed her arms and cocked her head. "But otherwise you *agree* with his methods?"

"Well, if—if we're discussing methods," I said cautiously, "you used the same oboes to gain access to police files. One might argue that the manner in which you coaxed Mr. Brunton to share his story of the crouching ghost—" I stopped there.

Vera turned again to face the window. "But to have that man come *stomping in* on my investigation—" She stopped there.

I took a moment to consider if speech or silence would better serve the situation.

Finally, I decided to say, "It's worrisome to think that the suspects might become more guarded in what they say if Friday's gathering fails to elicit a confession. Luckily, we speak to the widow this afternoon and Dr. James tomorrow." Seeing Vera continue to face away, I clarified my point. "We'll have met with all of our suspects before Friday. And that's fortunate."

She turned back. "We were making progress, but we'd have to be as fast as a frog to catch our fly by tomorrow. Do you think that's it? Do you think Mr. Watts wants to make sure he solves this case before a couple of *females* beat him to it?"

I stared at Vera. Finally, I replied, "As fast as a *frog*. Most people would've said something more like 'as fast as a *jackrabbit*.'"

"A jackrabbit! Jackrabbits don't *catch* things! A jackrabbit is fast to avoid being the thing *caught!* No, a *jackrabbit* wouldn't have served at all."

"I stand corrected. And dare I ask how your fascinating brain envisions Mr. Watts?"

Before Vera could answer, Miss Marchelli arrived with a plate of three Italian pastries called *cannoli*. They were comprised of rolls of fried dough filled with a creamy cheese that she referred to as *ricotta*.

"And, Lucille," she said while sliding the plate toward us, "you'll be pleased to learn that yours is courtesy of the clerk who assumed that a girl so pretty must surely be Italian."

I resisted an urge to nod my thanks to that flirtatious clerk.

Then Miss Marchelli said something unexpected. "Maybe

you're not Italian, but I'd wager your real name isn't Lucille Parsell. You were the first of us to step into this bakery, and you led the way with so much familiarity that I'd also wager that's why the clerk took you for a local."

I saw Vera sit upright as a smirk came to her face.

My own face grew warm. "It's true. My real name is Ludmila Prášilová. I must admit that this area of Boston reminds me a bit of the Czech neighborhood where I grew up in Chicago. The smells of food and the sounds of conversation in something other than English. Well, I suppose the language is different. And the storefront signs have *far* too many vowels."

Chewing her first bite, Vera muttered, "These pastries are a sweet antidote for a sour mood! And your drawing a correct conclusion from how a person enters a bakery is outstanding!"

Miss Marchelli shrugged and then faced Vera. "I also know that *your* mother took in sewing when you were a girl. You mended your nightgown yesterday morning like you were a seamstress in a mill."

Vera paused—swallowed—and then spoke. "How do you know I learned the skill from my *mother*? How do you know I haven't *been* a seamstress in a mill?"

"You don't talk like a mill girl, so the next most likely way you learned to sew is from your mother."

Vera tilted her head before saying, "Remarkable. And, again, completely correct. My mother *did* take in sewing, and I assisted. You see, my father always struggled to find customers for his candles."

"Because they made people sneeze?" I said with a giggle.

"Well," Vera replied softly, "some of our neighbors *did* sniff their noses at him."

Vera's eyes drifted to the window yet again. Her sour mood was returning, so I changed the subject.

"Given your deductive talent," I said to Miss Marchelli, "we might benefit from your company as we interview Mrs. Lapham this afternoon. I mentioned her during lunch, I think?"

"Yeah, the beautiful widow," she replied. "From what you told me, she's nervous about revisiting what happened there. S'probably best I'm not with you. Two's company—three's the start of a lynch mob."

Vera nodded. "Very astute."

"But I *will* give you a piece of advice," said Miss Marchelli, "that is—advice from a *maid.*"

"Oh, your occupation doesn't matter a scrap to us," Vera began.

I finished, "You've earned our admiration and, I hope, our friendship."

"Thank you, but that's not what I meant." Miss Marchelli brushed the crumbs from her fingers. "My *deductive talent* starts with knowing that most women"—and, here, she paused to gaze purposefully at myself and then at Vera—"*most* women have secrets in their pasts. I'd say it's from living in a man's world, but I calculate most men have secrets in *their* pasts, too. Now, if you've been trudging through the mud, no matter how hard you scrape your shoes, s'hard not to track some of it on the rug."

With her eyebrows high, Vera said, "I like how you think, my dear. If you ever relocate to Chicago and seek employment, *do* contact me."

Sophia dismissed the compliment with a wave.

I chuckled. Then, suddenly, I crossed my arms and cocked my head at Vera.

•

"The ducks are gone," I observed. "They were here when we passed by on Monday."

"That time of year," Vera muttered. Her thoughts were on more important matters, probably what should be said and what shouldn't be said to our next suspect.

We crossed Charles Street from the Common to the Public Garden. The day was almost as sunny and refreshingly cool as it had been on our arrival, but there was almost no breeze. The leaves were not rustling, and shoes—our own and those of passersby—clacked against the sidewalk. Instead of a park, I felt as if I were in a museum or a cathedral.

We spotted Mrs. Lapham on a bench near the Ether Monument. True to my memory of her stylishness, she was wearing a navy coat with ermine fur lapels and cuffs. Her hat, gloves, and scarf were all of a lighter blue and all trimmed with ermine. Her blonde hair was hidden by the wide brim of the hat.

She stood when she recognized us. "Miss Van Slyke! Miss— *Parsell*, isn't it? How lovely to see you both again. Thank you for indulging my wish that we meet outside. This is perhaps my very favorite spot in the city."

"I can see why," I replied while shaking her hand.

"With luck," said Vera, "the three of us can visit The Pitcher and Coach together before our trip is complete."

Mrs. Lapham knit her brow.

"A tavern by the bay," I explained.

She laughed. "No, I hardly think my husband would approve of *that*. But I would love to hear how it is you two remain in each other's company after four years."

Vera replied, "Do you see those squirrels chasing one another? A map of my life's wanderings would make them dizzy." Never one for chitchat, she led us back to the bench where Mrs. Lapham had been waiting. "So let's make better use of our time by seeing if we can't understand why your former residence is now home to a ghost."

Though the wide brim of her hat blocked her face when she looked down, it was still apparent that the topic of discussion agitated Mrs. Lapham. She needed a moment to settle herself on the bench between Vera and me.

The well-practiced reporter began the interview. "Can you tell us a bit about your childhood? We know that you've lived in Boston all your life."

Mrs. Lapham took a moment to arrange the layers of her apparel before speaking. "Yes. I was raised in Lower Allston, a neighborhood not too far from here. My father was a successful pharmacist there. It was a quiet life. Different from my life with Roderick, you know, in terms of—financial advantages. In many ways, though, preferable in its simplicity. Lower Allston is *not* Beacon Hill."

Our suspect directed her last comment to me. I was able to see her face more clearly, and I noticed that the barest lines had come to the outer points of her eyes and curled around the outer points of her lips. She was still very beautiful, if not more so, for the added humanity.

"You married Mr. Morley," Vera resumed, "and I was very saddened to learn about your loss of young Dorothy May. We spoke with Mr. Brunton yesterday, and I was struck by how he opposed the conversion of your daughter's room into what became called the Dawning Room."

Mrs. Lapham again hid her face beneath the brim of her hat. "Yes, Dottie endeared herself to everyone."

I knew that Vera was working to discover how our suspect felt about Mr. Sanderson's influence over Mr. Morley. With that goal in mind, I added, "My experience with those who've lost a loved one is that women often react to death differently than men do. Much as we better understand how the miracle of birth is, at best, a *messy* miracle, we are the ones who nurse the dying and wash their sheets afterward. I sometimes feel that death is less a mystery to us than to men."

She lifted her head to look back at me, but she remained silent.

I continued, "How did you feel about redesigning the room for a very different purpose?"

Mrs. Lapham spun her head to Vera and back. "Oh, I favored it! I think you're absolutely correct about how death affects men and women differently. Of *course*, I was devastated by the drowning. Of *course*, I was—but, oh, my late husband! He spent night after night in her room, grieving. He was drowning, too. It would have broken Dottie's heart to see him in that state— she was such a lively thing! She would have grown up to be a much stronger woman than myself. A woman who acted on her interests—as *you* do, Miss Van Slyke."

Vera grinned and softly replied, "Mr. Brunton described her as a 'delightful scamp.' Was she a bit of a—*prankster?*" With the final word, Vera angled her head to a new position.

"My, yes! No one was safe from her stunts, and no one was angered by them, either."

Vera asked, "What sort of stunts?"

"Well—I recall one time, after a day spent by the river, we discovered that a turtle had taken residence in her chamber pot. Dottie had sneaked it in by holding up a part of her frock to create a pocket."

Vera nodded. "Turtles are difficult. I only managed to sneak one or two past *my* parents."

"Another time, her father opened his closet to find all the legs of his trousers knotted together."

"Another irresistible temptation I know something about. Anything else?"

"Well, Dottie would sit in a room with someone, pretending to read. As soon as her victim left for the briefest moment or merely looked away—"

Vera cut in, "She would snatch a pencil or a scissors or some such, and place it somewhere else? And then return to reading?" She leaned forward to give me a slow nod.

We seemed to have identified one of the ghosts.

Mrs. Lapham chuckled. "You did that, too, when you were a girl? It certainly delighted Dottie! She'd laugh and laugh once the spoon or the handkerchief was finally spotted. Her glee made it utterly impossible to punish her."

"In that regard, I was never so charming. But to return to the matter of converting your daughter's room. You say you favored the change?"

"Yes. Yes—to distract Roderick from his melancholy. To relight the flame that Dottie's death had extinguished. That's what Mr. Sanderson had been hoping to accomplish."

I submitted, "And you agreed with the idea to make it a room for psychical research? I remember you did not share your late husband's interest in the Supernatural."

"Well, I would have preferred an ordinary library. But Mr. Sanderson convinced me that the *kind* of library was less important than the help that would be afforded Roderick."

"So you discussed this with Mr. Sanderson?"

"I did. It was a subject to avoid in front of Roderick, you understand, but we discreetly exchanged a few letters on the subject."

This time, *I* leaned forward and gave Vera a slow nod. This confirmed the clandestine letters, but also blew away their scent of scandal.

Vera inquired, "Were there any other instances in which Mr. Sanderson *did* raise your ire?"

Here, Mrs. Lapham took a moment to remove her hat and place it neatly upon her lap. Her hair was as no less golden than I remembered it.

She explained, "I confess I felt a bit *jealous* of his friendship with Roderick. I know it's not unusual for two men to share a bond that a wife will never know, just as women can understand one another in ways that a man never could. Still, a wife ought to have *some* influence on her husband's decisions. Isn't that one of the arguments made against women's suffrage—that we already *do* have a say in affairs outside the home—through our husbands?"

Vera nodded. "That surely is one of the arguments made. I wonder, though, if there had been anything more specific. Any particular decision that Mr. Morley made under his advisor's guidance with which you disagreed? Strongly?"

"I understand the question now," Mrs. Lapham said with a sudden twitch to her shoulders. "And I was very open with the police about this, following the, uh—following the *murder*. The alterations to the will made me feel resentment—betrayal—but not toward Mr. Sanderson. No, on that point, I strongly disagreed with my late husband. *He's* the one who left me with only the money from the sale of the mansion. *He's* the one who left me—well. Unlike yourself, Miss Van Slyke, I am not among those few blessed women able to make their own way in the world."

"So you remarried," I stated.

"So I remarried."

Vera touched Mrs. Lapham's arm. "I *do* hope it wasn't an act of financial desperation."

"Fortunately, no. I was not without options, and I choose a kind man who is patient and enjoys treating me to evenings out now and again."

"We all are blessed in different ways, I like to think," I mused aloud.

Vera sat forward and pivoted toward us, as if she were requesting our complete attention. "Speaking of the will, we know that Mr. Morley's revisions grew from the guilt he suffered for having benefitted so greatly from *slavery*. Now, I realize this is an odd question. But do you happen to know if slaves were ever *whipped* on the Morley plantation?"

At times, I was stymied by some of the questions Vera asked our ghost-plagued clients, but her reasons always seemed perfectly sound once she had time to explain them to me afterward. In this case, it crossed my mind that she was pursuing some explanation for the phantom slashing cloth. Was this ripping of fabric like the ghostly gunshot: a recreation of a terrible, violent action? Yet why would the echo of whipping follow Mr. Morley to Boston?

Mrs. Lapham sat still for a moment, her gloved hands folded on her lap. Gradually, she shifted to face Vera more directly. "I cannot say for certain. The few times I heard his parents discuss the race question when we visited Virginia, they held very different views. Now, Roderick's mother—well, she had a harsh opinion of what should be done about the Negros. But his father spoke of them as if they were a childlike people. Roderick did, too, when we discussed his past in the South. Both agreed that the obligation of white Christians is to provide colored people guidance and to keep them safe."

I suddenly remembered Vera's bold question about Mr. Morley possibly fathering a child with the daughter of a former slave. From behind Mrs. Lapham's back, I said, "If your first husband considered colored people to be childlike, his decision to fund their schooling suddenly becomes clearer."

She leaned back against the bench again to face me. "Especially when you consider the loss of Dorothy. I told myself that, when he signed the revised will, he was putting his name on the adoption papers for *thousands* of children." Turning back to Vera, she said, "And so I probably would recall any mention of *whipping*. Remember, though, that such a topic might have been far too painful for Roderick to mention. All I can say is that I very much doubt that *he* could have performed such a punishment."

"The whip *was* more common in the deep South," stated Vera with a ring of finality. She cleared her throat. "I fear my *final* question will prompt you to question my sanity."

Our suspect grinned. She nodded as she lifted her hat.

"Can you fathom any reason why *witches* keep appearing during this investigation?"

Mrs. Lapham gave her hat a small shake before repeating, "Witches? Do you mean—*witches?*" She resumed placing the hat on her head.

This time, I was stumped by Vera's question.

"Good, old-fashioned witches," answered Vera. "Of the black cat and broomstick variety."

"I'm afraid I cannot help you there," said Mrs. Lapham while arranging her hair under the hat, "other than to point out that Salem is only a short train ride away. Tell me, how has your investigation led to *witches?*"

"This morning," Vera explained, "I was in that library of the Supernatural, and a couple of books were brought to—excuse me, *caught* my attention. Both terribly outdated works dealing with ghosts and demons—and, interestingly, *witchcraft*. Now, I might be paving a road with soap bubbles here, but these books reminded me of a phrase used by the current owner of the haunted residence. 'A switch to switch a witch.' Before that, in the letter he sent to engage us, he had misspelled w-h-i-c-h as w-i-t-c-h."

"Amid several *other* errors," I challenged.

"Just so. An upbringing in rural Tennessee might best account for the misspelling. I mean to say that he might have been needed on the farm far more than in school. Still, I'm struck by how admirably Mr. Chillings has done for himself in other respects."

"Mr. *Childers,*" I interjected.

"Ah, yes. Mr. Herman Childers," replied Mrs. Lapham. *"There's* a name I haven't heard in a while."

"You've met our client?"

"He'd asked the estate agent to introduce us, and we met a few times." Mrs. Lapham now finished arranging her hair under the hat. With the trace of a smile, she added, "As I said, after I was left with only the money from the sale of the mansion, I was not without options."

Abruptly, Vera said, "He asked you to *marry* him?"

Mrs. Lapham giggled. "Yes. But I was already being courted by my current husband. And I barely knew Mr. Childers. And then there were those *teeth,* you know. Those alarming *teeth!"* She shivered with comic exaggeration.

The three of us surrendered to a hearty laugh. We all rose, and Vera and I gave the beautiful suspect our earnest thanks. We then cautiously asked if she had been contacted by Chief Inspector Watts or any of his men. She had not, and when she heard that she probably would soon, her shoulders drooped.

"I had truly hoped that this was behind me," she lamented, turning to walk away.

As we watched her depart, Vera said, "If only our murder suspects weren't so frustratingly *pleasant!* Perhaps we're out of our depth. It's entirely possible I'll want to visit The Pitcher and Coach again this evening."

•

Rather than go out for beer, Vera opted to soberly compose the next of her biographical sketches.

—

When the woman who called herself Viola Galt arose from the bank of the Charles River to be rescued by her future husband, it was as if she had washed away the mud of her past. Evidence of her earlier life is scant and contradictory. When speaking to the police, she claimed to be the daughter of a pharmacist in the Lower Allston neighborhood of Boston; however, a review of the city directories showed no man named Galt from that area. W.J., who attended her wedding, remembers that a small chapel had been chosen because no one from the bride's family was in attendance. The explanation was that Viola had been raised at the Boston Female Asylum for Orphans. No record of her was found there.

During the investigation of the murder, the detectives assigned to the case were approached by a fellow officer of lower rank. This officer recalled (with some murkiness) arresting a man named Martin Gatz several years prior. Gatz was an itinerate salesman of elixirs, tonics, and ointments. Several of his customers had registered complaints about his medicines: rashes, abdominal disturbance, and other unpleasant maladies appeared after using Gatz's cures. The curbside confidence artist had an accomplice—a blonde and beautiful girl—who "sawed on a fiddle" to draw a crowd. This accomplice fled as Gatz was being arrested and was never apprehended. The officer contended that Mrs. Morley looked like "a spruced-up twin" of that accomplice. The anecdote was recorded by one well-read detective as "more likely a memory of a Charles Dickens novel than actual evidence."

Mrs. Morley's fragmentary background ought not be a mark against her. Most lives are poorly documented and many erratic, and I know of more than one woman who is eager to hide her family history. If benefits are gained by passing for someone we're not— [I stray here. Retain focus.]

Thus, Viola Galt's biography begins in 1881 on the shore of the Charles River. She became Mrs. Roderick Morley two years later, and the couple gave birth to a daughter in 1887. Dorothy May was abundantly energetic and inquisitive, paying little heed to her parents or caretakers. At the same time, she won the hearts of all who knew her. Viola recounted one of the girl's favorite pranks: to slyly remove a small article and deposit it at another location nearby. Dorothy May would watch her victim's befuddlement without a sound, then burst into laughter when the item was discovered in its new, improbable spot. Is this, then, the specter who plays similar tricks?

Following the girl's drowning, the appearance of Silas Sanderson became a cause for some measure of marital tension. Mrs. Lapham claimed that she felt in competition with Sanderson for her then-husband's affection, even his attention. The final insult was the revising of the will. However, her ill feelings were aimed, not at the man who had advised the revision, but at the man who signed it. When questioned by police, she claimed to be in the parlor, on the first floor, of the mansion when the gunshot was heard. This accords with her being the third person to come upon the corpse.

Viola remarried in the latter half of 1902.

—

As Vera typed her sketch, I heard voices arguing on another floor. I assumed Mr. Childers was yet again working to prevent Miss Marchelli from quitting, and on the chance that there had been another manifestation, I crept into the hall to listen. I discovered my mistake. I recognized the voices rising from the first floor as those of Mr. Childers and Chief Inspector Watts.

Apparently, our client felt the city official's plan to reassemble the suspects was an invasion of his right to privacy. I could not discern the specific negotiations, but Mr. Watts was able to win approval for that Friday's experiment.

That was the last we heard from Mr. Childers that evening.

The previous evenings he had warmly bid us goodnight.
Not this time.

CHAPTER ELEVEN

I PREFER HUNTING GHOSTS TO WITCHES

On Thursday morning, Vera's silence was itself an expression of how she felt about competing with Chief Inspector Watts to discover who murdered Silas Sanderson. As we ate breakfast with Mr. Childers, I found myself obliged to review our findings of the previous day. Naturally, I avoided the subject of our client having proposed marriage to the widow of the man who formerly owned his house. I informed him, instead, that we had good reason to suppose this man's drowned daughter was among the ghosts lurking in the house. As I explained this, our client's former expressive enthusiasm appeared to have been replaced by tight-lipped toleration.

All and all, the crunch of the crispy toast had dominated the conversation at that meal.

Suddenly, Vera placed her hand on my arm. She faced Mr. Childers and asked, "I wonder if your groom might drive us to the train station after he returns from dropping you off at your workshop. Mrs. Lapham suggested we could gather some useful information if we pay a visit to—uh, to a town some miles to the north."

I did not know why Vera was sidestepping the mention of *Salem*. I could only guess that she was exploring the connection between Mr. Childers' two associations with the word "witch" and those books on witchcraft. It's true that our client was beginning to appear a bit more linked to this mystery than first impressions would have had it. Along with his having proposed to Mr. Morley's widow, there was the "Southern" warmth Mr. Brunton felt when he followed a phantom into the library. But this all struck me as, to use Vera's metaphor, a gray gull feather adrift on the gray ocean. Was she grasping at feathers in an effort to solve the murder before Mr. Watts' plans for the following evening?

Regardless of the answer, upon his return, Mr. Brunton drove us to Northern Union Station, and from there, our train arrived in Salem in time for lunch. We found a cozy restaurant, and our waitress suggested we visit the Essex Institute to learn about the history of the infamous witch trials.

In the Institute's library, we met a man named Mr. Giles. He was a nice-looking fellow with curly hair and a nervous habit of cleaning his spectacles with his handkerchief. It became obvious that he was frequently questioned about the Salem witches—or, perhaps, residing in that town had sparked his interest in the subject. He also had the strongest New England accent we heard on the entire trip. At times, I struggled to understand him, and I hope I have captured the shapes of his speech here.

"The mannah of treating suspected witches was in accahdance with the lahs of the land," he replied to Vera's first question. "And the very idear of that treatment might give you ladies nightmayhs!"

"We are both hardy women," Vera assured him. "Serve us the history with the gristle untrimmed, please."

After a deep breath, Mr. Giles proceeded. "Now, you must remembah that the Puhitans had an abiding belief in the *Devil*. He could appeah anywheh in the wildehness that engulfed them. The fihst suspects were simply put in jail." He directed his eyes toward the ceiling, as if consulting it when recalling details. "The women were Sarah Good, Sarah Osbawne, and Tituba, the slave. Now, the two Sarahs—they both denied the allegations. But Tituba—she confessed, saying that she'd signed the Devil's book and that maw witches were about!"

Vera nodded. "Perhaps Tituba had learned that *resisting* zealots only enflames their zealotry."

"Giving whiskey to a man raging for whiskey," I agreed,

"often puts him right to sleep."

Vera turned to me with eyebrows raised. She nodded once and gave me a pat on my shoulder.

Mr. Giles cleaned his spectacles. "Howevuh, the mattah grew and grew as accusations of practicing the Devil's magic grew and grew. Eventually, Bridget Bishop became the fihst hanged for being a witch. Regawding your question, Miss Van Slyke, *hanging* was, by and lawge, the means to deal with a witch. In the end, *nineteen* people died on Gallows Hill. Maw had died in jail—and then theh was the remahkable Mistuh Corey." Our well-versed librarian turned away and twisted his palms together, seemingly less to heighten our interest and more to contemplate how to proceed.

"Mr. *Corey*, Mr. Giles?" I encouraged him.

He smiled slightly before saying, "Mistuh *Giles* Corey."

Vera again looked at me with eyebrows high, and I returned the expression to her.

"I wrote my relatives in England to see if they could find some connection between the names—our suhname taken as a fihst name, perhaps. It seems to be nothing maw than an awdd coincidence."

"Disappointing," Vera commented.

"Curiously so," agreed Mr. Giles. He squared his posture and faced us directly. "Upawn being accused of witchcraft, Giles Corey *refused* to plead innocent—aw guilty. And so, accawding to the lah, his plea was, let's say, *elicited* from him in a prawcess called 'pressing.' His clothing was, uh, *removed,* and Corey was placed undeh a lawge, wooden plank. Rawcks and boulduhs were next placed on *tawp* of that plank of wood." Mr. Giles stacked his hands to illustrate how the torture worked.

Vera and I inched forward.

"Pressed under rocks and boulders?" I asked, as much to make sure I was understanding Mr. Giles's language as to encourage him to continue.

He nodded. "Rawcks and boulduhs."

"How long was Mr. Corey forced to endure this *process?*" asked the reporter.

"Days and days," answered the librarian. "He was fed stale bread and rancid watuh, but Corey still resisted. In fact, he ridiculed his punishehs by calling for *maw* rawcks! You two hit the nail awn the head—resisting zealots only *enflames* zealotry! Rathuh than confessing aw denying the crime, Corey was finally *crushed* to death!"

"Gracious," was all I could say.

"At least as regahds the *Salem* trials, jailing, hanging and pressing explains how witches wuh treated, Miss Van Slyke. Of cawse, the Salem witch hunts of the late 1600s had roots in Medieval Europe, wheh theh was also *dunking.* That involved submehging the accused in watuh. Witches floated, and the innocent drowned. I've neveh found evidence of dunking having crossed to the cawlonies, howevuh."

"To your knowledge, then, those accused of witchcraft were never treated to the sting of a bullwhip?" It was strange to hear a strain of lament in Vera's question. "Wasn't it shortly after the Salem witches when the Reverend Richard Dodge used a whip to drive evil specters out of Cornwall?"

"I'm nawt familiah with Richahd Dawdge. That might be maw a mattuh of hunting *ghosts* than witches," quipped Mr. Giles. "But—come to think of it—if you would—ah, could you give me a moment?" Rather than waiting for an answer, the librarian quickly retreated to the stacks of books.

I took the opportunity to ask Vera if we should ask about any possible witch hunts having been conducted in Virginia, since English colonists had landed there even before New England. She slumped and looked askance. Perhaps she was distracted by not yet being able to explain the spectral manifestation of the ripped fabric. But she then nodded to me. I wondered if she had been hoping that illuminating this corner of the mystery would reflect light on the entire dark chamber.

Mr. Giles rushed back with a book in his hand. Holding a

finger between the pages about three-fourths into the book, he announced, *"Witchcraft in Salem Village in 1692,* by Winfield Nevins! Nevins discusses Jawn Prawctuh, one of the few men hanged faw witchcraft, and—"

"I'm terribly sorry," I heard myself say. *"What* was his name?"

Vera leaned toward me. "John Proctor. Forgive her, sir— she's from the Middle West."

Mr. Giles gave me a short bow before continuing. "And, like Corey, he resisted the zealots. His whole family seemed to be tahgeted by accusers. Heh's what Nevins says about that: 'The reason for this, it was believed, was Prawctuh's intense opposition to the witchcraft prawsecutions from the very beginning, pahticulahly when he said he could *"whip the devil out of them."'* *Them,* it would seem, refuhs to anyone in league with Satan." He silently re-read the passage. "Now that I read it out loud—it's nawt much help, I suppose."

"Well," I offered, "it reveals that the notion of using a *whip* to drive away evil wasn't found only in Cornwall. It crossed to the colonies, even if dunking didn't. I have one last question, sir. The belief in witches certainly wasn't confined to Salem, I know. But have you ever heard about any such accusations being made in *Virginia*—perhaps when it was a colony?"

The librarian closed the book and cradled it closely. Again, he directed his eyes upward. "It wouldn't surprise me if, on a smalluh scale, witch hunts *did* happen in the Virginia cawlony," he said. "Howevuh, I don't pehsonally know of any cases. This institute is dedicated to Essex County, you see." He chuckled. "The only witches outside of New England with whom I'm acquainted is the rathuh ridiculous *Bell* Witch."

Vera jolted. "The Bell Witch—*of course,"* she whispered, after which she seemed too stunned to explain her reaction.

I didn't know who to ask the obvious question. I chose Mr. Giles. "What—or *who*—is the Bell Witch?"

"A decade aw so since," he said, "a book was published. It

told of the ghost of a witch that plagued a family named Bell. The book, I recall, was long on vocabulary and shawt on evidence. The author claims that, in the eahly 1800s, this ghost tawmented the Bells, especially the fathuh and his daughtuh. Then the ghost stahted to *talk*. And talk a *lawt!*"

"A chatty phantom," Vera commented. "The book is *An Authenticated History of the Famous Bell Witch*, by Martin Ingram. Very stupid of me to not have remembered it earlier. The manifestations accord with what the Germans call a *poltergeist* as much as the malevolence of a deceased witch. I agree with your assessment of the book's credibility, Mr.—uh—Mr.—uhm—"

"Mr. Giles," I said to Vera. Even though we had decided earlier against mentioning our investigation in front of the librarian, I asked her, "Is there something about this Bell Witch that relates to the Morley haunting?"

"Maybe not related to the *haunting*," Vera explained. "But curiously related to the *client*. Mr. Giles, do you happen to recall which state the Bell Witch called home?"

The librarian gambled. "Kentucky, wasn't it?"

"Very close, sir." Vera turned to me. "It was *Tennessee*."

We then thanked Mr. Giles and left him cleaning his spectacles amid a cloud of confusion.

•

On the train back to Boston, Vera appeared to be in a blithe mood. She grinned at the conductor, at the other passengers, and even at the scenery. Along the way, she grinned as she wrote a letter to Mr. Berry in Pittsburgh, requesting that our master researcher uncover whatever he could regarding Mr. Childers. I knew better than to ask what thoughts were sparking this delight. She would tell me in due course.

On debarking, she posted the letter, and we had dinner. In that we still had time before our appointment with Dr. James, we returned to The Pitcher and Coach for a beer. The bartender and barmaid recognized us from our previous visit and introduced themselves while asking for our names. Meanwhile, two gentlemen seated at the far end of the bar huffed loudly at the sight of two women in a tavern without male escorts. With a wink at me, Vera went over and asked that they stand guard at their post to ensure our safety. The two gents grew almost giddy at finding themselves knighted, and we also exchanged introductions. Already, the place was beginning to feel like home.

Once Vera and I settled at a private table, she explained why she had been grinning on the train earlier. "I honestly don't feel any closer to *solving* either the murder or haunting," she began. "However, I feel as if we *can* solve it now. Perhaps it's all these nuggets we've gathered. They seem unrelated, but if one piles enough rocks on a man, they will eventually make him a martyr."

"Vera! Shame on you! Poor Mr. Giles Corey inspired that metaphor."

"Yes, I suppose decorum dictates I replace the man with, say, a frozen pond. Either way, the deciding rock—or crushing boulder—might arrive at tomorrow evening's experiment."

"If I understand you, then, you're now hoping Inspector Watt finds *success* after strong-arming us to perform our 'trick' with the purple halos?"

Vera chuckled. "Let's just say that, if he finds success in strong-arming a murder confession, we benefit. And, if it all ends in failure—well, you'll have to remind me not to laugh too loudly."

We both grinned demurely.

•

The time arrived to ride the trolley across the Charles River to the Harvard University campus. Locating Dr. William James was easily managed. His office was rather small, though that might have been an impression caused by the many books jumbled on shelves and in random piles elsewhere.

The professor apologized for not remembering me, and I quickly forgave him, citing the many other psychic mediums he had revealed to be dubious or clearly fraudulent. To Vera, though, this was more a reunion than an interrogation. Perhaps it was my employer's *lack* of suspicion regarding Dr. James that urged me to be especially doubtful of him. Whether it can be blamed on his slow, careful way of speaking or his sudden glances at me as he spoke, I felt keenly aware that, of all our suspects, this man had the most intelligence and the most respectability—two valuable characteristics if one were to evade being charged with murder.

After the polite preliminaries, Dr. James led us to an empty classroom, a roomier setting for the interview. Vera and the professor remained standing between the blackboard and the podium. I took a seat at one of the front desks.

"As I'm sure I've mentioned by letter," Vera commenced, "strong feelings of guilt have become the anchor in my pursuits into haunted sites. The challenge is to start at the anchor, fumble upward along the line through rough waters and slippery seaweed, and finally locate the correct vessel."

"Another of your unique metaphors, Vera," said Dr. James. "Guilt *is* indeed a powerful emotion—a driving, psychological force—and I would assist with your experimentation into the validity of your idea, were I not so focused on finding evidence of true mediumship." Here, he glanced at me again.

Vera replied, "Oh, you're certainly far too busy to entertain *my* simple hypothesis about ghosts."

My neck grew warm at hearing Vera dismiss her remarkable discovery as a "simple hypothesis." She had ample evidence of its validity! I remained silent, though, knowing that false modesty was not typical of Vera. I watched her step toward Dr. James, which made him step backward. She rested her arm on the podium.

Was she strategizing?

"Tell me," said she, "do you think guilt is enough of a driving, psychological force that one can rattle it free? In other words, can a guilty person be *startled* into making a confession? A confession of *murder?*"

Dr. James allowed his head to loll to one side. "You mean

Inspector Watts' plan to gather those who were present on the night of Roderick's death, I trust. Yes, I've received my invitation—my rather insistent invitation. Is that what he's planning? Something to rattle free a confession?"

"I'm afraid so. The violet-edged ruptures I mentioned in my letters. Have you not found those interesting enough to try to recreate them on your own?" She lifted her arm from the podium.

Vera then stepped backward when Dr. James moved forward to take her place.

"To be perfectly honest—and I say this with heartfelt esteem for your efforts—the notion of harmonic tones tugging interdimensional ruptures into the color spectrum seemed so— so frankly *absurd* that I thought it best to give you time to rethink that particular element of your—your, uh, *hypothesis.*"

I almost lurched from my desk to insist that we've *seen* the violent ruptures!—on *several* occasions!—but Vera suddenly turned and gave me a decidedly expressionless look. An instant of reflection led me to suspect she was gaging the professor's knowledge of what would be happening the following evening. I then settled back into my chair, stifling a smile.

"But to answer your question," the professor resumed, "while I certainly do think a guilty party can be provoked into making a confession, I also know that it's far from guaranteed. A man who's committed murder *can* convince himself that the act was perfectly justified and, with time, even deny all culpability. It's surprising what the mind is capable of hiding from itself."

Vera casually picked up a piece of chalk. "I remember a mother whose boy had died in a factory fire. I spoke with her for an article, and she adamantly informed me that her beloved child had *survived*—and would return to her as soon as he overcame the fear of having narrowly *escaped* the catastrophe. All the while, the boy had been positively identified among the fire's casualties." She jostled that bit of chalk in her hand as if about to toss a die.

Dr. James stepped back from the podium. He crossed his

arms but quickly raised a tightly curled hand to his lips. "The death of one's child," he said from behind his fist, "to be sure, is a—a most *formidable* summit to conquer."

Gazing at the man, Vera awkwardly returned the bit of chalk to its shelf. "William," she said softly, "forgive me. I—"

The professor opened his fist to halt her. He then nodded, and Vera remained silent.

At that moment, I knew that Dr. and Mrs. James had also lost a child. The glistening of the professor's eyes was unmistakable. Perhaps this tragedy accounted for the bond between the professor and his student, Roderick Morley, who had experienced similar anguish. That attachment, in turn, accounted for Mr. Morley's deep feelings of having been betrayed by Dr. James on the night of the suicide.

Were the fatherly feelings Mr. Brunton had for Mr. Morley also felt by Dr. James, growing from a shared heartbreak rather than a shared background? More to the point, had such feelings spurred Dr. James to shoot Silas Sanderson for having taken advantage of Mr. Morley during the turmoil following the death of Dorothy May?

On the other hand, was Vera denying this possibility, even though she frequently reported on the complexities of human behavior? Or, if she were able to envision her friend capable of such an act, did she see it as a 'perfectly justified' murder?

I had many questions and few answers. My sharp suspicions of Dr. James eased somewhat. In their place came resignation to my role as a naïve student in this lesson in Advanced Psychology.

Vera next raised the issue of converting Dorothy May's playroom into the Dawning Room, a key point of contention for Mr. Brunton. However, Dr. James said he had agreed with the plan to divert Mr. Morley's attention away from his daughter's death and toward other subjects. That the library's subject—the Supernatural—was one Dr. James himself found fascinating probably bolstered his approval of the room's new purpose.

I was more interested in Vera's next topic: the revision of Mr.

Morley's will. Four years earlier, my brief eavesdropping had led me to believe Mr. Morley had assumed that Dr. James objected to his changing the will. After all, funding marked for psychical research—Dr. James's passion—had been diverted to the schools for Negro children in the South. As he had that night long ago, Dr. James now insisted that he had no objections to this. Indeed, the professor appeared sincere in feeling frustrated by his inability to convince Mr. Morley of this fact.

Was the professor's failure at teaching his student this truth years earlier that reason he retreated from the podium now? I waited for Vera to step toward it. However, she did not.

After a silence, I raised my hand and asked, "Was there anything in particular about Mr. Sanderson that *did* upset you, sir? Tensions between you and Mr. Morley were high on the night of the séance even before Vera exposed my fraudulence. What do you think *was* the cause of his ill feelings, if not his revising the will?"

Dr. James looked at me with a cocked head—and sighed deeply. I interpreted the expression as one of exasperation.

Vera stepped forward. "It's a fair question, William. *Were* you perfectly at ease with the influence the psychic advisor held over your friend?"

"Certainly not," he said.

"Did any of his advice in particular strike you as objection-able?" Vera was now behind the podium again.

Dr. James tugged at the cuffs of his sleeves. He glanced at Vera, then at me—then at the podium.

At last, he spoke. "What on *Earth* prompted Roderick to purchase that gun? Yes, I know that Sanderson claimed to've had a *vision!* Some waking dream about a sinister plot stemming from the revisions to the will. Now, I do my best to keep an open mind about premonitions—but good God, there was no iota of evidence to support this one! Yet, without a hesitation, Roderick went straight out and bought a *pistol!* A pistol that, in the end, led to not *one* but *two* deaths! Prophesy doesn't *forecast* future actions. It *encourages* them."

I again raised my hand. "As I understand it, Mr. Morley made it well-known that he had purchased the gun in order to block that sinister plot. Did you ever confront him about this?"

Curiously, Dr. James turned to Vera.

She added, "And, perhaps more importantly, did you ever confront his psychic advisor regarding the matter?"

Dr. James shifted his eyes midway between us as he answered. "I never confronted either one of them. Roderick probably sensed something, but no. No, I never confronted either of them about the gun."

"It was the gentlemanly thing to do," Vera said. "No doubt, your whereabouts on the morning of the murder have been established by the police, correct?"

It then occurred to me that I recalled nothing about Dr. James' whereabouts during the crime in the police records. Had they also assumed a man of his sterling reputation was incapable of such a deed?

"The *police* never had cause to *ask!*" scolded the professor. "Now, let me understand. Do you ask me these questions to determine why a house might be haunted? Or are these questions concerning my whereabouts during a murder and my animosity toward the victim—is this a way to rattle free *my* confession?" He raised his finger. Pressing his lips tightly together and exhaling sharply through his nose, he then let his hand drop.

Vera stepped forward to place her own hand on his shoulder. "I confess that we made a *list* of suspects, William. And, yes, your name was put at the bottom of that list. But we never intended to cajole a confession from anyone on that list. I'll gladly leave that task to Inspector Watts. Our sights *are* on the haunting. We are hoping to identify the ghosts by determining why they linger. Unfortunately, that seems to be so enmeshed with the murder that I'm no longer certain if I'm a ghost hunter or a private detective. I deeply apologize for the direction this meeting has taken."

The professor patted Vera's hand with his own. "Of course," he replied. "Let's place the blame on this ridiculous gathering Watts has arranged. It *does* weigh on my mind."

"And if all goes according to the Inspector's plan," said Vera, "I deduce that tomorrow's gathering will let me resume my more familiar role of ghost hunter!"

•

The remainder of our interview with Dr. James consisted of Vera reviewing our key discoveries in the case. The professor showed interest, albeit distracted at times.

Afterward, on the ride home, I pointed out that the irritation felt by Dr. James at Mr. Morley's purchase of the gun added yet another piece of evidence to our pile of ice-breaking rocks. Vera's only response was that the interview hadn't gone as she had hoped. She lamented her forgetting about the death of Dr. James's child and her revealing that the professor was among our suspects. When I asked if she still felt the confidence she had on the train back from Salem, she simply stated that she was tired.

We arrived late at Mr. Childers' mansion. Both our client and Miss Marchelli had gone to bed, but Mr. Brunton awaited our return. He informed us that, in our absence, the phantom gunshot had yet again sounded and one of the draperies in the parlor had been found ripped.

"I fear that you're already familiar with the only other news," said Mr. Brunton. "Mr. Childers is displeased that your ghost hunt—your *'four-day-old* ghost hunt,' as he phrased it—has turned his home into a laboratory for solving a murder. A *'four-year-old* murder,' as he phrased it."

Vera nodded and headed to the Green Room. I thanked Mr. Brunton for his trouble, and we bid one another goodnight.

When I entered the bedroom, Vera was retrieving a notebook.

"I must record some ideas for Dr. James's biographical sketch," she said. "I'll type it tomorrow morning—lest the noise of my typewriter make our client even more displeased."

—

William James was born in 1842 in New York City, afterward becoming the godchild of the esteemed poet and philosopher Ralph Waldo Emerson. Indeed, the social circle of William's family was comprised of prominent figures, and his father's wealth was such that his eldest son received an informal education on both sides of the Atlantic. Formally, William attended Harvard Medical School, from which he graduated in 1869. Medicine was not to be William's calling, however. His time spent in Germany prompted the ever-inquisitive man to pursue Philosophy and Psychology.

William's father had been an advocate of Swedenborgianism, a school of thought that branched off into Spiritualism and other mystical philosophies. The oceanic crossing—from a theological upbringing to a professional life in science—led William to develop a keen interest in humanity's predilection toward faith, conviction, belief—or, as he terms it in one of his essays, "The Will to Believe." He worked to understand this, not from a religious perceptive, but from a psychological one. His interest in mediums, clairvoyance, and ghosts, then, might well be founded in a fascination with what people *want* to believe.

Having similar interests, this reporter first became acquainted— [irrelevant]

William began teaching at his alma mater, Harvard University, in 1872. There, not long after 1879, he met a student named Roderick Morley. The two shared an interest in German metaphysics and formed a friendship. In 1896, this friendship would be severely tested when Mr. Morley lavished his trust and, one presumes, his money on a psychic advisor, Mr. Silas Sanderson. [Lucille reminds me that the friendship between teacher and student was likely deepened by their mutual grief for deceased offspring.]

It was discovered that William particularly objected to his friend obediently following the advisor's suggestion to purchase a weapon. The weapon was intended to deter retaliation for provocative revisions Mr. Morley had made to his will—

seemingly charitable and selfless changes—but also changes dictated by Mr. Sanderson.

Tallying the motives for murder:

a) The butler had a Southern sense of honor combined with deep feelings of guardianship for Morley. Love.

b) The unhappy but dutiful wife was deprived of a great deal of money. Revenge.

c) If the professor-turned-friend had as great an impetus, it is not readily apparent. Protecting a friendship born of shared intellectual interests—or sharply disagreeing with the purchase of a gun—seem unlikely motives for such a heinous crime. This is especially so when one considers that William is a man with a distinguished career and a loving family at stake.

[Am I unable to be objective in this regard? Must listen carefully to Lucille's reaction to this sketch.]

⚬ CHAPTER TWELVE ⚬

THE CURTAIN RISES

Friday morning, Vera typed her biographical sketch of Dr. James. I provided brief commentary on it, which she noted in the margin. We were still clearly in some disagreement regarding the professor's potential for being the murderer.

By the time we had finished, Mr. Childers had gone to his workshop, and we shared breakfast with Miss Marchelli in the kitchen. On the premise that we had been spending too much time investigating the haunting *outside* the house, we devoted the day to sitting in various locations inside it, hoping for a manifestation. None occurred before lunchtime, and Vera and I left to enjoy a large meal at a nearby restaurant.

We returned within an hour and spent an afternoon without any ghostly disturbances. Upon his return at 6:00, Mr. Childers curtly told us that he was going to the Drawing Room to remove his financial records and any other personal items from the desk there. We thought it best to remain in the first-floor parlor.

At 7:00, Inspector Watts arrived to prepare the house for the suspects' arrival at 7:30. He brought with him a patrolman named Officer Flynn. The tall, slender man seemed to be a fresh recruit, one who was slow in his bodily movements and reserved in his spoken replies. Mr. Childers agreed to guide them through the house, and bored with the front parlor, Vera and I asked to join them.

While in the kitchen, I noticed Miss Marchelli looking inquisitively at Officer Flynn, as if she recognized him. She said nothing about doing so, however.

"You mentioned that you're not hungry, sir," said Miss Marchelli to her employer. "But I know your two guests haven't had dinner. And I'd be happy to fix something for the officers, too."

The reluctant host turned to us.

"I suppose," Vera said, "something light might sustain us through what will hopefully be a productive evening. Lucille, don't you agree?"

"Uh—certainly," I uttered. "Perhaps sandwiches wouldn't be too much trouble?"

Mr. Childers then simply looked at the two men.

Inspector Watts replied, "Very kind, but we've eaten."

Our client continued the tour at a bit of rush. On the second floor, he indicated the locations of the Pink Room, his own bedroom, and the others without offering to open the doors to any of them. On the third floor, he merely pointed down to the Green Room while opening the door to the Dawning Room and bidding Inspector Watts and Officer Flynn to enter it.

"Now," Mr. Childers barked, "the fourth floor is empty except for the maid's room. If you have any reason to see it, I trust Miss Van Slyke and her assistant would be good enough to accompany you there. I think it best that I return to the front parlor and await *your* guests." He paused. "If that is *agreeable?"*

Inspector Watts thanked him. He waited for Mr. Childers to depart before saying, "He seems not to be getting into the *spirit* of the thing." After chuckling at his pun, he added, "I don't think we need to examine the top floor, but I *do* think you ladies ought to prepare your musical instruments. We might even have time for a—what's it called, Flynn—a 'dress rehearsal?'" He chuckled again.

Vera and I retrieved our oboes and, reentering the Dawning Room, I was struck by an odor that seemed out-of-place for a spot with such a solemn history. Inspector Watts was blowing cigar clouds into the air while leaning back in the chair I had occupied during the séance. Officer Flynn was scanning the book titles on the shelves, snickering as he went. Even though I ordinarily felt no disgust for cigar smoke or even derision at supernatural subjects, I suddenly felt in sympathy with Mr. Childers. It was as if this sanctum were being invaded by brutes.

We began to assemble our oboes, and Mr. Brunton arrived. On greeting everyone, he discreetly passed a folded slip of paper to Vera. She glanced at it, then passed it to me. Miss Marchelli was requesting that we both meet her on the second floor landing. No reason was given, and the note ended with "Mum's the word."

"I fear we might not have time for that dress rehearsal, gentleman," stated Vera to the policemen. "There seems to be a crisis involving sandwich meats and condiments that demands our immediate attention."

Inspector Watts grinned and puffed another cloud into the room. Vera and I placed our oboes upon the table, and our casual manner vanished once we were out of the room. We scurried to the staircase and down to the landing below. There, Miss Marchelli was bobbing in place.

"S'probably *nothing* at all," she rasped as she rushed to us. "But I felt I *had* to tell you."

"Yes, my dear?" replied Vera, catching her breath.

"I can't be certain—because I was way up in the balcony. But that fencepost of a police officer. Flynn. I'm almost certain that he's *not* a police officer."

"Not a—" I stammered. "Where did you see him? From what balcony?"

"The vaudeville house. In Scollay Square."

"Was he in the audience or—was he onstage?"

"Onstage."

"What was he doing?"

"He was throwing his voice. He's a *ventriloquist!*"

Vera and I turned to one another.

"Inspector Watts asked him to confirm if 'dress rehearsal' is the correct term," I said. "That suggests he performs in stage shows. Vera, what are we to do?"

She turned to Miss Marchelli. "Thank you very much. You

continue to surprise me."

"What *are* you to do?" asked the woman of continual surprises.

After tapping on the balustrade three times, Vera raised her finger. "Play our parts, of course. The farce must go on!"

•

Vera and I had returned to the Dawning Room, and around 7:20, Miss Marchelli arrived with Dr. James and two plates, each with a sandwich and pickle. The professor seemed to pay little attention to Inspector Watts, Mr. Brunton, and Mr. Flynn as he shook their hands. Instead, he gazed around the room, contracting his eyebrows, tilting his head one way and another, then raising his eyebrows.

Twisting to Vera, the professor remarked, "It's untouched! The room looks—as if frozen!"

"Yes, Lucille and I noticed exactly that a couple of days ago. Mr. Childers, it seems, keeps his own books at his workshop and uses the room only for figuring finances and finding solitude."

Dr. James nodded and wandered toward Vera and myself. As he had the previous evening, he glanced at me—but directed his conversation to the woman he had once entrusted to expose my fraudulence. I again became keenly conscious of how little the room had changed over the four years since I first spoke about *The Turn of the Screw* with Henry James's brother.

I decided to wander to look more closely at the lithograph. It was as isolated a spot as I could find under the circumstances. There, I chomped into my sandwich. Though the chicken was fine, the mustard was hot and even gritty against my tongue—but my mood accounted for that displeasure. I devoured the sandwich as if it might be my last meal for some time.

At 7:30, the room became much more crowded. Mr. Childers arrived with Mrs. Lapham, the woman to whom he had once proposed marriage. Even more worrying, Mrs. Lapham arrived with *Mr.* Lapham. Seeing this jagged triangle brought a queasy pang to my stomach.

Mrs. Lapham was dressed in a shimmering azure gown, adorned with a sparkling brooch and bracelets. Her husband provided an interesting contrast by wearing a simple brown suit and tie with no added finery. His wispy hair was dark, and his kindly eyes were blue. His wiry beard was long—but his moustache was lighter and fairly sparse—and the disparity resulted in the kind of lion's mane fashionable among an older generation. One might think of Abraham Lincoln to better envision this portrait, that is if the great president were of average height and build. As Inspector Watts introduced him to the many strangers in the room, Mr. Lapham's manner was polite, if a bit guarded. I noticed that he kept a gentle hand on his wife's back, and this helped to soothe my digestion for a moment.

"We are all arrived," announced the Chief Inspector. "I begin by noting the passage of *four* months and *four* years since a most tragic event occurred in this very room. I speak of the *shameless* murder of Silas Sanderson, faithful friend and trusted advisor to Roderick Morley, the latter being the former keeper of this household."

I glanced at Vera, ready to grin if she were as bemused by Mr. Watts' highfalutin language as I was. However, just then, she and Dr. James were exchanging grins, presumably for the same reason. Again, I felt a twinge in my belly. Nonetheless, I rallied my strength and stepped toward the oboes, leaving the protected spot by the lithograph.

That spot open, Mr. Childers sidled to it—away from Mr. and Mrs. Lapham.

"Within the shadow of this *atrocious* and *unpunished* act," continued the now effusive policeman, "I share with you a wondrous—dare I say, *miraculous*—exhibition. At the start of this very week, this worthy lady, Vera Van Slyke, disclosed to me a discovery she has made in her pursuit of—the *truth*. The *great* truth! The *truth* of the Hereafter!".

Here, I felt Vera step to the oboes and give me a gentle nudge in the ribs. We then exchanged grins.

"Yes, a decade or two since, people would have *laughed* at the idea of wireless telegraphy—of a ship far out in the ocean sending a message across the ether to those on shore. They would have been *frightened* by the prospect of X-rays—the skeleton of a living man photographed! Of course, we now acknowledge that these discoveries *do* work. Yet I suspect the average fellow cannot explain *how* they work. I am not a scientist. I cannot explain how *two* notes played on *two* clarinets—"

"Oboes," stated Vera.

"How *two* notes played on *two* musical instruments result in what you're about to witness. But witness it I have! And even if, for some reason, we are unable to recreate here what transpired at the Bureau of Criminal Investigation but a few days ago, it is *truth!* And unveiling the *truth* is exactly why I've asked you all here this evening. Miss Van Slyke, as you've just shown, you are much more knowledgeable about this procedure than I am. Will you please share with us your *startling* theory?"

As if rehearsed, Vera took the stage and, with occasional nods to Dr. James, reviewed her theory that intense guilt ruptures the membrane between the physical and spiritual realms. She summarized our experience with the musician who improvised with a phonograph recording in his dark room. She explained how the musician had discovered that a specific timbre and harmony triggered the phenomenon. Shrewdly or intuitively, Vera joined Inspector Watts in refraining from describing the specific appearance of those dimensional ruptures when nudged into the color spectrum. She didn't even mention that the phenomenon was a visual one.

The Inspector again took the stage. "And now, Officer Flynn—*extinguish the lights!*"

"One thing more," Vera interrupted. "It's vital that everyone remain perfectly still. Any movement can have dreadful results."

At this, Mr. Flynn put the room in absolute darkness. Vera and I raised the oboes. I inhaled deeply, and my abdomen reminded me of the unease of my situation. The brash Chief

Inspector's theatrics. The possibility that he had coaxed a ventriloquist to perform some stunt. The sight of Mr. Childers avoiding contact with Mr. and Mrs. Lapham. Vera's loyalty to Dr. James, one of the murder suspects.

And, of course—beneath it all—there was the horrible guilt that I carried for all that had happened in this house four years earlier.

As Vera sounded her B flat, I exhaled my high G.

•

The wobbling rings filled the darkened room, their violet hue aglow. I heard gasps, half-finished exclamations, even profanity. At the end of our first breath—and the sudden disappearance of the glowing circles—Mr. Watts shouted a single word.

"Again!"

Vera and I complied.

This time, the reaction was not quite so loud. Between the softer utterances, however, I heard a whisper.

"*You* did it. *You* did it."

I could not place the location from which the whisper was coming. It seemed to rise from different directions. And it was no longer a whisper. It was rising in volume and growing guttural.

"*You* did it. *You* did it! *You did it!*"

I heard a shuffling of feet and the rattling of something heavy—a bookend, perhaps—as someone collided with a bookcase. Still, the voice grew!

"*You did it! You did it!*"

Vera and I again reached the end of our breaths, and we were commanded to resume. After she scolded the group about remaining still, the violet forms swam and coalesced around us a third time.

"*You—did—it! Confess!*"

Almost simultaneously, I heard a piercing scream—a woman's—Mrs. Lapham's—her husband's cry for light—a stomping to the door. Vera and I had ceased the eerie harmony, and light streamed in from the hallway door. The silhouette of Dr. James appeared in the passage.

"Flynn," shouted the Chief Inspector, "relight the gas!"

As the light returned, we saw Mrs. Lapham slumped in the arms of her husband. She hadn't fainted, only collapsed. Someone dragged over a chair for her.

"It was him," she muttered. "It was Sanderson. I recognized him."

There was a moment of stark silence. Mrs. Lapham was pale. She blinked hard, as if her eyes were somehow misaligned with her brain. Vera rushed to crouch beside her.

"How—*how* did you recognize him?"

"It was him," was her dazed reply.

Inspector Watts approached slowly. "Forgive my being indelicate, but you need to tell me how you knew it was Silas Sanderson's voice."

Vera rose to her full, formidable height. She faced the policeman while speaking to Mrs. Lapham. "Before you say anything, you must know that the voice we heard was very likely a ruse. *Officer* Flynn, I was informed, looks suspiciously like a ventriloquist who has performed in a local vaudeville house."

I sensed more than saw a tremor pass through the others in the room.

"And *why* would that matter, Miss Van Slyke?" demanded Mr. Watts. "Our goal was to display a far more pressing *truth!* Now, Mrs. Lapham, what about that voice convinced you it was Silas Sanderson?"

Mr. Lapham knelt beside his wife and took her hand. "Do you wish to leave, darling? Say the word, and we'll leave right now."

"No," said the beautiful woman, touching her husband's cheek. "I mean—*no.* No, I didn't recognize the *voice* to be Silas Sanderson's. I *saw* him. I recognized him—by the way he *looked!*"

Vera crouched down again. "But how—how did you *see* him?"

"Through the holes. As they—floated by, he was *behind* them. There was *blood*." Mrs. Lapham trembled, then spun her head and clamped her eyes closed.

The Chief Inspector strode to where Vera was positioned. He put a firm hand on her shoulder to move her out of his way. I could see that Vera was too absorbed by the prospect of *seeing through the dimensional ruptures* to resist his efforts. In our past experiences, we had never glimpsed anything through the holes—only utter blackness.

Mr. Watts spun an adjacent chair so that he could face Mrs. Lapham closely. He assumed a gentle demeanor. "You say there was blood. How awful. But where *was* the blood?"

Mrs. Lapham turned to her husband.

Gently, Mr. Lapham asked, "Can you answer the question, darling? If you answer it, then maybe Mr. Watts will let us go." With deep creases in his brow, he turned to look at each of us.

The Chief Inspector did not comment.

Mrs. Lapham turned back to her interrogator. "The blood was all over his side." She placed her left hand on her right ribs. "Running down his side."

"Was it his *right* side, not his *left* side?"

She thought for a moment. "Yes. Yes, his *right* side. It was horrible." She again turned to her caring husband.

Mr. Watts looked down. With a tone of sincere sympathy, he said, "Viola Lapham, I regret to inform you that I'm placing you under arrest for the murder of Silas Sanderson."

Again, I felt a quake pass through those in the room, one that caused no palpable movement.

"Hold on one moment, Inspector," insisted Dr. James. "I recall that Sanderson was shot clean through the *heart!*"

Vera added, "The blood would have been on his *left* side, descending from his wound. That is—depending on his fall, I suppose."

"Mr. Lapham, sir? Please take your wife down to the parlor. Flynn? Accompany them."

We watched in silence as the man dressed in a police uniform stepped forward and Mr. Lapham helped raise his wife. The husband put his arm around her back, and as she did the same, she paused.

As if searching for some distraction from what was occurring, she asked, "Ernest? What's happened to your coat? How funny."

He checked to find that, without explanation, there was a slash in the back of his suitcoat. "We—will—we'll take care of that *later*, darling. Let's go down to the parlor now."

While they departed, I noticed Mr. Childers move to the back of his desk. Instead of sitting down there, he stood and crossed his arms. One might have inferred that he was saying he had business to do and it was time for the rest of us to leave, too.

The Chief Inspector, however, leaned back in his chair.

Dr. James spoke. "I hope you haven't been overly eager to make an arrest, sir. As I say, there wouldn't have been blood on Sanderson's *right* side."

"Unless we were misled," said Vera quietly.

Mr. Watts nodded. "The bullet that struck Sanderson penetrated the liver with enough force to damage the right lung above and the duodenum below. Not shot through the heart, as reported by the press. No, that was a dramatic flourish invented, I suppose, to add some gory romance to the crime." He turned to Vera. "To sell *newspapers*. I do admit, however, I allowed the falsehood to persist in the hopes that, one day, it would help us catch our murderer."

"The only one who could've known where the blood *truly* was," reasoned Dr. James aloud, "would be the killer."

"But for one alternative," Vera stated. "Suppose she saw the actual ghost of the man shot."

"Did anyone else see it?," asked Mr. Watts.

We acknowledged that none of us had seen it.

"Nor did I," stated the Chief Inspector. "I honestly wish I had. It would delight me to add evidence to defend your beliefs,

Miss Van Slyke. However, phantoms do not carry much weight in a court of law. Whether Mrs. Lapham actually saw a ghost or only thought she saw—"

A piercing *blast* rang out!

And what felt like *fire* in my belly crumpled me forward.

And one side of my face *hit* the back of a chair, then the other side of my face *hit* the carpet.

And the stage went *dark* again.

ACT THREE

THE MASTERMIND
(Immediately Afterward)

CHAPTER THIRTEEN

NOT SHOT—
MERELY POISONED

While some might contend that the gunshot occurring simultaneously with my collapse was an astounding coincidence, over the next few days, I began to wonder if the former hadn't been a spectral warning related to the latter. That evening, I had been attributing my abdominal agitation to the relationships of those in the Dawning Room—particularly, my own relationship with the room itself—but these were aided and abetted by a more culinary culprit.

"Something—a bad taste—or *sensation*—in my sandwich. The mustard?" I sputtered as I felt my shoulders being lifted from behind. Gradually, I noticed Vera's face very near to my own. "How was yours?"

She was kneeling beside me, cradling me in her arms. "Fortunately," she replied softly, "I had only nibbled on the crust before putting mine down." She caressed my cheek. "You gave us quite a scare."

I then noticed Dr. James stooping beside me. He spoke to someone else, though. "I still think it best to fetch the doctor."

"And *I* still think it best that Brunton rush her to the hospital!"

I recognized that as Mr. Childers' tenor voice, though the table blocked my view of him. Mr. Brunton's baritone spoke next.

"I will gladly do whatever you gentlemen decide."

Vera said, "Dr. James has a degree in medicine, sir—a medical degree from Harvard."

"He just said he doesn't *practice* medicine," insisted our host.

Dr. James stood. "That being so, let's get the opinion of a

173

physician who *does* practice. The girl is conscious. She seems to have just doubled over from a cramp, hitting her head on the chair and falling over. There will be a bruise, but there's no blood. She's not cold, not pale—her lips aren't blue. Let's allow a man more qualified than either of us to decide if she needs hospital care."

After a silence, Mr. Brunton decided: "I'll fetch the doctor."

Dr. James continued, "In the meantime, sir, would you be good enough to bring us some ipecac?"

"Very well," Mr. Childers spit. "We'll have it *your* way! I'll send up some with Sophie."

"Here's the sandwich Miss Van Slyke didn't eat." That was Inspector Watts's voice. "I don't smell anything funny about it. Do *you*, doctor?"

Dr. James rose. "Let me—Childers? The ipecac please? The sooner the better, sir."

As Mr. Childers exited, he grumbled, "I keep a *clean* kitchen!"

Dr. James waited a moment before grunting. "Can't say I would be any less cantankerous if *my* home had been subjected to tonight's, uh—*events.*"

"Speaking of that," said Watts, "if you're confident everything is fine here, I really must see to Mrs. Lapham."

Dr. James must have nodded. I saw the legs of the Chief Inspector depart.

I turned to Vera. "Tonight's events. Ask him what he thinks about your purple holes *now.*"

Vera only grinned and patted my cheek again.

"I think your purple holes are mystifying," admitted Dr. James as he crouched down again. "Truly spectacular. I'm ashamed of myself, Vera, for having been skeptical about your letters. I can only plead that many, many ridiculous claims are delivered to my doorstep."

Vera nodded. "An actual veil between the living and the dead. Stabbed by guilt. The perforations *seen*—by using *sound.* It *is* entirely absurd. I wouldn't have believed it, either. Not if I read it in a letter. But that's a topic for another time. Don't you think we should help Miss Parsell to bed now? It's only the next room over."

Shortly after I was escorted to the Green Room, Miss Marchelli arrived with the medicine, and soon all undigested toxin in my stomach was duly purged. Next, a neighborhood physician arrived. Neither he nor Dr. James were able to identify any specific poisons in the remaining sandwich. He deemed Mr. Childers' suggestion that I go to the hospital to be overly cautious. A diet of oil, milk, and raw eggs—along with bedrest and careful watching—were prescribed. Vera and I were to remain at the mansion.

Upon hearing this, Mr. Childers bared his fangs while rocking on the balls of his feet. He muttered, "It's been close to a *week* now. Had I have known that ghost hunting was so *prolonged* a process, I wouldn't have troubled you."

Vera walked to him and touched his arm. "This road of deprival will rise to survival."

He sneered.

Vera amended, "Or should it rise to *arrival?* The rhymes are promising, but there's no rich reward. Oh dear, I'm exhausted. I had intended to say that, given a few more days, I can ascertain if apprehending the murderer tonight will put your ghosts to rest. If so, *all of us* will rest."

Only then did Mr. Childers appear agreeable to the situation by attempting to form a smile around his obtrusive teeth.

•

Having slept soundly, I was feeling more like myself again in the morning. Barely awake, I found Vera already dressed in a wool, slate-colored jacket with gray-checkered skirt, a white blouse with no lace or frill, and a cameo brooch at the neck. This was the outfit worn when there was serious work to be done. Vera explained that, according to Miss Marchelli, Mrs. Lapham was almost certainly being detained at the Suffolk County Jail. It was located on Charles Street, surprisingly close to the elegant homes of Beacon Hill. With a slight quaver, she asked my permission for her to walk over to the jailhouse. The widow, having made her criminal confession, might now provide details helpful to resolving the haunting.

"More importantly," Vera said with two fingers touching her jaw, "we might uncover something that shows Viola to be less villainous than the Prosecution will certainly portray her. Her early history is murky. She's beautiful. She twice married wealthy men. All the materials for some shyster to invent a villainess like those found in your silly novels."

Ignoring the poke at my tastes in reading, I replied, "But what if you uncover proof that Mrs. Lapham actually *is* a villainous—uhm—villainess?"

Vera tilted her head. "Then we leave Boston assured of that."

With a mutual nod, Vera and I shook hands to officiate our new mission.

Of course, I was not present at the conversation Vera went on to hold with Mrs. Lapham at the jailhouse. However, immediately upon her return, Vera supplied the details of what had transpired, often checking her notes. I am confident, therefore, that what follows is largely a correct record.

Vera found the woman's complexion wan and her posture sagging. Her honey hair was disheveled. Mrs. Lapham was grateful for Vera's visit, and she repeatedly apologized for having kept her terrible secret during the séance of long ago and during our much more recent interview in the Garden.

"No need to apologize," said Vera. "In fact, thank you for not sharing it with me—I have quite enough secrets of my own! But has making your confession brought you any relief? Any sense of unburdening?"

Mrs. Lapham kept her eyes closed for a long time. "I've upset Ernest. Deeply. He said we should both leave judgement of my sin to a Higher Power." She opened her eyes. "Yes. Yes, I told Ernest a week after he proposed—and a month before I accepted his hand in marriage."

"He *knew?*" replied Vera. "And still he *betrothed* you rather than *betrayed* you by contacting the police? Extraordinary man! Was there something in the motive for the—uhm. The reason for the—"

"Murder?"

"Something behind the *crime* that convinced your husband to keep it concealed? I assume you gave him a full account of the deed."

"Yes. He says it was an act of maternal passion, and no man has the right to punish a woman for that."

"*Maternal* passion? But hadn't Dorothy May already, uhm— I wonder if you might tell me what you told him. I assure you that my goal is to use whatever power I have—the power of the press, if need be—to ensure that you receive a fair trial."

"Thank you. At this point, though, I'd find great comfort in a *quick* trial."

Vera paused from opening her notebook. "Let's strive for fair *and* quick, shall we?" She then readied her pencil.

Mrs. Lapham began her account. "I've already told you about the letters passed between Mr. Sanderson and myself regarding the plan to convert the old playroom into an occult library and séance parlor. The *Dawning* Room. Well, the last of those letters was a demand, an ultimatum that I meet him in that very room. Its tone was uncharacteristically blunt for Sanderson, whose usual manner was gracious. For instance, he stipulated that I meet him *alone* on that Sunday morning. He was well aware that almost all of our staff would be out at church or wherever else they pleased.

"Now, this letter arrived in the wake of Mr. Sanderson's premonition of danger, which led to Roderick's purchase of the gun. With this in mind, I assumed Mr. Sanderson had plans to accuse me of conspiring against Roderick in response to his changing his will. I suppose I went to that meeting prepared to do battle.

"By this time, Sanderson had so ingratiated himself into the household that he could come and go as he pleased. If I was ready for battle, imagine my state when I found him in the library, tipped back on his usual chair at the table with his legs crossed on another chair. Before I could object to that, I was immediately affronted—not by accusations that I posed a threat to my husband—but by something far more reprehensible! You see, he—Sanderson—had designs to use the letters we had written about converting the playroom against me.

"First, he rose to pull me into the room and close the door behind us. Next, he reminded me that I had asked my maid to discreetly deliver those letters. She had no idea what was in them. He then asked me to read *another* letter, one he handed to me. I only had to read the first page to see that it was—well, it was a *love* letter. A love letter addressed to *him*. His lover wrote about her unflagging devotion to him. And about her loathing for her husband. If not for the husband, I would have dismissed it as the work of a starry-eyed schoolgirl.

"Then he—Sanderson—told me to look at the signature. I saw *my own name!* He told me to look at the penmanship. I saw my own *hand*. However, and here I beg you to believe me, *it was not a letter I could ever have written!* Yes, it's true that my marriage had grown stale. Especially since the death of our little girl. I admit that. And, speaking woman to woman, I also admit that Silas Sanderson was a very charming man. But I *never* had the feelings expressed in that letter. I repeat: *it was not a letter I could have written—not ever!*"

At this point, Vera interpreted Mrs. Lapham's eyes as belonging to a person yearning to cry, but too exhausted to do so. Regardless, her narrative continued.

"Miss Van Slyke, I know your reporting must have exposed you to the very worst of humanity. As a girl, I was not sheltered from thievery, maltreatment, even depravity. I am not the delicate hothouse flower some might judge me to be, but perhaps years of living leisurely had softened me. I beg you to believe me when I say that Mr. Sanderson's next step was astounding to me. You see, he was planning to *blackmail* me!"

"Blackmail is indeed an ugly matter," said Vera, "However, you're correct in saying I have been witness to many crimes, and there are darker ones than—"

The glare that Mrs. Lapham aimed at Vera made the angelic-looking woman appear diabolical.

"To use blackmail," she stated, "to force me into *murdering my own husband!*"

"Ah. Yes. Well. That is unquestionably a—a damnable crime. Please proceed. What did the blackmailer say after he had shown you the forged letter?"

"That Roderick had admitted that our love was over. That the only thing left in our marriage for me was a comfortable life. Then he—Sanderson—told me that, after Roderick's death, he knew a way to split the money intended to go to the Negro schools. All I had to do was pull the trigger—the trigger of the gun that Roderick himself had brought into the house so overtly.

"The monster even walked behind the desk and removed the weapon from the top drawer. He brought it over and lifted my hand, the one not holding the letter. He placed the gun in my empty hand so I could feel the heft of it. Then he lifted my hand holding the letter as if I were to weigh one against the other. To choose between what would come of each. Everything, he assured me, was arranged so that neither of us would be suspected if I chose the gun.

"Suddenly, I had the grand idea of simply tearing up the forged letter. I put the gun on the desk beside me, and I did exactly that. I slowly ripped the letter in half. In quarters. As I did so, he shook his head with mocking sorrow. He explained that, knowing I would do so, he had given me a practice copy. More convincing forgeries—several of them, all different—were hidden within the library, he said.

"If I didn't do as he said, he would tell Roderick where they could be found. Even if I devised some way to convince Roderick to banish Sanderson from the house, those letters would remain somewhere in that room. Hidden in that room walled with shelf after shelf of books and books and books.

"I remain astounded at my own composure at that point, to tell you the truth. Apparently, my childhood *had* prepared me to show no weakness, and Sanderson was not counting on that. I stated flatly: 'I am not going to murder my husband. Not for half of his money. Not for *all* of his money. I would rather endure a scandal. I would rather Roderick divorce me and leave me penniless. I am *not* going to murder my husband.'

"Just as I did not flinch, neither did he—not quite yet. Sanderson took my hand and looked pityingly into my eyes. I let him. I did not feel seduced. I did not feel outrage. I don't believe I felt much of anything. I felt nothing when he said he would give me a week to make my choice: a life of infamy and poverty or the life of a wealthy, not-so-very-old widow. I felt nothing when he reminded me that my fairytale marriage was over—the girl whom the sad prince had rescued from the waters of the Charles River, the woman who now spends each evening alone in the castle, listening to Gramophone records.

"I pulled my hand away. Still devoid of emotion, I repeated, 'I am *not* going to murder my husband.' In anger, he repeated, 'I'll give you *one* week to choose!' Then he turned to leave—but he stopped. He wanted me to crumble before his might. He wanted to show how repulsive he could be if I *refused* to do as he demanded. To horrify me. To master me.

"Still facing away, he said, 'You know, Viola? While we're on the subject of fairy tales, I recently learned something rather interesting about women and water—and *witches.*"

Vera froze—but for letting her pencil droop.

"Yes, Miss Van Slyke. Good, old-fashioned witches of the broomstick and black cat variety—just as you said near the Ether Monument. I was able to hide my surprise behind my hat that day."

"What was it?" Vera whispered. "What had Sanderson

learned about witches?"

Mrs. Lapham shut her eyes. "He said he had learned that witches don't drown. If you dunk them in water, they will float. And then he suddenly turned around. And then he said it was unfortunate my *daughter* hadn't inherited that characteristic from me."

"And then you shot him?"

"And then I grabbed the gun beside me—and—and I shot him."

•

My first question after listening to Vera recount Mrs. Lapham's shocking narration was: "How did she get away with it? After she shot him, how did she—what did she do?"

Vera dragged the dressing table chair to the bedside and made herself comfortable on it. She reminded me, "It was Sunday morning, and no one had seen the blackmailer enter the house or pass to the Dawning Room because he knew the house would be close to empty. As you recall from your séance, the door between the Dawning Room and *this* room was kept unlocked. She slipped from there to here—and waited. She waited until the cook came down and discovered the body. She waited until her husband joined the cook. Only then did *she* walk out of this room, into the hall, and around into the Dawning Room, claiming she had rushed up from the parlor. Indeed, she *was* flush and panting, but it wasn't because she had charged up two flights of stairs."

"No. Because she had just—*gracious!* But—but how did Mr. Sanderson know he wouldn't run into Mr. Morley? The police reports say he was in the house. He was down in his bedroom. What if he had been in the Dawning Room—or roaming the house?"

"We know now Mr. Sanderson took risks, but this was a calculated one. Did you see the report on what Mr. Morley himself had told the police after the murder? The millionaire admitted that he and his trusted friend had partaken of certain merriments that Saturday night. Who knows exactly what that means? Even Puritanical Boston must have an opium den or two."

"Poor Mr. Morley. Very likely drunk and possibly drugged. It's surprising he woke up at all!"

"We now have a much clearer picture of the crime, and now we can put another rock on top of the martyr. Oh—forgive me— on top of our pile on the frozen pond. We now know we're dealing with a *forger!*"

I exclaimed, "Mr. Sanderson was a huckster of many talents if, along with his psychic advisor scam and his blackmailing, he was skilled in forgery!"

"That *is* a lot to expect from just *one* man." Vera rose from her chair. "Let's not rule out his being in cahoots with a specialist. A minor figure in the mystery—someone Sanderson turned to now and again when he needed, say, a letter of reference from someone of high standing." She began to pace.

"Well, one thing is certain. Even if he had outside assistance, Mr. Sanderson learned a lesson in overextending his reach. A lesson in *greed.*"

She halted. "*And* a lesson in attempting to control a woman by attacking her most cherished memory. Now, I see what Viola's current husband meant by her committing a crime of *maternal passion.*"

"Oh, I wonder how poor Mr. Lapham is holding up. From what I saw last night, he seems like a caring man."

"He was there at the jail. Only one visitor is allowed at a time, so we only crossed paths. Yet he appeared to be standing firm. I told him I would help in any way that I could, and he gave me his calling card."

I sighed. "Why do you suppose Sanderson said that awful thing about Dorothy May drowning? Was it an attempt to *break* Viola?"

"Another calculated risk, I suppose. Drastic measures are required to provoke someone to commit murder. Perhaps he wasn't expecting to be met with so steadfast a refusal from Viola. Perhaps he spun around and said what he did out of desperation."

"Perhaps he was *also* being coerced. I wonder if we can uncover any debts Sanderson had. Gambling or otherwise."

Vera squinted. "Secret debts from four years ago. That's a greasy gopher. We might more easily pursue another clue Viola provided. She said that Sanderson knew a way to split the money that Mr. Morley had willed to the Negro schools. Do you remember seeing anything in the police reports confirming the legitimacy of this charity? Does it even have a name?"

I did my best to recall the many, many files I had surveyed. At last, I answered, "No. Not even a name."

"The American Missionary Association has been a leader in building schools for freed colored students since before the Civil War. There's the Hampton Institute—and the Tuskegee Institute. But I don't recall seeing any of those mentioned anywhere."

"Nor do I," I admitted, wondering how Vera was able to easily extract these names from her memory while she routinely forgot the names of people she'd met a minute earlier.

"It's possible a *new* philanthropic organization was created, maybe one named for Morley himself?"

"If so, I don't recall it."

Vera sprung from her chair. "Over a million dollars went *somewhere!* Surely, this was investigated!" She began to pace.

"It *must* have been verified—if not by the police, then by the attorney who executed Mr. Morley's will. It *must* have been!" I touched my lower lip. "Mustn't it?"

"*H'well,*" Vera huffed, "if it *h'wasn't,* I certainly intend to uncover the reason *h'why!*"

∽ CHAPTER FOURTEEN ∾

AN EVENTFUL SATURDAY

Vera left me to ask Mr. Brunton if he remembered the name of Mr. Morley's attorney. He did not. On her return to the Green Room, she ran into Mr. Childers. Though working on Saturdays was his usual habit, he remained home this day. Vera inquired if she might borrow his groom for a couple of hours, assuring him that I would remain behind to act as her "spectral sentinel." He smiled at the phrase and politely granted his permission. Apparently, the debris stirred the previous evening was settling.

Vera then came in and apologized again for leaving me. She explained her plan to return to Mrs. Lapham to ask the name of her late husband's lawyer and, thereby, to hunt down the name of the lucky charity the millionaire had endowed.

"I wonder if Mr. Lapham would feel more useful if he had more to do than simply wait at the jailhouse," I suggested.

"You mean I should let his standing in the community add some pressure in case the lawyer tries to hide behind client confidentiality? Very astute."

"Not *exactly* what I meant," I murmured, "but you know how to deal with lawyers better than I do. Now, you won't forget to take time for lunch, will you?"

"I have never *once* forgotten to take time for lunch, my dear. But thank you for the reminder. I honestly don't know how I could function without you," Vera said with a gleam in her eye. "But, for now, it's *fare thee well!*"

Again, I shift my narration to recording Vera's account of what happened next. In doing so, I feel similar to how I felt having been left behind in that bed—as if I had become a ghost.

Vera and Mr. Brunton found Mr. Lapham still at the Suffolk

County Jail. Mrs. Lapham informed them that her late husband's attorney was a gentleman named Leonidas Varney, Esq., and the freshly formed trio of modern musketeers went to work in locating the correct office. That is, they did so after Vera had convinced them that lunch was a prerequisite to all serious investigative labors.

By early afternoon, the team had discovered the attorney's business address in Winthrop Square. Fortunately, Mr. Varney was another independently employed gentleman whose work ethic included resting only on Sundays.

Vera described the lawyer as "a living daguerreotype, born about the time when Victoria was crowned—as proven by his snowy beard, which was expansive enough to be called glacial. In fact, Mr. Lapham might have been a bit cowed by its contrast to his own beard, and Mr. Brunton, too, if he hadn't stayed with the horse." Instead of a bright office with crisp corners and efficient organization, Mr. Varney toiled in what was more a dark catacomb of uncanny angles interrupted by pillars of law books and ledgers. Despite the room's stifling heat, the man huddled within a shawl of faded brownish plaid.

Vera realized how fortunate it was to have included Mr. Lapham on the outing when she noticed Mr. Varney's beaming smile upon hearing the affluent man's name. The attorney clearly hoped he might be welcoming a new client. Vera realized this was one time when she would be wise to curb her desire to conduct the interview, a task she found nearly impossible.

"We'd very much like to learn about a probate case," Mr. Lapham said, "one you handled four years since for a prominent man named Roderick Morley."

Mr. Varney cupped a hand over his mouth, either to suggest he was unable to discuss the matter or to give himself a moment for consideration. "Ah, yes," he eventually said, "I recall the case. Wrapped in a scandal of some sort."

Vera could not stop herself from reporting the specifics. "The murder of Mr. Morley's friend preceded his taking his own life."

"Ah, yes—a suicide." Mr. Varney clicked his tongue a few times. "I knew a sin was involved."

"Well—a murder *and* then a suicide. A *sequence* of sin—I would say," Mr. Lapham stammered. "But we're here regarding the execution of Mr. Morley's will. We understand that his widow was bequeathed the house, and there might have been a few similar allocations, too. However, the bulk of the deceased's fortune was bestowed upon one particular charity."

Vera added, "An organization dedicated to building schools for colored children in the South." She then caught herself and settled back into her chair.

"Ah, yes," repeated Mr. Varney.

"I wonder if you might give us the *name* of the charitable association," said Mr. Lapham.

"And tell us if there was any investi—" Vera started. "The name. Let's begin with the name."

"I must ask what you plan to do with the information. To challenge the will after four years—"

"No, no," interrupted Mr. Lapham, "we have no intention to challenge the will. We're simply interested in the charity itself. One is always scouting for worthwhile causes."

"Were the beneficiary an individual, I'd have to respect my client's privacy. But I see no potential harm with divulging the name of a benevolent society." He placed both hands on the respective arms of his chair, inhaled, pushed himself upward, wobbled slightly, exhaled, and finally checked his stance. He then hobbled to a cabinet of drawers. *"Morley,"* said Mr. Varney. After taking some time to remember where 'M' falls in the alphabet, he withdrew the correct file and returned to his desk chair. The process of sitting reenacted that of standing, albeit in the opposite order.

Vera exchanged a polite smile with Mr. Lapham.

Mr. Varney scanned the documents. "Ah, yes! Its office is down in Quincy. Here, allow me to copy the address for you. If it's not untoward of me to ask, Mr. Lapham, are you considering adding this society to your *own* will? I am, you see, well acquainted with the practice and procedures of probate law."

"I will certainly remember this courtesy, should the occasion arise."

Vera was unable to wait. "Given the criminal circumstances surrounding the death, sir, I must ask if the charity had been duly investigated prior to delivery of so much money."

Mr. Varney grinned as he finished jotting down the address. "Duly investigated? It's hardly a crime to leave money to a charitable cause. All of the documents were in order. Had there been any evidence of criminality regarding the beneficiary, certainly the police would have performed an investigation."

Vera found herself dumbstruck.

"But surely," said Mr. Lapham, "you made inquiries regarding the charity? Quincy is barely ten miles distant. Did you at least deliver the check in person? Out of deference to the memory of Roderick Morley?"

The aged attorney passed the slip of paper to Mr. Lapham before speaking. "You must understand, sir. I had been employed to execute Mr. Morley's final wishes. I did so as instructed. I felt no further obligations afterward. My relationship with my client was contractual, not convivial. I genuinely doubt I *could've* felt such duty to a man whose life ended by—"

Vera found her voice again. "Sin?"

Mr. Varney's only response was to straighten his dingy shawl beneath his magisterial beard.

Vera and Mr. Lapham thanked the man for his assistance but found themselves with nothing to say upon leaving the office. They found Mr. Brunton keeping warm within the carriage. He quickly exited, and Mr. Lapham handed him the paper with the address scribbled by the attorney.

The groom read the address and asked, "Is there some mistake?"

Vera stepped forward. "This is the address of the charity. The organization overseeing the building of the Southern schools."

"No," replied Mr. Brunton, "I don't think so."

"Whatever do you mean?" asked Mr. Lapham.

"This is Mr. Childers' workshop. That's the address. Down in Quincy."

Vera put her hand against the carriage to support herself for a moment. "The rock that makes a man a martyr!" she announced. Rather than explain the statement, she stood straight and insisted, "Quickly—we must get back to poor Lucille!"

•

About the time that Vera was lunching with Mr. Lapham and Mr. Brunton, Miss Marchelli brought a bowl filled with warm cream of tomato soup to me in the Green Room.

"May I keep you company?" she asked, placing the tray over my lap.

"Please do. Bedrest is always a relief, but not when Vera is hard on the heels of a solution to some mystery. Then it's a chore."

"I made your soup as bland as I could. But just in case—" Miss Marchelli retrieved a salt shaker from her apron pocket, displayed it to me, and placed it on the nightstand. She then sat on the edge of the mattress.

The soup was indeed very bland—more cream than tomato—exactly as prescribed. After a spoonful or two, I noticed Miss Marchelli was being curiously quiet. I asked, "Have you had any ghostly encounters since all the commotion of last night?"

She shook her head to indicate she hadn't.

"Nor have I. But it's too early to be certain they're not still lurking somewhere." After another period of silence, I inquired, "Would it be all right if I called you 'Sophie'?"

She shrugged. "S'fine. And what should I call you?" There was a trace of a smile on her lips.

"Vera calls me 'Lucille.'" I chuckled. "'Ludmila' is a name I thought I had laid to rest. But ghosts leave when they're ready to leave, I suppose."

This was met with more silence.

I felt impelled to say, "Is there something on your mind, Sophie?"

With half-playful anguish, she carefully collapsed across my legs. "I feel *awful* that I gave you a poisoned sandwich! It wasn't on purpose, I promise you!"

"Oh, Miss Marchelli! *Sophie!* You mustn't blame yourself! It's not proven that it was poisoned at all—and even if it were, I know it was an accident!"

"You forgive me, then?"

"Oh, yes! I forgive you—if there's anything that needs forgiving. Please don't feel guilty. Gracious, this house has *enough* guilt soaked into its walls."

Sophie pushed herself back into a sitting position. "I gave a lot of thought to how that sandwich might've gone bad. I bought the meat that morning, and the bread was maybe a day or two old. The mustard—well, maybe something had gone wrong with the mustard. But I had a spoonful after I'd heard what happened, and I was fine."

"You *tried* it? You darling! You're taking this too seriously."

"I was curious. You've seen that about me. I notice things and look for explanations. S'just how my mind seems to work."

"Have you ever read any of the Sherlock Holmeses?"

"No, but I've seen William Gillette play him on the stage. Yes, I see what you're saying. But you know what's a funny thing? You know what's a *very* funny thing?"

"What's a very funny thing?"

"I had just ladled a bowl of soup to bring to you, and Mr. Childers asked me to go out back to shoo away a cat that had wandered into the yard. Mr. Childers has never explained to me why he's so afraid of cats. That's not the funny thing, though."

"That's *not* the funny thing?"

Tim Prasil

"No, he's got certain quirks, that man. The funny thing is that, when I went out to shoo away the cat, there was no cat to be found. Anywhere."

"Why is that funny? It probably kept wandering."

"Agreed. But I came back and sampled a bit of your soup. I wanted to make sure I had added enough cream to cut the acid of the tomatoes. Well, the soup had an oddness to it. Not the taste so much as—"

"An odd sensation against the tongue? Almost like hot sand?"

"Yes, that's a nice way to describe it. I had to wash it off of my tongue! But there's nothing wrong with the soup in the pot I made for this evening's meal—just in the bowl that I had ladled for *you.*"

I immediately dropped my spoon.

"No, *that* bowl is fine. I checked it, too. And then it struck me. Last night, when I came up to tell you about how that cop looked like the ventriloquist I'd seen, Mr. Childers was downstairs. The sandwiches, Lucille! *I'd left the sandwiches!*"

"Down in the kitchen," I thought aloud. "Is it possible? Is it possible Mr. Childers is trying to—to *poison me?* If he doesn't want us to continue our ghost hunt—if he wants us to *leave*—but—*poison me?*"

"I can't believe he was trying to *kill* you, Lucille. Or Miss Van Slyke, either. He probably wants to make one or the other of you sick so that you'd both leave. I know he wants to be rid of the ghosts, but now that he sees it's not like exterminating rats, he wants to be rid of the ghost hunters."

Now, *I* was the silent one.

Sophie continued, "As I say, he's got certain quirks. He doesn't seem to know how a grown man handles a problem. When things don't go his way, he's liable to have a conniption fit like a spoiled child. You've probably heard us caterwauling a few times."

"I have, but—but I understood that it was Mr. Childers

191

attempting to prevent you from quitting because of the ghosts."

"No, I've come round to finding the haunting fascinating, even though I've given up trying to figure it all out. No, our spats are all due to Mr. Childers throwing a fit about one thing or another. At times, s'like I'm his mother instead of his maid. Still, as I say, I can't believe he was trying to *kill* anyone."

I managed to whisper, "He *did* take the side of my going to the hospital. He *claimed* to be considering my best interests."

She sighed. "Only if your best interests would serve his own best interests. Once Miss Van Slyke returns, you two should discuss moving to different lodgings."

"Should've stayed in Chicago," I heard myself say. "Vera asked me if we should take the case. We should've stayed in Chicago."

Sophie grasped my hand. "Do you want me to get rid of the soup? I will if it scares you."

I looked at the bowl of rich, red nourishment, and I thought of Vera's philosophy on lunch. "I don't think that's necessary. Quite honestly, I—I'm *famished*. I'll go ahead and eat it. If you're—if you're very certain it isn't poisoned."

"Very certain." She smiled and let go of my hand.

I smiled back. Then I giggled a bit. "But it truly *could* use a dash of salt, if you don't mind."

"I don't mind." She turned and reached for the salt shaker she'd placed on the nightstand.

It wasn't there.

She looked at the floor.

It wasn't there.

Slowly, she pivoted to face me. "I—I *swear* I just put it down right there!"

I stated, "The ghosts aren't done with this house, so it would seem."

"So it would seem," said Sophie while nodding pensively.

•

"We must leave this place *immediately!*" Vera shouted as she charged through the door. She then halted and rebounded as if the horse she was riding had reared at the sight of a snake. "Wait. What are you doing out of bed?"

"Packing," I stated. "I've opened your trunk, but your dresses are still hanging in the closet."

After a considerable pause, Vera said, "Have you gotten to know me *that* well, my dear? I haven't had a chance to tell you what I learned about our host."

"Is it that Mr. Childers is very likely poisoning me to get us out of his house?"

"Well—yes. Yes, that *is* what I learned. Exactly that. But you seem to have gotten to Scotland a'fore me." Vera cocked her head. "How do you feel?"

"Emotionally?"

"Digestively first."

"Physically, I'm operating at half-steam—but strong enough to pack our things. Emotionally, however, it's *full* steam ahead."

"And we shall go, my dear. We shall." Vera marched to the closet and began to transfer her garments to the trunk. "However, we don't want Mr. Childers to get off without due punishment. I'm not certain what you've learned—or how you learned it—but this afternoon, I learned that he's enmeshed far more deeply in this mystery than I had suspected. Perhaps it would be prudent for us to exchange information. To form a plan of action."

I sat on the edge of the bed and related what Sophie had told me. While listening, Vera continued to transfer her dresses to her trunk. Once I had finished, she sat beside me, carrying a blouse. It was one of her favorites, ivory-colored with a lacy jabot.

"Look," she said, "this slash along the sleeve wasn't there this morning. Still more confirmation that the ghosts continue to have unfinished business."

She then told me *her* afternoon's discoveries.

"On the way back from the attorney's office," Vera added,

"the wealthy fellow said that, if need be, he would gladly offer us rooms—or put us up at a hotel."

"Mr. Lapham is a kind man. Has he gone back to the jailhouse now?"

Vera nodded and then nibbled one her fingertips. "But he has enough worries at present, hasn't he? Let's decline that offer. What do you say to our staying with my friend William. I don't think he or his wife would find it an imposition. Or would you prefer a hotel?"

"It's kind of you to consider everyone's wishes."

"Blame the panic of my having put you in danger."

I chuckled. "A hotel is probably best. I've received the cold shoulder from your Dr. James. Understandably. He's only known me as yet another fake Spiritualist. The one present when his friend took his life. And now I associate with *another* of his friends. Come to think of it, it's a wonder the good doctor doesn't outright despise me."

"Oh, I don't think he's capable of that. He just doesn't know you as I do. You know, it would be wise for you being under the roof of a man with medical training. Until you're fully recovered, I mean."

I saw the wisdom in that. "Then we shall arrive in a basket on Dr. James's doorstep and hope he takes pity on us. But what do we tell Mr. Childers, since we don't want to let on that we're close to uncovering his dark secret?"

"Simple!" said Vera with a clap of her hands. "We pretend his plan to get us out of the house has worked. We tell him you've had another bout of abdominal cramps and so we're taking you to the hospital. For propriety's sake, I'll be staying with Dr. James and his wife, but I'll return daily as I devise a means to evict the ghosts. The maid here is very clever—she'll understand the ruse. And, if the groom takes us, we can explain everything to him then."

"So that they'll be aware they're living with a scoundrel?"

"So that they'll serve as our *spies* and keep a close eye on that scoundrel! I ought to stop off and inform the Chief Inspector what we've discovered about our host's *charitable* workshop. Shall we do that on the way? No, we should get you safely back into bed, and *then* I'll go. But it *is* on the way." Vera nibbled another of her fingertips.

My only reply was a gentle caress.

CHAPTER FIFTEEN

THE RARITY OF COMPLETE TRUTH

The next morning, I exaggerated when I told Vera and Dr. James that I was 'fit as a fiddle.' In truth, I felt more like a wheezy accordion, but I wasn't about to remain loafing as the investigation of Mr. Childers' workshop proceeded. Twice now, I had lain in bed as Vera had made key discoveries in the case. I confess I was envious.

The previous evening—after we had settled in at the James house—Vera had gone to the Criminal Investigation Bureau to leave a message for Mr. Watts. She informed him that the "charity" to which Mr. Morley had left his fortune had the same address as Mr. Childers' workshop. She also told the Chief Inspector to meet her there at 10:00 the following morning, a Sunday, on the assumption that Mr. Childers would be absent.

"Is it a *safe* assumption that Mr. Childers will be absent?" I asked Vera as we rode to Quincy and passed a church welcoming its congregation. "I now wonder if he's a man who honors the Sabbath day."

"Haven't the maid and groom both said it's his habit to work Saturday and take off Sunday?"

"Yes," I replied, "but he stayed home yesterday—presumably so that he could give me another dose of arsenic or whatever awful stuff he's using. I wonder if he might go to work *today* as a result. And we now know he can be dangerous."

"Very astute, my dear. But I have *you* with me again. We'll keep each other safe."

"And hopefully Mr. Watts will be joining us, correct?"

"At 10:00. Unless there are signs that our suspect is there, that'll give us about a quarter hour to snoop around on our own."

"Vera! Is *that* safe? What if Mr. Childers *walks in on us?"*

Vera cocked her head, patted my hand, and turned to observe the passing scenery through the carriage's window. I began to feel less like a wheezy accordion and more like a guitar crushed by our wheels. Remaining silent, I gazed out at the cold, cloudy morning.

As Vera had planned, shortly after 9:30, we arrived at the address. Around us were the mechanical grumbles and billowing chimneys of manufactories. At some distance, a smattering of workers walked and chatted and smoked. These buildings overshadowed Childers' brick workshop, which bore no signboard and was small enough to be a garage. While it matched how I would imagine an inventor's studio, it looked nothing like the office of a charitable organization.

We approached it slowly, and Vera put her ear close to the front door. She shook her head to indicate no noise. Next, we carefully peeped through smudged windows on the sides and in the back. Still nothing.

"Well," decided Vera aloud, "I'll go ahead and knock to make absolutely certain. It's best you stay out of sight."

Before I could contest the plan, she strode to the backdoor and knocked loudly. "Mr. Chitlins?" she sang. "Oh, Mr. Chitlins?"

"Childers!" I hissed from behind the corner.

"Oh—Mr. *Childers!* I have important news, sir, regarding your haunting!"

No one answered the door, so I crept very cautiously forward.

"Try not to look like a burglar, my dear. You'll draw attention."

Vera then searched her handbag and extracted a ring of skeleton keys, a useful weapon in her ghost hunting arsenal. Upon finding one that unlocked the door, Vera then glanced both ways and entered the workshop.

Glancing both ways, I followed—feeling as if the carriage had reversed and crushed the guitar a second time.

Lit only by an overcast sky filtered through dirty windows, the workshop looked much like a storage shed. There were three dusty desks pushed beside one side wall, the accompanying chairs placed on top of them. Opposite to these was a drafting table cluttered with numerous instruments, such as pens and rulers, and beside this was a bookshelf of what appeared to be technical books of some sort. I noticed an icebox standing in one corner. As I breathed the stale air, I shuddered as I recalled that Mr. Childers said he used to live here, sleeping on a cot.

I stepped toward Vera and whispered, "I don't suppose this was *formerly* the charity's office. Perhaps those unused desks are evidence of that."

With no attempt to hush her voice, Vera explained, "The coincidence is too great. He lives in the millionaire's house, *and* he works in the spot where the millionaire's money went? No. That drafting table is not used by an inventor. It belongs to a *forger*. I'd gamble that, four years ago, those desks were used to make this place *look* like a charitable organization. Our Mr. Childers might have paid a few conspirators to appear officious, should anyone come to investigate." She resumed her snooping.

I muttered, "Seldom, very seldom, does complete truth belong to any human disclosure."

"What's that, my dear?"

"Jane Austen," I replied, "from one of those silly novels I read." I walked to the bookshelf and withdrew one of the books. The title was *Edison and His Inventions*, J.B. McClure named as editor. As I leafed through the volume, I found several envelopes wedged between the pages. These envelopes has been slit open, I saw, and each still contained a letter.

I checked another book and found letters inside it, too. A third and a fourth book convinced me that this collection of books about technology and invention was a disguise. The shelves were actually being used to conceal samples of handwriting.

"Vera?" I said. "I think we've got him." I noticed she was peering into a waste basket beside the drafting table. I also noticed she wasn't moving. "Vera? Did you hear what I said?"

"Lucille? I think *he's* got *me.*"

She stepped aside, and I moved to see that there was a single scrap of paper in the bottom of that waste basket. I reached down and raised the scrap to better see what was written on it. It appeared to be a list.

"After his initial letter," whispered Vera, "we communicated via telegram. When we first arrived, though, the letter I'd written to Vitellius Berry—the letter asking for additional information on our murder suspects—I'd left it with *him.* The *forger!* He had offered to post it for me. Remember?"

"I remember." I held up the scrap of paper to the dim light coming through the filthy window.

It was a column of attempts to copy Vera's signature. The first four were crossed out. The fifth was left as is. I had come to know Vera's penmanship well enough to recognize the accuracy of the facsimile.

Then we *jolted* when we heard a male voice boom: *"Miss Van Slyke?!"*

Vera grabbed my elbow to steady me.

"Must be 10:00," she stated. "The Chief Inspector has a deeper voice than the forger. I'll let him in."

●

"What I *ought* to do is charge you with breaking and entering!" said Mr. Watts after we had ordered our lunch. "That's what I *ought* to do!"

Vera retorted, "Your uncovering a case of million-dollar fraud and forgery hinged entirely on the apprehension of one snooping reporter? A snooping *lady* reporter? Wouldn't that news distract from what may well be your most celebrated arrest since Jack the Slugger?"

Mr. Watts tightened his lips. "We preferred to call him 'The Slugger!'" He narrowed his eyes. "I'll take liberties when innocent women are being clubbed—sometimes, to *death*—for whatever jewelry and cash they happened to have on them. A crime such as *this*, though, needs to be handled strictly by the book." Behind the slits of their lids, his eyes rotated. "I'm confident I can get a search warrant and *legitimately* enter Childers' workshop on the basis of it being at the same address where Morley's bequest was delivered."

"No doubt, you'll handle the case with the same ethical standards I've seen used by the Police Departments in New York and Chicago," replied Vera with a sly curl in her lips. More sincerely, she added, "I promise to take no credit in resolving the case. Knowing I provided crucial evidence is reward enough."

I added, "And it was foolish of us to enter the workshop before you arrived." I aimed a sharp sneer at my friend.

Vera added, "However, sir, I implore you to remember that this is not simply a case of high-society fraud. Childers is not our only concern. His machinations have placed Mrs. Lapham in jail. Clearly, he's the crook who fabricated the phony love letters Sanderson claimed were hidden in the Dawning Room while attempting to blackmail the former Mrs. Morley. Childers was assuredly Sanderson's conspirator. Given the outcome, he may have been the backstage mastermind of the entire operation!"

I've often marveled at how Vera's inability to recall names vanished when her mind was racing with all sails hoisted.

"Here's my theory," she declared. "Childers was either Sanderson's unseen partner from the start—or became so once the psychic learned of the marital difficulties between the Morleys. Together, they hatched the scheme to convince *Mr.* Morley to revise his will and then coerce *Mrs.* Morley to murder her husband. The plan was dodgy from the start, but it took an alarming detour when Sanderson was murdered instead of Morley. Childers was safe, though, so long as he could continue to make his workshop pass for the office of a charitable organization.

"Unfortunately for him, Childers might've had to sustain

that charade until Morley died a natural death. That's when Fate rushed to his rescue. Morley committed suicide. His money went to Childers. Childers cleverly bided his time a couple of years before embarking on the life of a millionaire. And he did so in a surprisingly unoriginal way. Not only can Childers mimic another man's signature, he decided to mimic another man's *life!* It's the ultimate forgery."

Mr. Watts nodded with his brow raised. "So the man who now lives in Morley's house—is the man who appropriated Morley's wealth."

"Is the man who asked Morley's widow to marry him," I added.

"Is the man from whom Sanderson learned that *witches float!*" exclaimed Vera. "And innocent women drown. And an innocent man's bones *break!*"

"Huhm?" muttered Mr. Watts. "You've walloped me there, by God."

After a good laugh, Vera explained, "From the start, our investigation has had witches flying by it. A misspelled word, a country colloquialism, a couple of books on the subject, and then Sanderson's fatal taunt about the Morley girl drowning. I sought to link the whipping of accused witches to the slashing of fabric that haunts the mansion, but as yet, that pocket watch has no stem for winding it."

"What do you think?" I asked Mr. Watts. "There aren't any connections between forgers and witches, are there?"

He replied in a very measured way. "Tell me—about—the misspelled word."

Vera straightened her back and leaned forward. "It appeared among several other errors—some of them corrected—in the original letter sent to us. The letter inviting us to rid the house of ghosts."

The Chief Inspector pressed his hands together. He laced his fingers together—all but his index fingers, which he moved back and forth like a single pendulum pointing skyward. "Now, one method used to narrow down a forger's trail is to look for what we call 'forgers' footprints.' We have little to work with if they're simply signing checks with someone else's name, of course. But *letters* are a different matter. Some rascals, unaware of a rule in spelling or even punctuation, reveal themselves by making the very same mistake across several letters."

"Our rascal strikes me as too smart for that," commented Vera. "He's managed to do quite well for himself, after all."

Mr. Watts now separated his index fingers and began to tap them against each other. "*Expert* forgers do something similar—yet also very different. With them, forgery is a game of poker, and the method of winning is to bluff their opponent. When I say 'opponent,' I mean an officer of the law. To make that game all the more thrilling—they drop hints. They'll hint that the work is, indeed, a forgery. They'll even hint at *who* the forger is by, oh—putting their personal stamp on a counterfeit letter. It might be a design, such as a star. This seems like a variation, and 'which' is such a common word, this man almost always has an opportunity to sneak in his special spelling of it."

"I've read about such a thing happening in forged paintings," Vera noted. "It follows that it occurs in written letters, too. Furthermore, if he deliberately misspelled 'which,' then the other errors were very likely used as camouflage—a way to make that word look like just another error."

I said, "But that letter wasn't a forgery. It was signed by him."

Mr. Watts offered an answer. "He's still a game player. The slip of paper left in the wastebasket is proof of that. It was his way of warning you, Miss Van Slyke, that—if you happened to be a shrewd enough opponent to, *ahem*, break into his workshop—he'd have the power to retaliate. To ruin your reputation, perhaps, or even to steal your savings."

Vera angled her head to stare at the table's floral centerpiece.

"But *we're* winning the game now," the Chief Inspector assured her. "I'll ask our man who scours all of the works of forgery that come into headquarters if he's noticed any with the word 'witch' slipped into it. If so, that's very likely Childers' stamp. His strategy to *bewitch* his opponent."

Vera agreed with me that Mr. Watts' pun was a clever one, an affirmation that clearly pleased him.

"While I disapprove of *how* you made this discovery," said the Chief Inspector, "it *is* a very valuable one, and on behalf of the Boston police force, I wish to thank—"

"Why didn't the Boston police force investigate the phony charity *four years ago?*" Vera demanded as much as asked.

Mr. Watts smiled at first, but then he must have caught the very serious expression on Vera's face. "Well—well, first off, there's no crime in leaving money to a charity. For us to pursue such a thing, a complaint would need to be registered, and Mrs. Morley certainly wasn't going to draw any more attention to the case. Besides, if the charity had a stink to it, Mr. Morley's attorney certainly would have looked into it—or contacted us to do so."

"Uh huh," Vera said with a sigh. "I see." Clearly, she had solved that mystery to her satisfaction.

Only a few minutes passed before our meals arrived. I looked with longing at Mr. Watts' ham and potatoes, and Vera's seabass and carrots in contrast to my scrambled eggs and milk. When I reached for the pepper, Vera snatched the shaker and placed it at the far end of the table.

"You're still recuperating, my dear," she said. "Here, let me help you resist temptation." She then placed a napkin over the pepper shaker.

I considered the hidden spice. "Merely a thought. A notion. Mr. Childers keeps the Dawning Room almost exactly as it was four years ago. What if he's searching for the phony love letters? What if he knows that his stamp—his use of the word 'witch'—can reveal that he's the sole prizewinner of a secret game that included murder and suicide?"

Mr. Watts snorted. "He's lived in the place for a few years now. If such letters ever actually existed, surely he would have found them by now!"

Vera and I exchanged expressions of astonishment.

"Not if there's a ghost that likes to play games, too. But her game is moving things from one place to another."

"And to silently look on as her opponent becomes utterly baffled."

The Chief Inspector put down his fork. "You've walloped me once again. What does all of this mean?"

"It means," announced Vera, "you mustn't arrest this rascal for forgery just yet. If you give us a couple of days more, we can find evidence of his involvement in a crime even more serious. Though this will not exonerate her, it will at least ensure a fair trial for—for, uh, the millionaire's widow. I'm very sorry—could one of you remind me of the woman's name? I'm not very strong with names."

•

That afternoon, I returned to bed while Vera went to the Boston Criminal Investigation Bureau. She was gone for several hours, but on her return, I learned that Mr. Watts had uncovered nothing at all about Herman Childers and only slightly more regarding forged letters with the word "witch" in them. The detective tasked to record and collate such forgers' footprints did not work Sundays, but after hours of searching, Vera and Mr. Watts found three letters with the misspelling. The Chief Inspector was going to have their specialist continue the search on Monday, allowing Vera only a day or two to prove Mr. Childers' direct involvement in the murder and suicide.

At dinner, I became better acquainted with Alice, the professor's wife. She was a Bostonian from birth, and she believed Spiritualism had a thread of truth tangled amid all the chicanery. She had excused herself from our company after dessert, and it occurred to me that the quiet woman might have been weary of engaging me in conversation while her husband directed all of his toward Vera.

A late October gale had developed that night. After dinner,

we retired to the parlor, where a robust fire and walls covered with pictures of Europe blanketed us against the storm. Once settled, we sipped sherry and gazed at the hearth.

"Vera?" began Dr. James. "I enjoyed reading your book—your *Spirits Shouldn't Sneeze* exposé. How are the sales going?"

"Not very well," she chuckled. "Too long a train of authors doing the same work, I imagine, from *Spiritualism and Charlatanism* to *The Bottom Facts Concerning the Science of Spiritualism.*"

"Unfortunate," the professor said. "I understand you contributed what you knew, Miss Parsell." It was the first time that evening he had referred to me by name.

I put down my sherry. "I was very ready to confess my transgressions."

Mr. James tilted his head, held his glass just below his lips, and peered into my eyes. He nodded and then sipped his wine. I wondered if there were a glimmer of reassessment in that moment.

Perhaps sensing this warming of our host's view of me, Vera raised the temperature another degree. "Lucille here is very well read, you know. In fact, my dear, you said something very intriguing this morning at the forger's workshop. A passage from a novel, you said. What's the quotation?"

"I said, 'Seldom, very seldom, does complete truth belong to any human disclosure.' It's from Jane Austen's *Emma*. There's more to it, but that first sentence often recurs to me—especially when confronted by the worst cases of complete *untruth*."

Dr. James grinned at this. "That's exactly the feeling I have as I explore psychic phenomenon. Man's character is too, uh—*sophistically mixed*—for the alternative of *honest* or *dishonest* to be a sharp one. Even good scientists cheat to demonstrate that an experiment is successful rather than admit their failure. Perhaps I'll confide this to readers one day in an article about my experiences in psychical research."

Vera flicked her fingernail twice against her sherry glass, the clink seemingly intended to draw our attention. Brusquely, she challenged, "Forgive me if I misunderstand. Are you both implying that we should see the forged love letters and the phony charitable society—the entire blackmail and murder plot—as merely a somewhat clearer example of the fraud we *all* commit each and every *day?*"

Any attempt my friend had made to increase the warmth was now whisked away by a chilly gust.

"Wuh-well," Dr. James began, "it's hardly an isolated—I mean—" He turned to me.

I turned to Vera. "Think about our own history at the Morley Mansion," I suggested. "There I was, pretending to be a medium. There you were, pretending to be someone *other* than a reporter intent on debunking me. Even Dr. James was playing along with that ruse."

The professor shrugged. "And then, all these years later, there's the police charade that induced poor Viola to confess. Granted, it *worked!* But our point is that the truth is tweaked and twisted and, yes, *contorted* on a regular basis—from committing a felony to sparing a loved one's feelings. Isn't that our meaning, Miss Parsell?"

"It is. Thank you, Dr. James. Put simply, Vera, whether it's our own or that of others, fraud haunts us each and every day."

Vera grinned at us. *"Fraud Is a Phantom.* There's an awful title for a novel." She chuckled.

"Do you get the sense that we've just been duped into finding common ground, Miss Parsell?"

"I do indeed, Dr. James."

"Lovely sherry," Vera noted as she lifted her glass to us.

This was followed by a peaceful period of gazing into the fire. It and the sherry were fulfilling their mission of facilitating contemplation.

Eventually, I asked our host, "If Vera's theory regarding the case is correct, sir, what do you make of Mr. Childers's curious desire to *become* Roderick Morley. He has your friend's money, his house—he wanted his wife. Speaking as a leader in the field of Psychology, how do *you* explain the man?"

Dr. James resettled himself in his chair before speaking. "The original scheme was most likely sparked by simple greed. Childers and Sanderson probably saw the girl's drowning in the newspaper and developed their plans at that point. Or Sanderson did on his own and brought in Childers afterward. Either way, Viola made it unmistakably clear that—despite her unsatisfactory marriage—her husband's wellbeing meant more to her than did the prospect of acquiring half of his wealth. Even if it meant her own downfall, Viola was going to keep Roderick *safe.*"

"A semblance of safety and security," said Vera, "are probably what held the marriage together, since the love seems to have died."

Dr. James nodded. "Now, what if that semblance of safety and security fascinated Childers? What if it became his obsession? Perhaps he had lived his life without such things."

Vera affirmed, "He divulged that he had grown up in a Tennessee cabin, sharing a room with—how many brothers?"

"Three brothers," I said. "Financial security must certainly have fascinated him."

Dr. James smiled. "Financial security, but also emotional security. Both exert a powerful attraction."

"They pull with as much power as guilt pushes," I commented.

"That's very observant, young lady."

"Kind of you to say so, sir. You see, I read *novels,*" I turned to Vera and blinked slowly.

She smirked and turned away.

Dr. James said, "Yes, my brother Henry contends that his profession and my own are not all that dissimilar. You asked me to speak as a leader in the field of Psychology. Now, Miss Parsell, I'll ask you to speak as a reader in the field of Literature. What do you think of my analysis of Childers?" He rose to fetch the bottle of sherry from the shelf.

"I certainly agree that envying his financial security is the best explanation for Mr. Childers daring to purchase his victim's house, and his attempt to marry his victim's widow is undoubtedly tied to a yearning for emotional security. Of course, the life of any criminal is hardly a safe one—and forgery, at its heart, requires mirroring the identities of those who have something deeply desired. Something *coveted.* I'm curious about what made Mr. Childers covet another man's entire life. What made him so dissatisfied with his *own* life? Does it boil down to shame? Was he ashamed of his life?"

Returning with the sherry, Dr. James added, "*And* did Mr. Childers feel that shame—that is, did he only sense the evil of the blackmailing scheme—*after* he learned it had resulted in his collaborator's death?"

I wondered how seeing Mr. Sanderson's dead form standing before him—be it my mother in disguise or whatever Mrs. Lapham claimed to have seen—might affect Mr. Childers. Would it evoke an expression of horrified guilt?

Vera held her glass so that Dr. James could refill it. "May *I* speak as a journalist in the field of Journalism now? Effects matter more than causes—*what* happened, not *why* it happened. And the effects here have been *monstrous.* Whether or not he can be judged guilty of *murder,* he's complicit with one! Complicit with a *suicide!* Complicit with landing that poor woman in *jail!* Let's not turn this man into a mere victim of circumstance, someone worthy of our sympathy. Would either of you say the same of the trusted psychic advisor?"

"I would not," asserted Dr. James. "Sanderson knew Roderick's soul better than I did, and still he could execute a scheme to have him murdered. That requires a hardening of the heart I've heard described by scarred veterans of the Civil War forced to do battle with their own cousins. Childers, however, had a great advantage. I imagine it's far easier to kill a man one has never met—especially when someone else pulls the trigger."

Vera moved to the front edge of her chair. "Why, he met Lucille, and there are strong indications that he fed her *poison!*" Yes, perhaps he was only *trying* to make her sick. Yes, his maid says she doesn't *think* him capable of murder. But what if all that is a gross *miscalculation?*"

Seeing our bookish analysis had irritated my friend, I spoke softly. "All crucial points, Vera. But my saying that Mr. Childers feels shame does not mean I would find it easy to forgive what he's done. If he apologized with tears in his eyes, I would not be very Christian in my reply. But I do wish to *understand* him. Sophie—she's Mr. Childers' maid, sir—said her employer often acts like a child and she must act like a mother to him. I think this indicates an adult whose maturation was thwarted. Who never learned how to cope with shame. And who struggles desperately with the evil within himself."

"A Jekyll and Hyde?" said Vera with an edge of derision.

"Something like that. Mr. Stevenson exaggerated the division between Jekyll and Hyde to illustrate his point. But, yes, it would not surprise me to learn that Mr. Childers struggles with the evil within him. Thank you, sir."

Our host had put another splash of sherry in my glass. He returned to his seat to refill his own glass and then put the bottle on the floor.

He asked, "Could this struggle with his own evil have something to do with his using a *witch* as his secret signature? Is it merely part of his game—or part of his inner conflict? Is the witch a muffled expression of him crying to get *caught?* I fear such questions are often unanswerable."

Again, we stared into the flames.

Vera spoke next. "I hope my previous comments didn't sound dismissive. How the man's mind works and what made him the monster he is will be terribly interesting to me—*after* he's convicted for his crimes. *Then* we can investigate why he chose the cipher of a witch. What I want to know *now* is how we find evidence that might be of some value to the drowned girl's mother. We only have a day or two to find it."

Dr. James grunted heavily. "Unless we stage another spectacle with your oboes and a ventriloquist to coerce a confession, I don't—"

"As we've seen," Vera interrupted, "a confession might be coerced from someone who definitely has a sense of shame—who is capable of feeling guilt. I am deeply fond of you both, but I do *not* share your view that he has such feelings. I do *not* see him as a thwarted child in a grown man's body. I do *not* see him as Jekyll struggling with his Hyde."

"How, then, do you see him?" inquired Dr. James.

"Monstrous effects, not causes. Hyde standing alone." Vera thrust a finger forward, almost spilling sherry from her glass. "Not a man who struggles with the evil within himself. A man who *relishes* the evil games he plays."

This sparked an image in my head. The vision was of Mr. Childers facing, not Mr. Sanderson's dead form, but the apparition of the young woman he had sickened with poison. If Sophie were correct in saying her employer wasn't a murderer, he would be shocked by the vision and horrified by what his actions had wrought. According to Vera's assessment, though, he would remain an unshaken, cold-blooded monster.

At this point, I knew I would have to become a ghost.

I knew I would have to become my *own* ghost.

CHAPTER SIXTEEN

A DESPERATE PLAN (OR TWO)

I had discussed my idea with Vera and Dr. James by the parlor fire before we retired for the night, and both had received it with half-hearted interest. This made sense to me the next morning, when I awoke and realized the plan woefully lacked in crystal clarity. However, the gale had passed, and the frigid air behind it had left frost on the window. Frost melts with the rising sunshine, however, and the glaze obscuring my scheme began dissolving, too.

As it did so, I had a welcome visitor. Mr. Brunton, after driving Mr. Childers to his workshop, decided to stop by and see how I was recuperating. Fortunately, I was already dressed and had eaten breakfast, and I could meet him in the parlor.

"Where is the great ghost hunter?" he said by way of a greeting, his triangular eyes wide with delight upon finding me out of bed and chipper.

"She's gone for a meditative walk on the Harvard campus. We're both hoping to hatch a plan that will—now that I think of it—a plan that will put you out of work, I'm afraid." I clasped my hands and pressed them to my chin.

Though his eyes remained wide, one of his eyebrows crept slowly higher. I invited him to take a seat. Usually, his face was usually very animated, but now Mr. Brunton's expression turned to stone as he listened to me recount our findings at the forger's workshop and Vera's theory on Mr. Childer's involvement in the suicide of his cherished Mr. Morley. I ended by saying that we were racing against time to unearth proof of this involvement and that doing so meant finding the forged love letters hidden in the Dawning Room.

"He spent most of yesterday in that very room," reported my guest. "I heard a few unsavory outbursts from there, too. I assumed he was still riled by Friday night's intrusion into his sanctum—as well as its lack of results regarding the specter. If anything, our supernatural resident has become more adamant in reminding us of his presence. We've heard the gunshot four times, and Miss Marchelli has had to mend six or seven of the linens and garments because of the rips. Some had to be tossed in the waste bin."

"I see. You've known Mr. Childers longer than anyone we've spoken to in this case. How would you describe him? You mentioned he enjoys his privacy, but are his outbursts common? Is he a volatile man?"

Mr. Brunton stroked his beard. "In my company, he's professional and courteous. Never especially warm, mind you, despite my years in his employ. I've heard stories from the maids, though, about his tantrums. Fortunately, he's easily calmed by a feminine hand. Well, *some* feminine hands. I don't think he quite knows what to make of Miss Van Slyke!"

"Many people don't. No, Vera isn't one to mother any man."

"But she'll mother *you* if you're in danger—I saw *that!* I suppose that's motherly in its way. Not as a mother dotes on her babe, but—but—"

"As a mother grizzly protects her cub?"

"Exactly. Perhaps, though, that's more a sign of loyal friendship."

For some reason, I felt myself blush. "I'm sure Vera will be flattered by being compared to a snarly bear. If you don't mind, could you tell me about *your* loyalty toward Mr. Childers?"

"*P'huh*," he popped, "vastly diminished *today*, given what you've told me! If there's any way I can assist in exposing his role in Roddy's suicide, please consider me your ready soldier. I don't care to tell lies on general principle, but I *did* find it rather easy to tell Mr. Childers I had driven you to Mass General instead of bringing you here."

I smiled—then winced. "Might I ask you to tell a bolder lie? Do you suppose you could tell him that things look bleak? Regarding my condition, I mean?"

A look of heartbreaking sadness weighed down his face and shoulders. "I would be very sorry to say those words—if not for the lie, then for the picture they paint." Suddenly, he rebounded. "Hold on. Are you plotting yet another confrontation with the dead? But with *you* as ghost this time? You certainly are your mother's daughter, aren't you!"

"I fear it might be the only way to induce Mr. Childers to confess."

His green eyes sparkled. "Yes! I will tell him—how's this?—I'll tell him that your constitution is simply too delicate to rally. And then, when he spots your specter, well, seeing such a ghost surely broke Mrs. Mor—uh, Mrs. *Lapham!* Oh. Mrs. Lapham. That poor, poor woman." Just as quickly as the man's bearing had risen in glee, it again fell back to sorrow.

"Of course, Vera might return with an entirely better plan. In fact, she doesn't believe my plan will work. She feels it all hinges on Mr. Childers feeling some small twinge of guilt for his actions—at least, when they result in the death of someone he's known—and she is firmly convinced that he's incapable of any such feeling. What do *you* think?"

Mr. Brunton looked downward. "If he felt nothing upon facing the death of a young woman—one who has so corrected the path of her life as you have—then he would truly be a monster."

"Thank you, sir. *Monster* is the word Vera used. But is he a monster—or is he a terribly troubled man?"

Again, he rubbed his beard. "I don't know him well enough to make that judgment. Your plan might allow us all to do so."

"Unless Vera comes up with an entirely better plan," I whispered as my eyes wandered to the windows. On this side of the house, I noticed, the frost had only started to melt.

"As our time is limited, would it make sense for us to meet

again this evening to learn whose plan will achieve the best results? I can invite Miss Marchelli, if you think she'd be useful."

"Yes," I responded, shaking off my distraction. "Yes, a wonderful suggestion. Vera and I have become fond of you both, and we would like to keep you informed of developments. Oh dear, if all goes well, Sophie will be losing her job, too."

"She'll have another within a week. She's endlessly resourceful, that girl. And I've been looking forward to retirement for years now. Don't let us hinder you." He took my hand. "You know, Miss Van Slyke might have been correct in saying that the crouching figure I saw lurking by the Dawning Room *wasn't* a demon. However, there's one there now by the name of Childers—and our first priority is to send him to where his kind belong."

As we strolled to the door, Mr. Brunton and I agreed to meet at The Pitcher and Coach at 8:00 that evening. He bade me adieu, and my eyes wandered again to the frosty windows.

"A *demon* by the name of Childers?" I muttered. "Or a man plagued *by* demons?"

•

"I have a plan!" Vera proclaimed upon her return. "It's not a perfect plan. It's a plan that depends upon the cooperation of our spies to let us into the house and into the library. I think we're safe in that regard. But the plan also requires the cooperation of the drowned girl. Do you think the little prankster would behave herself long enough for us to search the library for the precious letters?"

"Actual ghosts are *your* area of expertise. *Fake* ghosts are mine." I then told Vera about how my own plan was becoming clearer and how I had already asked Mr. Brunton to take the next step toward convincing Mr. Childers that he was responsible for my death."

Vera's pursed lips told that she was still skeptical.

I asked, "Are our plans mutually exclusive?"

Her lips relaxed, and her head eased backward.

216

"What if—" I improvised, "what if we spent this afternoon and most of tomorrow searching for the letters while Mr. Childers is off doing whatever he does at his workshop. However, *this evening,* you tell him that you need to perform a ceremony much like the one that prompted Mrs. Lapham to confess."

Vera bit her lip.

"Yes," said I, "much too straightforward. How can we arrange something that would rattle him in the way that Mrs. Lapham was rattled? Rattle a *confession* out of him?"

She rested two fingers on her jaw, but remained mum.

"I have it! An *exorcism!* You tell him that, since the haunting isn't related to the apprehension of Mrs. Lapham, you've come to conclude that it's something else entirely! Maybe not *demons*—that's a bit Medieval. How about—how about—"

Vera raised a finger before finally speaking. "On the surface, the manifestations can pass for a poltergeist. Of course, poltergeists create random havoc while these manifestations are very focused and persistent. But he probably doesn't know that—so, yes, he *might* allow us to blow our oboes again if he thinks it'll end his spectral annoyances. I'll concoct some malarkey about a remedy for poltergeists to tell him this evening."

"And tomorrow evening, if need be, my ghastly form will float in from the Green Room and accuse him of murdering me. And Mr. Sanderson. And Mr. Morley! That should evoke *some* kind of response from him—hopefully."

Vera again pursed her lips. "I will agree to this chicanery *only* as a last resort. *Only* after we've spent this afternoon and all day tomorrow scouring that library for the forged letters. If my plan fails, we shall implement yours."

"Perfectly reasonable. Thank you, Vera. I know how opposed you were to Mr. Watts using such devious tactics to evoke the confession he wanted."

"But he *got* what he wanted, didn't he?" Vera admitted.

"From a woman with a *conscience,*" I conceded.

•

Since Mr. Childers kept the key in his pocket, Sophie was unable to admit us into the Dawning Room. Vera tried her skeleton keys in the hallway door, but the locked room remained impenetrable. When we tried the door leading to the supernatural library from the Green Room, though, we heard the click that signaled success.

Immediately, I lamented, "The Chief Inspector won't be pleased with us."

"He seems to mind less if he's given accolades for the arrest," Vera reminded me as she led the way. "Our concern right now is to ask our naughty friend for her help. How are you at managing children?"

Vera pulled the curtain aside and filled the room with afternoon light. I sat at the table, where I made my best efforts to cajole the invisible ghost of Dorothy May into guiding us to the forged letters. I borrowed a letter opener from the desk and invited her to give us a hint where they were, much as she had used a key to draw my attention to the books on witchcraft. Vera and I kept our eyes shut to a slow count of ten, hoping that when we opened them, the letter opener would be moved.

It remained exactly where I had placed it.

Two more trials ended with the same result.

"Disappointing," Vera stated. "The best we can hope for is that the ghostly girl *is* teasing the forger by moving the letters from place to place as he searches for them—and that she won't pull the same stunt with *us*. If you start at that end, I'll start at this one. We'll meet at the Mississippi River."

We went to work, pulling out one book at a time, carefully leafing through and shaking it, then moving to the next. We checked behind each row of the books. The cracks along the undersides of each shelf. Between, beneath, and behind each tower of shelving.

An hour passed in silence.

"I'm sorry to be discouraging," I said as we both continued the search, "but we should consider the possibility that Sanderson was lying when he told Mrs. Lapham about the phony letters being hidden here. Or that Mr. Childers found them long ago, and we're mistaken about why he still guards his sanctum? Surely in the years he's lived here, he's had time enough to page through each and every one of these books—to scrutinize each and every one of these shelves—possibly several times. There *are* an impressive number of volumes here, but this is hardly the Boston Public Library."

"Yes. I know. I have considered all of those points. But if we deliberate too long in choosing the best oil paints, all the fruit in the bowl will have turned brown. Sally forth, my dear! Sally forth!"

By the end of the next hour, we had arrived at the muddy banks of the Mississippi, so to speak. Once we had completed the final shelf together, Vera sat at the table. With sharp intensity, she surveyed each shelves in order. I sat down beside her.

She rose. "Have we been thinking about this all wrong?" She slowly approached Mr. Morley's beloved Currier and Ives lithograph hanging on the wall. She stretched to reach it, and she was tall enough to do so without a chair.

Lifting the picture from the wall and bringing it to the table, she inspected the back of it. She quickly found a slit made in the paper glued to the frame's edges. Gingerly tugging the slit open, she peered between the paper backing and the lithograph itself.

"Disappointing," she repeated. "No letters, but the fact that this has been cut open supports the hunch that the forger has been searching the room for them."

"Explaining why he keeps his sanctum so unchanged," I added softly.

After replacing the picture, Vera announced, "It's time for us to go. We must walk to the Criminal Investigation Bureau to inform the Chief Inspector that he might be needed to make an arrest tomorrow evening. Once that's arranged, I'll come right back to meet with the forger and tell him about my plan to expel his poltergeist tomorrow evening."

"And I'll remain out of sight. After we meet with Mr. Watts, I mean."

"Of course. I'll be sure to mention that you're on death's doorstep, my dear. We'll both return again late tomorrow morning to consider other hiding places. I haven't given up on that yet. However, as it stands, *your* plan is looking more promising."

•

"*VERAAA!*" cheered the bartender, the barmaid, and the same two jovial gents we had met on our previous visit to The Pitcher and Coach.

She had just entered and now she halted. "Are you people intent on recalling the names of *everybody* who frequents this establishment? Such a goal strikes me as unfathomably futile."

"We do our best," replied the bartender. "Lucy and your party are waiting over there. We'll take your drink orders after you're settled."

Once Vera arrived at our table, she greeted us by saying, "I certainly will miss *this* place!"

"Aww, but you won't miss the Hub altogether?" Sophie protested.

"She's from New York," Dr. James explained. "If she *did* miss Boston, she'd never utter a word of it."

Vera sat down with no comment beyond her grin.

"You Yankees are such a pugnacious breed," teased Mr. Brunton.

Our team was now fully assembled.

"How was your meeting with Mr. Childers?" I asked Vera.

"Successful. I stayed true to the theory that extreme guilt opened a dimensional breach, especially in the Dawning Room. However, I fibbed about how we *now* know that it wasn't former inhabitants who returned through the breach to haunt the house. Rather, it was a poltergeist. And that very spot is where we shall have to exorcise this errant elemental. Did Lucille or Dr. James explain to both of you what a poltergeist is?"

Sophie and Mr. Brunton indicated that we had.

Vera continued. "Now, our visit to his workshop revealed that he's read up on Thomas Edison, presumably to help him pass as a fellow inventor. To prey on this knowledge, I found myself using the word *energy* a lot. Psychical energy. Odic energy. Even Ouija energy. All malarkey, of course. Nonetheless, he was impressed enough to agree to tomorrow evening's spectral eviction."

"How did he take the news of my failing health?"

"He seemed *genuinely* sympathetic—which I assume was more malarkey. I left him with the recommendation that he read the 'Ghost Laying' chapter in Thistleton-Dyer's *The Ghost World*. It's in his library, and I know it well enough to cobble together some corresponding ceremony. Have you cast the rest of our roles?"

"Yes," I answered. "We were just discussing how Miss Marchelli and Mr. Brunton will be responsible for the oboes. I can teach them how to play a B flat and a high G while you continue to search for the forged letters. When Mr. Brunton leaves to fetch Mr. Childers around 5:00, I'll move to Sophie's room, where I'll transform into a ghost."

Sophie winked at Vera. "I'm borrowing my grandmother's wedding gown. It's old and dingy and downright ghastly! That and plenty of face powder should make our Lucille look like she's fresh from the tomb."

After we all laughed, I turned to Dr. James.

"Sir, I hope you don't mind if Mr. Childers comes home to find you waiting in his parlor. You'll be there with the terrible news of my demise."

The creases in his brow deepened as he turned to Vera. "If you ever doubted the sincerity of my loyalty to you—" He stopped there.

I resumed. "Now, you won't *directly* tell him that I've died.

Instead, you'll say that you knew Vera is due to arrive, and you'll ask Mr. Childers to let her finish her business there before he tells her she's wanted at the hospital. This way, you'll say, Vera can finish climbing the hill before confronting the mountain. After all—and it's vital that you mention this to Mr. Childers—the news you have for her will be the same in three or four hours as it is now."

"Ah *ha,* he'll naturally assume that news is of your death— but the slim possibility of it being something else will nag at him. He'll grow anxious and unsettled. Honestly, Miss Parsell, I simply *don't* know what to make of you."

The professor's comment sparked a chuckle from the others in the group, but he only stared at me, offering no suggestion at all if he had spoken in jest or in sincerity. Perhaps this was reinforcement of his point from the previous evening: the alternative between *honest* and *dishonest* is not a sharp one. At that point, I realized that my being a mystery to Dr. James was the best explanation of why he remained a mystery to me. He didn't let me know how he felt about me—because *he* didn't know how he felt about me.

I didn't know quite what else to say, so I replied, "Well, sir, your task will be complete at that point."

The barmaid arrived at the table. I ordered a beer, and Sophie asked for a glass of red wine.

Then it was Vera's turn, and she said, "The same please."

"Really, Vera?" I interrupted. "You're having wine instead of beer?"

"Uhm—oh," she stammered. "How silly of me. Make mine a beer, too."

As Dr. James ordered his wine and Mr. Brunton his beer, I looked closely at Vera. When she blinked, it was a slow movement, and this was the only sign of nervous fatigue that I could discern. I wondered if this particularly complex ghost hunt was taking a toll on her.

For now, though, I resumed outlining my plan. "Vera, what

time did Mr. Childers and you agree to conduct the exorcism?"

"7:00. I assume you'll already be hiding in the Green Room by then. Our two friends will be with me to play the oboes—so how will the Chief Inspector make an arrest, assuming all goes well?"

Sophie offered a solution. "He was introduced to the layout of the house the evening he arrested Mrs. Lapham. S'easy to find the way to the Green Room. We'll have to remember to close the library door, though."

"Excellent," Vera stated. "Let me remind you all that, ideally, we'll never have to enact this wild ruse. If I find the letters and they bear the 'witch' cipher, *that* should be enough to convince a jury of the forger's complicity with the blackmailing scheme, the murder, and the suicide."

Mr. Brunton commented, "Still, wouldn't a confession from Mr. Childers himself better serve that purpose?"

"Yes. Yes, I suppose. If he's *capable* of confession."

"You disagree, then," replied Mr. Brunton, "with the adage that what is good for the goose is good for the gander? The goose here is Mrs. Lapham, of course, and the gander—"

"In this case," Vera interjected, "I think we have two *very* different creatures. Not a gander so much as a spider. Perhaps a jackal. Or a buzzard, if we must stick with birds. Come to think of it, a mockingbird might be said to *forge* the calls of other— but—oh, please forgive my rambling."

At this point, I felt certain that Vera was more nervous than she wanted us to know.

Yet it was Sophie who came to her rescue. "Well, another common saying is that lightning never strikes twice in the same place. That cop was darned lucky to get his confession. Mr. Brunton told me that, even with the ventriloquist's help, things didn't go quite as planned. Isn't that right?"

"Very true," Dr. James said. "Viola didn't confess because she thought she *heard* the murder victim. She claimed she had *seen* him. Watts attained his desired result, but not in the manner he had anticipated. This Childers is unpredictable, as shown by his possibly using *poison* to achieve his ends. I'm not discouraging you from pursuing this plan. Indeed, as this group's member with the safest assignment, I applaud the fortitude of the rest of you. But on that same point, let me caution that you're about to do something terribly dangerous."

"Dangerous is only half of it," Sophie amended. "I'm with Miss Van Slyke in thinking Mr. Childers will be much tougher to crack. Sure enough, he gets riled—but he's choosy about who he lets know it."

Mr. Brunton nodded slowly.

Sophie continued, "You let me know, Miss Van Slyke, if I can help you search for those letters."

"While your assistance with this investigation has been exemplary," she replied, "I think your time is better spent practicing your oboe. There's a knack to blowing those horns."

Here, the barmaid returned with our drinks on a tray. We stopped talking as she placed each one before us.

At her departure, we shared a silent toast. It struck me then that, despite Dr. James' warning of danger, no one expressed hesitation to proceed with the mission. I was among courageous, if motley, company.

Vera was the first to speak again. "I now think Lucille and I went about things unwisely while searching for those letters today. We marched into the library with blinders. First, we assumed that our ghost who plays hide-and-seek had made finding of the letters nearly impossible. Second, we devoted most of our time to looking through the pages of the *books*, perhaps because we had seen that technique used in the forger's workshop. And I imagine the forger himself has been operating that way, too."

It dawned on me where Vera was heading. "According to Mrs. Lapham, Mr. Sanderson claimed the letters were hidden *in the library*, not *in the books*."

"And so, when the books proved fruitless, I looked behind

the lithograph, instead. Still no luck. Therefore, we're left with a question."

I believe all present except Vera uttered some form of that question: "Where would *Sanderson* have hidden the letters?"

Despite all of us fully grasping the question, not a single one of us could offer a promising answer.

Not even after another two rounds.

ᐁ CHAPTER SEVENTEEN ᐂ

A HAND FOR A HAND

On Tuesday morning, Vera appeared poorly rested. Dark crescents appeared under her eyes, and there was an ashen hue in her cheeks. She had brief moments when she seemed to be lost in choosing between first buttoning her cuffs or pulling on her shoes. I had hoped a good breakfast would improve her condition.

However, during our ride to the mansion, her posture sagged and she remained silent. I was unsure if, beneath her weariness, she was contemplating. Rather than disturb her, I carefully ensured that our two oboes were in proper order.

Only upon our arrival did Vera speak. "I forget if I said this—last night—at the tavern, you know—but it's challenging to learn how to make an oboe reed, uh—*resonate*. And then there's the—" She twiddled her fingers.

"The fingering. Yes, I believe you *did* mention that."

She nodded. "Let's start with you teaching that to the maid and the groom. I'll head directly to the Dawning Room."

"Certainly."

"Oh—but I'll need the gentleman's help."

"For moving the furniture?"

Vera stopped. "Hmm? Oh, no. Not for moving the furniture." Without further explanation, she proceeded to the door.

We arrived late enough that Mr. Brunton had returned from Mr. Childers' workshop. He greeted us and accompanied Vera to the Dawning Room while I proceeded to teach Sophie how to play a B flat. She mastered it with almost no difficulty. As we waited for my other pupil, Sophie and I went to her room to look at her grandmother's wedding dress.

"I'm surprised it's already here," I said as we climbed to the fourth floor.

"I had Mr. Brunton pick it up on his way back from Quincy. Soon as he told my mother I wanted it, lickity-split, it was in his hands. He said there was no convincing her that I wasn't thinking about *finally* getting married. Mothers, huh?"

"Mothers, indeed."

Sophie held the garment against my body. The fit was good, and its silken sheen, tanned with age, gave it a ghostly glimmer. The veil was sheer enough that Mr. Childers should be able to recognize me, but I decided that my whisking it aside upon my entrance would add a dramatic flourish.

I gazed at myself in a small mirror hanging on Sophie's wall. I began to think of my own mother. How she would wear costumes to impersonate the dead. How this was very amusing when I was twelve—but terribly embarrassing by the time I turned seventeen. How four years earlier—

"Lucy? S'everything all right?"

I smiled at Sophie. "I hope it will be."

"Mr. Brunton is calling from the landing below. The stairs, you know."

"Gracious, I didn't hear him. I was remembering how my mother—well. Yes, of course! Let's go down! I must teach him his high G."

Once the three of us had returned to the kitchen, I assembled the second oboe. Sophie displayed her virtuosity on the first, improvising a tune that might have come straight from Tin Pan Alley. Meanwhile, I asked Mr. Brunton what Vera had wanted with him.

"You remember that crouching figure I witnessed when I lived alone in the house, yes? Well, she asked me if I could recall the spots where that figure had appeared. She was attempting to follow the squatting ghost's line of vision. I fear she didn't have any luck, though, and she wasn't very talkative. Speaking of that, does she look slightly the worse for wear to you?"

"She does," I said. "Since I've been her assistant, no ghost hunt has lasted quite this long. And the complexities and uncertainties of this case! It's taken a toll."

Mr. Brunton gently touched my shoulder. "I'm sure it's taken a toll on you, too."

I nodded—then I handed him the oboe.

He was not as adept at playing the instrument as Sophie, but after a brief time, he grasped the technique. I taught them both the finger positions for a high G on the chance that Mr. Brunton needed help when it came time for their debut that evening.

I chose the second-floor hallway as a suitable area to rehearse the harmony. It was lit dimly enough that the violet holes would be visible. I cautioned my oboists about the danger of moving swiftly when the violet holes were visible, and I then raised my hands as if I were an orchestra conductor. I signaled them to play.

The hall became a slow stream of floating, florescent violet halos. Though there were fewer here than had appeared in the Dawning Room, this was Sophie's first experience with the phenomenon. Her eyes seemed about to burst from her head, but she still managed to sustain her B flat. Mr. Brunton—who knew what to expect—kept his eyes tightly shut while blowing.

"S'a doughnut-maker's *dream!*" shouted Sophie after she had refilled her lungs. She placed her hand over her heart as she searched the hall to find where the grape-frosted pastries had gone.

Spotting a vase of dried flora mixed with peacock feathers, I selected one of the roses. "The holes *are* enchanting—but they're also very hazardous. They mark tears in the membrane between the ethereal realm and our own, and that skin serves a good purpose. Would you mind blowing again?"

Once the holes reappeared, I slowly and cautiously inserted the stem of the dried rose through one. As I withdrew it, I whispered, "Stop now."

This time, both pairs of eyes grew wide as I displayed the crystalized segment of the stem that had returned from the Other Side. I gently lifted the flower to my lips to illustrate how even the slightest puff of air turned the silvery glass stem into a shower of dust.

To my astonished audience, I said, "My apologies to whoever arranged that lovely bouquet." I then did my best to return the much shorter rose to the vase.

When I turned around, I heard someone prancing down from the floor above. We all saw that it was Vera.

Yet it was not the same Vera whom I had seen earlier, the woman befuddled by how to dress herself or frustrated by finding the correct word. It was not the same Vera that Mr. Brunton had described as "the worse for wear." *This* Vera moved with a confident stride, even a bounce of smug pride. Her cheeks had turned from grayish to pink.

"It's usually easier to go *around* the thicket, but what if the thicket is around *you?*" she exclaimed. Upon receiving no answer, she explained, "Well—well, in that case, you thrash right *through* the thicket. You see?"

Disregarding whether or not we saw, all of a sudden, Vera took me into her arms and gave me a firm caress. Pulling back, she giggled and gleamed at all three of us.

"Is it too early for lunch?" she asked. "Oh, what am I saying? Is it *ever* too early for lunch?"

•

It was hardly difficult to conclude that Vera had located the incriminating letters. Nonetheless, she was refusing to confirm this fact—and refusing to divulge *where* she had found them. All through lunch, whatever she had ascertained was kept masked behind the same giggle and gleam that she had exhibited earlier.

"All I shall say," said she, "is that our witch failed to consider the fundamentals of magic. And, very stupidly, so did I."

"Until this morning?" I asked.

"Until this morning. I promise I shall share everything with all of you before bedtime. For now, allow me my fun. Our forger enjoys his version of poker, and it seems I'm caught up in playing the game, too."

Following lunch, Mr. Brunton drove us to the Harvard campus. We stopped first at its Psychology Department. Next, Vera took a note written by Dr. James to the Lawrence Scientific School, specifically, its Electrical Engineering wing. There, she borrowed a piece of equipment, one that she said would serve as a prop in this evening's ceremony. They were kind enough to cushion the fragile item in excelsior and place it in a discarded apple crate.

Vera next instructed Mr. Brunton to drive her to the Hotel Touraine, which was across the Common from Beacon Hill. She would stay warm in its lobby while deciding the final details of an imaginary ceremony to expel a poltergeist. Meanwhile, the three of us were to return to the mansion. Vera said that we should keep the oboes there, and Sophie and Mr. Brunton could tell Mr. Childers that *she* had spent the morning teaching them how to play their notes.

Though I offered to help Sophie and Mr. Brunton with their usual chores, they required little assistance—especially since they had an eye on waking the next morning to find themselves unemployed. This meant I would have to wait alone—for *hours*. As I had when bedridden while Vera was out and about, I again felt like a ghost. I decided, therefore, I might as well look the part.

I climbed to Sophie's bedroom, where I put on my costume and powdered my face. I used soot around my eyes and down my cheeks to look more cadaverous. As I checked my work in the mirror, my mind returned thoughts of my mother masquerading as a wide variety of spirits. She had never admitted that these performances gave her a curious thrill, but her eyes and her voice intimated that she did. I confess that I also experienced a strange swirl of excitement amid anxiety.

I recalled Mr. Watts explaining how some expert forgers drop hints about their craft or their identity to enhance the "game" of crime. I also remembered Dr. James' question regarding how these hints might be as much a cry from their consciences to be caught. Whether it was rooted in a desire to fool one's opponent or to be beaten—or the paradox of wanting *both*—the mad mix of emotion I felt was exhilarating, and I took a step toward better understanding why my mother had raised me to be a Spiritualist fraud.

I then descended to wait in the Green Room. Once there, I confirmed that Vera had left the door to Dawning Room unlocked. Afterward, I sat on the bed and was briefly amused to see myself across the room in the dressing-table mirror. I wondered if the skills of deception I had learned as a medium could be redirected toward noble ends. Was I returning to my previous transgressions to aid a good woman, one driven to a rash act by a miscreant cruelly provoking her? On the other hand, was I merely returning to my previous transgressions, drawn back by the same house where I had sworn to end it forever?

Was I capable of redemption—or would my ghost drag its chains through eternity?

I turned away from the mirror. Again, I checked the door to the Dawning Room. Of course, it was still unlocked. But perhaps unlocked doors were a good sign—a symbol of open possibilities. I turned again to the mirror and wondered if I were desperate for hope. An unlocked door, after all, is merely an unlocked door.

I decided to stop looking at my reflection.

I cannot say how much more time passed before Mr. Brunton stopped in, and after expressing his approval of my spectral visage, he informed me that he was going to fetch Mr. Childers. Later, when I heard Dr. James arrive, I stayed put rather than risk exciting heart palpitations in the venerable gentleman by going down to wish him luck. I then listened to Mr. Childers' arrival and the murmurs of his conversation with the professor. Dr. James departed, and I assumed dinner followed.

At last, Vera arrived.

•

When I heard her come up the stairs with Mr. Childers and the two oboists, I crept to the wall between the door to the hall and the door to the Dawning Room. I wondered if perspiration might be streaking the powder on my face, yet I was too jittery to risk checking it in the mirror.

"Sir, you may place the box on the table," said Vera from the other room. "Before I reveal what it contains, I'll explain the procedure."

I heard a sound of wood against wood, and I assumed it was someone closing the door so that Mr. Watts could pass by and join me in the Green Room. At this point, I gently opened the hallway door for the Chief Inspector, then sidled toward the other door to listen. Perhaps those previous hours spent in a somber mood hindered me from laughing out loud as I listened to Vera's tall tale about how to catch a poltergeist.

"Now," she began, "did you have a chance to read Thistleton-Dyer's chapter on ways to lay a ghost?"

"I did," said Mr. Childers with his distinctively nasal voice. "Am I right in thinking the author is a collector of *beliefs about ghosts* instead of a believer himself? Some of what he says about eliminating ghosts seems much like centuries-old folklore, not time-tested experience."

"Absolutely correct—and, yes, those first few pages about using a stream or the sea to banish ghosts strikes me as laughably impractical. However, the next section is of more use. There are several instances of a ghost being lured into a *bottle*—a bottle that is quickly corked and disposed of with the ghost inside it. The notion seems as absurd, but it's here that we see the brick of *truth* around which fanciful legends are so often built. Would you remove the piece of equipment from the box now?"

I heard some shuffling.

Flatly, Mr. Childer stated, "It's a condenser."

"Is that the technical term these days? It's probably better known as a *Leyden jar* to your employees. Perhaps you could explain to them what one stores in these ingenious jars. Not

Granny's stewed tomatoes, but what?"

"Electricity," was all Mr. Childers had to say.

"Yes! Exactly! *Energy!* And, if you recall the discussion we held yesterday, what is the major substance of a poltergeist?"

"Energy," Mr. Childers repeated. "Miss Van Slyke described a poltergeist as a ball of energy that bounces around a house, shoving the china from the shelves, yanking blankets off the beds, pounding on the walls—"

"Ripping cloth?" offered Sophie.

"Thundering like a gunshot?" added Mr. Brunton.

"And even showering a house with stones in some cases," concluded Mr. Childers.

It was about this time that I began to worry about the Chief Inspector. The Green Room's door to the hallway was ajar now. Why hadn't he joined me? Had he come to the house at all?

Vera continued her lecture. "Unlike sentient ghosts compelled to communicate their unfinished business as best they can—and unlike the less sentient echoes of traumatic events—the insentient poltergeist does little more than wreak havoc and make mischief. The instances of small items being moved from place to place that you've experienced with the other manifestations strike me as unbridled rage subsiding to vindictive spite, if only for a moment."

"Like a child who's been horribly misused and retaliates with anger," said Mr. Childers.

Vera took a moment to speak. "Very astute. A poltergeist, however, is disembodied—as if that anger has burst forth from the child and is now ricocheting here and there all on its own. My *revised* theory is that, when Mr. Brunton encountered *his* ghost in this room, that actually was the former type, namely, a phantom with unfinished business. However, instead of finding new means to communicate, that ghost did as most ghosts eventually do—it proceeded to the next state. Perhaps it recognized the futility of remaining. Meanwhile, the very same dimensional ruptures that had been utilized by that beleaguered specter *also* permitted the entry of this poltergeist. You see, we didn't simply have more than one ghost. We had more than one *kind* of ghostly visitor."

As Vera was stitching together the evidence to make the poltergeist theory convincing, I was becoming increasingly worried that Mr. Watts hadn't yet appeared. Even if we were able to shame Mr. Childers into confessing, how much weight would be given to the testimony of four people who staged an elaborate trick to illicit that confession? The Chief Inspector's presence was a *vital* to our success!

My nerves worsened even more when I heard that Vera might have been underestimating her opponent. Mr. Childers raised a formidable problem for the scenario she was creating.

"This all fits with the little I've read about ghosts, but how do we transfer this angry energy *into* the Leyden jar? The charge must be *conducted* into it, usually from an electrostatic generator. That's what this electrode sticking into the jar is for—it functions roughly like a lightning rod. Once the charge passes into the jar, it's stored in the dielectric."

"Dielectric?" inquired Mr. Brunton. He might have been hoping to steer attention away from the problem raised.

Sophie joined him. "It's the two sheets of foil on either side of the glass. The glass acts as an insulator between the positive and negative charges."

Breathily, Vera commented, "What an *utterly* remarkable woman you are!"

"S'nothing. I helped my brother prepare when he wanted to leave Boston Gas Light Company for a job with Boston Electric Light Company. He figured—"

Mr. Childers gently cleared his throat before resuming his challenge. "As I say, these devices can *hold* a charge once it's conducted inside, but they don't *trap* it. It's not a rabbit snare."

"Well—in that regard—uh, sir," fumbled Vera, "you are—of course—better versed than I am. Does your idea of lightning being drawn to a lightning rod apply? Well, I cannot explain the, uh, specific *dynamics* of this procedure. I can merely vouch for its effectiveness. And, if it fails this time, you can continue to experiment with it—and possibly become the world's first inventor to *confirm* a connection between the supernatural world and our own."

"Wouldn't *that* be a triumph!" Mr. Childers replied with enthusiasm enough to suggest he was now distracted from the problem he had raised. "Maybe I can discuss the feasibility of such a project with Mr. Edison!"

"Yes!" Vera encouraged. "And, at some point—in the not too distant future—you two might even collaborate on a *telephone* to the Great Beyond!"

There was a moment of silence, and I pictured Mr. Childers struck speechless by the prospect.

"For the present," continued Vera, "let's see if the violet holes are alluring enough to at least tempt our poltergeist into the room. I remind you all of the dangers these holes pose. Remain as still as you can so long as you hear the oboes. Are we ready? If you would darken the room, sir? Players, please wet your reeds."

This was my cue. I moved into position to appear at the door and—with very slow, very steady movements—float among the violet punctures.

But Mr. Watts was *still* not in position!

•

When I heard the eerie harmony of the two instruments, I carefully grasped the doorknob. Fighting a wave of wooziness, I twisted the knob and pulled it toward me. I saw the Dawning Room awash with the violet glowing rings. Immediately afterward, even before stepping into the room, I noticed that the other door—the one connecting the Dawning Room to the hall—was *not* closed! Mr. Watts would have risked being noticed if he had passed by it! The sound I had interpreted as the door closing? Probably the apple crate being set on the table.

All of these thoughts had flashed through my mind before I glided into my ghostly character and drifted into the room. Ever so slowly, I spotted Sophie and Mr. Brunton close to the door, Vera nearer the table, and Mr. Childers toward the far end of the room. I let my head loll to the side as I cautiously lifted my arm and pointed at the poisoner—the horrible man who had killed me with poison!

"*Yoooou!*" I wailed as I brushed the veil covering my face to the side. "Confesssss! *Murdererrrrr!* Confess your *crimmmmes!*"

Sharply aware of the purple-edged holes surrounding me, I inched forward, heading toward Mr. Childers. But I halted—halted in place.

Not from the danger of the holes.

From an outburst of *laughter.*

It was Mr. Childers—*he* was the one laughing. Instead of horror at my appearance, he found it laughable. Hilarious! At what point had he realize this was all an elaborate prank? When he recognized my face? When Vera suggested a Leyden jar could capture a poltergeist? Even before then?

As I stood there, frozen and dumbfounded, either Sophie and Mr. Brunton was struggling with sustaining the note.

Vera commaned, "Deep breath—and *again!*"

The room became completely dark. I heard sharp inhaling, then the notes—and the glowing circles—returned.

Through it all was the unbridled laughter. A high, nasally guffaw edged with the cruelty of a mocking boy. To Mr. Childers, the tragedy I was enacting was the pinnacle of comedy.

In my shame, I glanced aside. Doing so, I spotted something incongruous. A hazy but *human* figure—shorter than Mr. Childers and on the other side of the room. I was on the brink of recognizing who it might be—

Then the staccato of Mr. Childers' laughter elongated, and its throatiness deepened, and the sound transformed into *screaming!*

The oboes' drone vanished simultaneously with the glowing halos. In the last instant of light, I lost sight of the short figure and glimpsed the laugher's form drop to his knees. The screaming cascaded over sounds of scrambling. Mr. Brunton's back appeared—he had managed to relight the room with his oboe under his arm.

Mr. Watts then rushed in from the hall. *"By God!"* he yelled. He ran to the collapsed body of Mr. Childers. "His *arm!* What the hell's happened to his *arm?"*

Sophie also approached Mr. Childers. "I saw a hand. It—it reached from out of one of the holes—it passed *through*—a hand—it reached out and *grabbed his elbow!* He was laughing, and the hand from nowhere *grabbed his elbow!*

Mr. Brunton had now lit the gas in another lamp, and I discovered that Vera was seated at the table, twitching her head as if she were whisking away flies. I knew she was actually shaking off a fainting spell.

"Yes," Vera muttered. "A hand from the Other Side reached out. It pulled the elbow *into the hole.* As if it wanted to grab the whole man. As if it wanted to pull him to his *death."*

"I saw it, too," Mr. Brunton said. He turned to me.

I could only move my head from side to side. I hadn't seen the reaching hand. I felt incapable of describing the short figure I had seen with articulate speech.

Mr. Childers' screaming had now become a gurgly groaning.

"By God," Mr. Watts exclaimed, "get me something we can use as a tourniquet! His arm is severed at the joint. But—but there's—where's all the blood? There's not enough blood! *Get me something we can use as a tourniquet!"*

"It's been cauterized," said Sophie.

Vera managed to say, "It's been *crystalized.* Is it cold?"

Mr. Watts, now kneeling by the collapsed man, put his fingers near the wound. "It's frozen!"

"It won't last," Vera explained. "It will thaw, and the blood will be released."

I realized the gossamer veil I was wearing could be twisted into a sufficient tourniquet. I ran over, and still unready for coherent words, I mimed the idea. Once Mr. Watts had tightly bound the stump, he and Sophie lifted Mr. Childers into a chair.

"I'll ready the carriage" said Mr. Brunton. "Give me a few minutes, and we'll rush him over to Mass General." He departed.

Before following him out, Sophie stated, "I'll get some bandages for when the bleeding begins."

The pain had subsided enough for Mr. Childers, on one end of the table, to raise his face enough to glare at Vera at the other end.

"Why!" he demanded.

After a deep inhale and exhale, Vera returned his stare. "To get you to *confess,* of course."

"Confess." With a glance at the Chief Inspector, he spit, "I have nothing *to* confess!"

"You've forgotten your deep involvement in a plot to blackmail Mrs. Lapham into murdering her husband."

"No *proof!"* Mr. Childers snarled.

"The letters with your mark on them. The mark of the witch. I *found* them."

"Letters? Don't know what you're talking about!"

"The letters you've searched for—for how long?" Vera rose. She walked to the lithograph that had touched Mr. Morley so deeply. *"Good Times on the Old Plantation,* if I recall correctly." She glanced in my direction.

I nodded to confirm the title. I then did my best to avoid looking confused. Vera knew the letters weren't there.

Vera reached for the picture. "You failed to look behind the picture, Mr. Childers."

"You're *wrong!"* he insisted with a groan that sounded more like a growl. "I looked there a hundred—"

Mr. Watts stepped forward. "You mean to say that you *have* looked for the letters, then?"

Mr. Childers refused to answer. Instead, he hissed while rocking forward and back, forward and back. With more of a whine than a growl, he said, "You *neeeed* to get *meeee* to the *hospitaaaal!"*

Sophie returned with lengths of linen to use as bandages. Indeed, despite our tourniquet, the end of Mr. Childers' arm was starting to seep with blood. Only then did I think to look at where he had been when his laugh became a scream.

On the floor, a hand with a bit more than its wrist was covered with a fine powder. I knew it was the dust of what had been the elbow. Like the still-attached upper arm, the end of this appendage had thawed enough to start dripping blood, too.

The hand of a ghost, reaching across the dimensions, had taken a forger's hand in retribution. Had this been the final earthly act of Roderick Morley—or of Silas Sanderson?

Some mysteries must forever remain unsolved.

•

When I looked away from the hand, Sophie and Mr. Watts had their arms around either side of Mr. Childers. They were guiding him out of the door. Noticing my arms and legs were trembling, I sat down in a chair close to Vera.

After a minute or two, I found my voice. "Vera? I've changed my mind. I'd rather we *didn't* take this case."

She was able to smile at that.

After another moment, I asked, "Did or didn't you locate the incriminating letters?"

"I did. And I'm very disappointed in *you* for not having thought of it."

"Disappointed with *me?"*

She smiled again. "Where does a Spiritualist medium hide the trinkets she wants to have magically materialize during a séance? That is, a medium who doesn't have a mother handy in the next room."

"No!" I whispered as I rose and ventured toward the chair where Mr. Childers had just sat. The chair where I had led a séance on the night of Mr. Morley's suicide. The chair where Mr. Sanderson had led his séances earlier. "No, it can't *be!* I checked there! On the afternoon before my séance, I checked under the

table to confirm that this was the medium's chair. But there were no strings, no wires—nothing to hold *anything.*"

"Take a look at how the psychic advisor had improved upon the strings and wires."

It was difficult to spot at first. In fact, it looked almost exactly like the underside of the table top. Nonetheless, beneath that end of the table—spanning the supporting cross-boards—there was a spring-hinged plank. The medium would simply have to reach below and lower the closer edge of this board. Whatever was clamped between it and the tabletop would roll into his palm. It was a variation on the "clandestine clothesline" that only a medium who had designed a room and who would spend months in it would have bothered to install.

"Mr. Sanderson clearly didn't travel as much as my mother and I did. He could use a more elaborate method for the trick."

Vera nodded. "And he needed a method that wouldn't be discovered even if someone looked from under the table. That spring hinge is strong enough that, even if one were to tip the table on its side, it would hold the letters in place."

"Well, I have a new respect for Mr. Sanderson," I admitted. "But he seems to have known how to conjure a spirit far better than he knew how to manipulate a woman."

Vera grunted as she pushed herself up from her chair. "I had hoped to manipulate our forger by confounding him. After I found the letters hidden under the table, I propped them behind the lithograph. My hope was that Inspector Watts would witness our host admit he had been searching for them." She stretched to pull the frame from the wall, and the letters—neatly bound with a gold ribbon—dropped neatly in her hand.

She returned to the table. "My original plan was to dazzle our forger by producing the letters from behind the picture. I assumed *that* would get him to blurt out that he had already looked there. My timing was off slightly, yet I'm pleased with the outcome."

I remarked, "Wasn't it Sophie who pointed out that the Chief

241

Inspector's plan didn't work out *exactly* as intended? I guess plans rarely do. I panicked when I saw that the door to the hall wasn't closed as we had discussed."

"Ah, yes. Mr. Childers was gracious enough to enter last after he had lowered the gas in the hallway."

"Well, I should've known that Mr. Watts would simply wait out in the hall. Isn't it interesting how nerves can rob us of our better sense?"

After a moment, Vera asked, "You mentioned Sophie. Who is Sophie?"

"Miss Marchelli. The maid here."

"Of course, of course," she muttered. "Remarkable woman."

I grinned, knowing that life with Vera Van Slyke was returning to normal. She slid the letters toward me.

I examined them, the pivotal evidence in our case against Mr. Childers. "You checked to see that they substitute 'witch' for 'which'?"

"Yes, and assuming the Chief Inspector finds other forgeries with the same cypher in that workshop, I believe they'll displace some of the blame for the murder onto the forger himself. Our lovely friend is still in terrible trouble—but so is that man who will never again commit forgery."

"Never again—*if* the ghost grabbed the correct arm, that is."

Vera sighed. "Very astute. I wish you hadn't mentioned that. Now, we have another mystery to investigate. And I think I'm very much in need of a vacation."

I saw my friend's eyes blink slowly and then stay closed. The excitement was concluded, and the morning's exhaustion had returned.

"Shall we go to the parlor to wait for the others to return from the hospital? I can make you some tea."

Vera consented, pushed herself up, and led the way out of the room.

Before leaving, I turned to look at the room—for the very last time, I hoped. I gazed at the Dawning Room and dwelt on all that had transpired within its walls.

Until Vera interrupted me.

"By the way," she called from the staircase landing, "don't you want to get out of that fearful dress and wash your face? You're quite a sight, my dear."

⊱ CHAPTER EIGHTEEN ⊰

THE GHOST IN QUESTION

We spent the following morning answering questions at the police station. While there, we were informed by Mr. Watts that Mrs. Lapham had been released on bail. We visited her elegant home in Back Bay, where she invited us into her parlor. Once settled, we told her all that had transpired and how we hoped it might bring greater fairness to the court trial.

As Mrs. Lapham reacted to our narrative, I was unable to spot a single trace of the woman's time spent in jail. No redness in her eye, no slump to her shoulders, no stray strand of her golden hair. Either this was a very resilient woman, made strong by life's adversity, or she was an expert in disguise. Perhaps she had learned to combine those qualities.

At one point, I noticed the distinctive eyepiece and mount of a stereoscope on the corner table. Beside the device was a pile boxes containing stereographs, and I imagined they depicted far-off locations. I wondered if this entertainment had become Mrs. Lapham's replacement for her Gramophone.

Mr. Lapham joined us after a while, and he pointed out that—as our receiving payment from Mr. Childers for our services was highly unlikely—he would gladly double the sum. Vera refused, explaining that she was especially well-positioned to write articles about the case that promised to garner her more than any ghost hunt.

"Unfortunately," she added, "I shall have to excise the supernatural elements to give the articles credibility."

"Will you be able to *do* that?" asked Mrs. Lapham. "Your solving of the crime seems so very interwoven *with* the supernatural elements, I can't imagine how you'll tell the story without them."

Vera sighed before speaking. "I keep my pursuits as a ghost hunter quite separate from my career as a journalist. Professionally, I sidestep it as easily as I sidestep being a woman."

Mr. Lapham then asked, "Along those lines, how do you suppose the police and the lawyers will deal with the way Childers lost his arm? There's no sidestepping the supernatural there!"

"It *will* be a challenge," agreed Vera. "However, I never underestimate the ability of the *rational* to prevail over the *empirical*. Your stereoscope over in the corner illustrates the point. You insert a card that presents *two* pictures, taken at slightly different angles. Your *two* eyes peer into the eyepiece—and the brain convinces you you're seeing *one* solid picture with a depth that neither picture has by itself. Let me offer a better example. At breakfast, my friend William James told us he's already lit upon a notion that grounds our observation of the violet holes in the natural world. Our oboes, he contends, generate a vibration that tickles and misleads the optic nerve. He was quite pleased with the idea and crowed about testing it with a former student of his, a woman by the name of—uh—"

"Mary Calkins," I said.

"She's explored a phenomenon she termed *synesthesia*. It seems some people have the marvelous experience of *seeing* a fragrance or of *tasting* the prick of a thorn. In time, I'm sure the combined intellects of my friend and his former student will strip every flavor out of a sunset and drain each hue from those symphony concerts you two enjoy attending."

Mr. Lapham chuckled, but his smile suddenly fell into a pout. "'Every man takes the limits of his own field of vision for the limits of the world.' Who were we reading who said that?" he asked his wife.

"Schopenhauer," she told her husband.

I realized then that the stereoscope was probably not Mrs.

Lapham's—the couple very likely shared it as they shared what they read. At the same time, though, I noticed Vera working very hard to mask a yawn. I asked if the couple might recommend a seaside spot for her to plan those articles while we both relaxed for a week. They suggested a Cape Cod town by the name of Granger, and Vera granted Mr. Lapham's plea to pay for our hotel expenses there.

As it turned out, in late October—when the few year-round residents of a town that depends on summer tourists learn that ghost hunters are visiting—they naturally bring up the subject of their own haunting. But that's another story.

At long last, we boarded the train bound for Chicago. Heading west, I returned to Mrs. Wilkens' *The Wind in the Rose Bush*, which I had been too mentally distracted to read on the trip east. This time, I was able to concentrate well enough to complete the book. While the tales are beautifully written, I found their subject matter a touch wearisome: it is a collection of ghost stories, you see.

Now, typically, a house is haunted by one who has *returned*. On occasion, though, a home is haunted by one who had gone away *permanently*. As I related earlier, upon my return to my rooms in Chicago, I discovered that my mother had used my absence to fulfill her wish of returning to Prague. Over the ensuing weeks, I came home to empty lodgings, and I came to better understand why she was unhappy there during the times I was with Vera.

I then moved away from the Pilsen neighborhood with its familiar bakery and butcher and church. I found smaller accommodations on the city's West Side and settled in at a cozy rooming house for working girls.

The residents there knew me only as Lucille Parsell.

•

A very different sequence of events occurred at Vera's office in the Hotel Manitou upon her return. First, to our surprise, we found waiting for us a reply from Mr. Vitellius Berry, the master researcher from Pittsburg, regarding our first four suspects. Addressed to and forwarded by Dr. James, the return letter must have arrived while we were staying on Cape Cod. We thought that, in order to copy Vera's handwriting, Mr. Childers had kept her letter to Mr. Berry and hidden it in his workshop. However, the forger apparently posted it once it had served his purpose — presumably to cast off any suspicions arising from a lack of response. Regardless, Vera used the information sent by Mr. Berry to put the final touches on her four biographical sketches.

Second, about a week afterward, I opened an envelope from the Criminal Investigation Bureau. Surprisingly, the letter it contained had been signed by Sophie Marchelli. Vera then informed me that, during our vacation, she had dashed off a recommendation for our friend. She mailed it to Mr. Watts, who obviously offered her a job. It was a clerical position, but Sophie told us that the detectives were already finding her abilities went far beyond keeping records and brewing coffee. With predictable male discretion, they had utilized her sharp skills of observation and her shrewd insights into character to assist with more than one investigation.

Sophie also mentioned that Mr. Brunton had retired to Virginia, where he promised to take walks along the long, flat coastline and never again climb even a single stair. It struck me that it would have been nice to receive a picture postcard from my giant elf, but we hadn't had the opportunity to exchange addresses.

Finally, our friend gave us news about the Morley Mansion and its last owner. Though she and Mr. Brunton both departed the residence in a matter of days, neither witnessed any of the manifestations that had previously plagued it. Indeed, in the years that have followed our investigation, neither Vera and I have come across any report of supernatural intrusions at that address. It appears that the apprehension of Herman Childers has freed the ghosts.

Sophie's letter ended with a startling clue regarding one of the manifestations. According to the doctor who attended to Mr. Childers' severed arm, the patient had a proliferation of scarring on his back and his legs, the disfigurement of deep lacerations. Not his first experience with such marks, the physician speculated that Mr. Childers had been whipped in his youth or had been raised to practice self-flagellation. As Sophie mentioned, the parallel between this and the slashes in fabric left by one of the ghosts was unmistakable.

"We knew that the ghost responsible for ripping the cloth was Mr. Sanderson," I reminded Vera after she had finished reading the letter. "If he was trying to prompt us to look for a man with scars, the two must have confided very much in one another."

She replied, "Deepening the feelings of betrayal by his partner in crime. The ripping ghost was doing his best to expose the man who *alone* had reaped all the rewards with scant regard for his confederate's death."

"Do you suppose the crouching figure was another manifestation of the same vengeful ghost? Was he attempting to divulge the location of the hidden letters? When that failed, perhaps he shifted to convey the identity of the culprit himself."

"That's one possibility, I suppose," Vera admitted. "Another theory is that your giant elf was *en rapport* with the millionaire, who had learned about the hiding place somehow once he had reached the Other Side. As you know, though, I'm not an advocate of ghost-seers or mediums or any other specialists being *en rapport* with the spirits. Call me an egalitarian among ghosts. When all's said and done, I'm still not fully convinced that crouching figure wasn't simply a hallucination."

I was flabbergasted. "But then—but you—you called upon Mr. Brunton's memory of the crouching figure to locate the hiding place of the forged letters!"

"I needed to consider that room from a very different perspective." Vera shrugged. "It worked. The way I see it, the psychic advisor ripped the cloth. Then the sad millionaire produced the gunshots. Finally, his drowned daughter joined him to play her favorite prank."

I recalled what Vera herself had said about stereoscopes and Schopenhauer during our final visit with Mr. and Mrs. Lapham. I then replied, "Well, that's a very *orderly* way to see the haunting, I suppose. Whether the crouching figure were a hallucination or one of the ghosts, we can at least agree that the ripping pointed to Mr. Childers. And do you remember the phrase he used? 'A switch to switch a witch.' Clearly, *he* had felt the bite of a switch while he was younger. But did he take the word 'witch' as his personal cypher solely on the basis of that silly saying? Was *that* enough to inspire him to secretly mark himself as a witch?"

"There's too much water in that plaster for it to stick to the wall," Vera replied. "However, it now seems entirely likely that the psychic advisor had learned that absurdity about witches not drowning from his bewitched partner. It must have sprung back into his mind when he was failing to convince the millionaire's wife to commit murder. Still, I cannot make all the connections. I'll track down Ingram's book on the Bell Witch and see if there's anything there."

•

In the end, the key didn't come from a book about a witch haunting the Bell family in Tennessee. Instead, it came *again* from Mr. Berry. It was his reply to the letter Vera sent him after our Salem visit. Vera had expressed doubt that Mr. Berry would be able to locate any useful information due to Mr. Childers' undistinguished origins and his life of deception and evasion. We had every reason to question if his name was actually Herman W. Childers!

However, a purebred bulldog does not easily relinquish a bone, no matter how deeply buried it might be. After an exhaustive effort—including visits to the newspaper archives in Knoxville and Nashville—the stalwart Mr. Berry completed his quest. His reply arrived in Chicago about three weeks after we had returned.

The information unearthed by Mr. Berry inspired Vera to write yet another biographical sketch, not for publication, but for the sake of completion. It is supplemented by information gleaned from Ingram's book on the Bell Witch legend and from Miss Sophia Marchelli of Boston's Criminal Investigation Bureau.

—

Extensive research on a man named Herman Warrick Childers starts with a short series of newspaper articles, the sensational nature of which led to their rapid republication in prominent Tennessee newspapers over the summer of 1872. According to the reports, a Robinson County minister was taken into police custody for the manner in which he handled a case of church embezzlement. The perpetrator was a boy, eleven years of age. The details of the crime strongly suggest that this child, identified only as H. Childers, is the same man arrested for forgery in Boston some thirty years afterward.

The pastor, left unnamed, was a proponent of a Protestant denomination rooted in the Millerist movement, though branching in a different direction from the Seventh-day Adventists. The minister taught that the duty of every Christian is to assist in the sharp separation of the good and the wicked, thereby preparing for—if not accelerating—the Second Coming. When the boy was found responsible for having forged the pastor's name in order to gain some of the church's funds, the punishment was dire.

Indeed, the minister whipped the boy until medical attention was required. Dr. Clyde Rawls, whose treatments probably saved the boy's life, insisted that the minister be charged with criminal conduct. The minister claimed—even under oath—that the boy had fallen under the sway of witchcraft. Whether the pastor truly believed that the Childers boy had been a witch or was possessed by one is unclear. Regardless, the accused man was subsequently acquitted of all charges.

Martin V. Ingram discusses a comparable case that occurred about the same time. He quotes a local resident as saying: "The Bell Witch was, and is still, a great scapegoat. Every circumstance out of the regular order of things is attributed to the witch." This source then mentions the court trial of Thomas Clinard and Richard Burgess, and Ingram reports that a jury exonerated these men from murdering a coworker who boasted of his ability to cast spells on others. The author interviewed a member of the legal counsel, who recalled that "the lawyers handled the Bell Witch affair for all that it was worth in the defense of their clients, presenting the analogy or similarity of circumstances with good effect on the jury."

It seems the minister used a similar defense with the same outcome. The minister was found innocent, and apparently, the reporters turned to more timely events. No further information regarding the Childers boy was located.

Exactly how the experience affected Herman Childers and shaped the course of his life can only be guessed at by his criminal activities in Boston thirty-one years later. As of November, 1903, he remains at Suffolk County Jail, awaiting trial for committing fraud as well as being an accomplice to blackmail and an accessory to manslaughter. He is unable to sign affidavits or other documents because of the loss of his right hand. This being the case, the deeply-rooted belief that left-handed persons are prone to be servants of the Devil is less refuted than extended: right-handed persons can be, too.

•

In the first week of the last month of 1903, Vera and I were enjoying a few glasses of beer at The Foiled Gelding. I spoke of how turning the calendar to December reminded me that I'd be spending Christmas without my mother for the first time. This topic meandered to another and then another. By the time Vera and I ordered more beer, we had resumed the debate we had held about Mr. Childers' capacity to feel guilt. Was he a *monster*—a Hyde with no remnant of Jekyll? Or was he a very troubled *man* with a deeply buried desire to be caught?

"His seeing your ghost certainly didn't provoke the pangs of remorse you had hoped for," Vera said with a hint of triumph.

"It surely did *not*," I acknowledged. "My elaborate attempt to overwhelm him with shame only provoked unrestrained laughter. Your own deception had better results, but even so, his confession of having searched for the letters was a slip brought on by rage and pain. It certainly wasn't the outburst of guilt that we saw with Mrs. Lapham."

Vera raised her glass as if toasting. "Still, there were a tremendous number of violet holes in that room, and he seems a very likely source of some of them."

"I hadn't thought of that. That's—very astute," I replied softly as I raised my glass in return.

"Can we ever truly know the soul of this man? I suspect all we can know is that, while he was able to depart Tennessee, he was never able to depart his past." Vera took a swig of her beer.

In the quiet that followed, I remembered my mother returning to the land of her birth, the past to which she was entwined. I also considered my having relinquished the name Ludmila Prášilová and wondered if I would be able to escape my own. I took a sip of my beverage, too.

"May I make a confession," I said.

Vera raised a finger. "Kindly refrain from admitting that you've committed *murder*, my dear. The aftermath can be very messy, and I'll have to hire that remarkable maid to help me tidy up things." She then cackled at her own quip.

It was her third beer.

"No. No, this concerns something much more ghostly than bodily. Do you think Mrs. Lapham *actually* saw the phantom of the man she shot—or do you think that she hallucinated under the terrible pressure of the moment?"

"As you well know," Vera said seriously, "I don't share the ghost-seer theory my mentor did in his ghost hunting. I supposed I did when Harry first introduced me to the idea of being *en rapport* with the ghost in question. But no longer. Since the good woman was the only one in the room to witness the specter—and she might have been very much predisposed to such a vision—I lean toward judging it a hallucination. In an odd way, I think she saw what her guilty conscience *willed* her to see. A dreamy sort of message."

"But did you see the hand that yanked Mr. Childers' elbow through the hole to the Other Side? I didn't."

"I saw it for the briefest instant. But both of our oboe players witnessed it, too, and I would wager that Mr. Childers himself at least glimpsed it."

I remained quiet.

Vera resumed, "What did *you* see that no one else saw?"

"It was the same moment as you and the others saw the reaching hand. It was on the other side of Mr. Childers. Off a ways. Closer to the desk. It—it was short. It *might've* been the crouching figure."

"But you don't think it was the crouching figure?"

"No. No, I don't." I looked at the foam remaining on the top of my beer. I took a swig. I put down the glass and watched the amber liquid in it sway and settle. "I think it was Marianne. She was waving—"

"Wait. Remind me who Marianne is. I'm not very strong with names, but I know *that* wasn't one of our ghosts' names."

"Did I say *Marianne?* How silly. I meant to say *Dorothy May*. She's the girl—the daughter of the Morleys—the child who drowned. The one we think hid things as a prank. Not *Marianne."* I did my best to laugh at my mistake.

Vera raised her eyebrows and tilted her head.

"Marianne was the name of my spirit guide at the Morley séance. When we met. I *had* been using a control called Uncas, but shortly before I abandoned my life as a Spiritualist, I switched it to Marianne. A twelve-year-old girl. Dorothy May's age, if she had lived. Since I had to be my mother's sister with better sense— she's a character from a Jane Austen novel." I stopped babbling.

"Let's let these be our last beers, my dear. But you said the short ghost was *waving?"*

"Yes. Waving to me. Looking directly at me—and waving."

"To get your attention? Because of the danger you were in?"

I slid my beer away from me. "No," I answered. "I got the impression that she knew what was about to happen and—and perhaps—she was waving *good-bye.*"

Vera guzzled the last of her beer. She leaned back in her chair and put two fingers to her jaw. After careful—albeit, slightly teetering—meditation, she repeated, "A dreamy sort of message."

POSTSCRIPT

In my Introduction, I mention that this chronicle written by my great-grandaunt is the only historical record I've found concerning the murder or suicide at the Morley Mansion. Documents about the court trials of Viola Lapham or Herman Childers have also eluded me. Unless a researcher better than myself finds something conclusive, the verdicts passed in these trials are left to my readers. It's certainly easy to guess at how things turned out for Childers. The Lapham trial, though, is a trickier matter. I like to think that Vera Van Slyke's investigation worked to the advantage of the accused. (Very likely her husband's wealth did. It's hard to decide if her beauty would have helped or hurt her. Remember that, in 1903, her jury would have been made up entirely of males.)

Though I've hit an impasse in tracking the life, death, and possible return of Roderick Morley, I'm very happy to report that more of Van Slyke's ghostly explorations *have* come to light. In response to my publication of *Help for the Haunted*, the companion volume to this one, I have received an email from a descendant of Vera Rose Bergson, the daughter of Ludmila, a.k.a. Lucille. My distant relative explained that she inherited additional manuscripts written by our mutual ancestor. She mentioned that there's a sequel, set in the 1920s, along with a collection of Van Slyke's reminiscences of investigations conducted in the second half of the 1880s, cases shared with her mentor in ghost-hunting, Harry Escott.

The email ends by suggesting we discuss these manuscripts over *lunch*. Very fitting. It seems likely that, in the not too distant future, these stories will join with the two books now published.

Maybe, one day, they will all be included in a library of the Supernatural—a collection of books similar to what once was assembled in the Dawning Room.

I imagine Vera and Lucille lifting a spectral beer to that possibility.

Tim Prasil

This is the only known photograph of Vera Van Slyke (seated) and Ludmila "Lida" Bergson, née Prášilová, aka Lucille Parsell.

ABOUT THE AUTHOR

Tim Prasil writes fiction, plays, and the occasional limerick. He also researches quirky genres of fiction from the 1800s and early 1900s, from occult detective fiction to tales of sinister hypnotists. From this research, Tim edits entertaining and informative anthologies.

In 2017, he started Brom Bones Books as a publishing "cottage" for his work. Visit brombonesbooks.com to learn about Tim's upcoming projects. The site also has a page titled "The Life and Ghosts of Vera Van Slyke," which reviews the verifiable history underlying many of the cases chronicled in this book and in *Help for the Haunted: A Decade of Vera Van Slyke Ghostly Mysteries*.

One more thing. *Tim Prasil* rhymes with *grim fossil*. Flattering, aint' it?

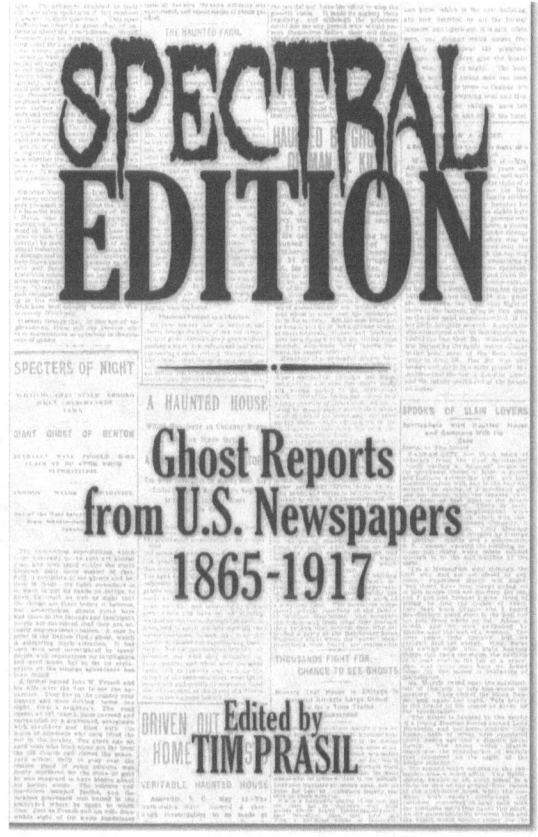

www.ingramcontent.com/pod-product-compliance
Lightning Source LLC
Chambersburg PA
CBHW020740250626
47155CB00003B/841